LEG LOVER

And I loved mirrors. Loved to see a guy holding a fist full of my hair while he banged me from behind. I was slim and very pale, and it was so sexy to see a hard, muscular male body thrusting away at a pretty girl wearing too much make-up. With glossy stockings on her legs and her high heels still on like some actress in a porn movie. Men didn't even need to ask me to leave them on. I never took my shoes or stockings off, ever, unless they got carried away and wanted to lick the soles of my feet, or suck my toes naked.

And I started to meet a lot of men with a real thing for legs. You know, they would take time to caress my legs. Lick them. Rub their erections against them. And just hold my ankles up in the air and stare at my shiny legs while they were fucking me. Like they couldn't believe their luck.

LEG LOVER

L. G. Denier

The LAST
WORD *in*
FETISH

enthusiast

This book is a work of fiction.
In real life, make sure you practise safe, sane and
consensual sex.

First published in 2006 by
Nexus
Thames Wharf Studios
Rainville Road
London W6 9HA

www.nexus-books.co.uk

Typeset by TW Typesetting, Plymouth, Devon

ISBN 0 352 34016 9

Penguin Random House is committed to a sustainable future for
our business, our readers and our planet. This book is made from
Forest Stewardship Council® certified paper.

MIX
Paper from
responsible sources
FSC® C018179

Printed and bound in Great Britain by Clays Ltd, St Ives plc

One

'So I'd like you to tell me in your own time, why you feel you need to see me.'

I laugh in a way that irritates me, then stop laughing and feel embarrassed. I don't know where to look. Certainly not at her legs. They are long and taper from knee to toe within tight leather boots, mounted on elegant square heels. Her feet are long and thin. The boots look new. The leather is supple and unmarked by wear or wrinkles. It's a leather skin; a thin, clinging leather skin over a second skin of shiny flesh hose. Her knees look polished. I can't help thinking about how warm and slippery her calves would feel when unzipped and withdrawn from the fragrant interior of those boots. And in turn, once her well-worn hosiery had been rolled down her pale legs, how her flesh would taste. Of soap or moisturiser. Tangy with perfume. Warm with salt.

Twice already she's crossed her legs in a routine but demure manoeuvre, carefully tucking her black skirt under her thighs. Of course, it's a perfectly innocent movement and she wears this tailored suit and the tight boots because she likes to look chic and feminine. An intelligent, professional psychotherapist dressed in clean, simple lines and dark colours. Bespectacled. One string of pearls hanging neatly across her silky white

1

blouse, peaking between the lapels of her jacket. She has no idea that I have come here to confess everything about my fetish – a desire for certain things she is actually wearing.

I secretly and guiltily confess to myself – even at this stage of my addiction and considering where it has led me – I am glad my therapist is a woman. I liked her voice on the phone. Well spoken but soft; a voice to put a man at ease, a man with much on his mind. And I would be lying if I claimed I was insensitive to, or unaware of, the erotic value of talking to a female doctor about a sexual fetish. Even now, when seeking professional help, I am incorrigible. Despite the trouble it has dragged me into, the slump I have slipped into, and the ruin I face because of my passion for female legs and feet, I felt a sudden and electrifying jolt of excitement when I knew my therapist was going to be a woman – an older, educated woman too. Perhaps I am beyond hope. Maybe I already know this.

I came here for analysis, confession, advice, answers, solutions, and yet I am still compelled at an instinctive level to seek the friction of arousal. Everywhere. In even the most innocent and ordinary of situations.

She prompts me. Smiles. 'It's important you relax. I'm not going to judge you. Just listen to what you have to say.'

'Sure.' But I am in an awkward position, considering her outfit and the way she has presented her legs. 'But it's difficult.'

'That's perfectly natural to feel self-conscious and wary. But we must develop a dialogue. We must start somewhere. Anywhere you're comfortable with really. Anywhere at all. And this begins by you talking to me.' She smiles, which seems to project a mist of lipstick scent and perfume towards my chair.

I swallow, nod in agreement, go to speak, then stop. Clear my throat. 'I have . . . I have an addiction.'

She nods, lowers her eyes to allow me the space to talk without her direct scrutiny.

'But not an ordinary addiction.'

She looks up at me, her face impassive, but somehow prompting me through its apparent neutrality at the same time.

'I . . . I have an attraction to certain things that have . . . well, that have taken over my life. It's something that makes me take risks. Makes me impervious to the feelings of others. A powerful compulsion to something . . . something women wear.' My face colours and a sudden panic fills my head like a fire in a confined space. I pull at my shirt collar. Sweat seems to be pouring down my back and swamping my armpits.

Through the reddish confusion that seems to have filled my head, the room and the imploding world beyond it, I hear her clear, impassive voice. 'Am I wearing it today?'

'Yes.' My voice is barely audible. A pitiful rasp at best. I noisily clear my throat again and begin to get irritated at my own reticence. 'Yes.' I look at her face. Use all of my concentration to keep my eyes level with hers. To not look down and give myself away.

She smiles in the way a mother does when she forgives and soothes the conscience of a child clearly tormented by its guilt over something trivial but all-consuming to that child. I warm to her immediately for that smile.

'And you feel embarrassed about discussing this with a woman.'

'Ashamed would be more precise.'

'I see.' She frowns, as if fascinated by some engaging discourse I have just begun on a cerebral topic. Which of course I haven't.

'Most people would think me silly. Foolish. I really am an absurd man. Not unique in any way, but I may have taken things further than other men who share my

3

interest. You see, I've dedicated my life to something of a sexual nature. On every level. Romantically, professionally, intellectually. I am obsessed. And trapped by it.'

'This addiction, as you call it, you feel it is ruining your life? Or has ruined your life? I'd like to know why you think of this in such epic terms.'

'Well, I've read an alcoholic cannot live a normal life when he's drinking. Can't function properly. You know? I feel the same way.' A long silence follows in which I am profoundly uncomfortable.

She nods in agreement. 'There are common traits in all addictions. I can tell you have given this desire of yours a lot of thought.'

'Yes, I have. Virtually my whole life. I've always had it. There's nothing I don't know about my fetish. I've read a great deal about the psychology of sexual difference too. I think that's what it's called these days. I have lived a life of self-examination. Self-interpretation too. But, I'm still here.'

'So why now?'

'Because ... I've hurt someone. And been hurt by someone else. Emotionally. It's supposed to be about pleasure. This fetish of mine. Harmless pleasure, but things have got out of hand, I feel. You see, I am addicted to my own pleasure. I live what could be called a self-pleasure lifestyle. Utterly selfish, though harmless. But I feel things have changed. Can I truly say what it makes me do is harmless now? I have to change, if I am ever going to have a shot at a normal life. At happiness. Isn't that what we all want? Happiness? But the means we pursue to get it are often counterproductive.'

Doctor Kim nods. 'Perhaps, Algernon, you need to start being more specific.'

I frown.

'About your interest, we will call it, without assigning names and classifications you may have come across in your reading. And you mustn't feel foolish. You are not foolish.'

'No?'

'No. We will leave the expectations and opinions of others at the door when we meet. We will just talk about your feelings. Your thoughts.'

'And will you . . . you know?'

'What?'

'Tell me things?'

'In time, I may give you my thoughts and share my experience. But you can only understand yourself and realise why you are here by talking. That is what is important. So?'

'So?'

'Your interest?'

I clear my throat. 'Legs.'

Not a flicker of surprise or discomfort in her face. Without me realising it, my eyes move to take in her gleaming boots and compact, shiny knees. 'And feet. Women's legs and feet.'

'Do my legs and feet make you feel unable to talk freely?'

'No. Not at all.'

'Do they arouse you?' Again, save an intense curiosity, her face is inscrutable. She doesn't seem disgusted or repelled by me.

I nod. 'They are very beautiful. Just what I like.'

She looks down, at her legs, as if suddenly surprised by the sight of them. Nods.

'The way they are presented. Boots. Tight leather boots. And hosiery. Sheer hosiery. I like it.'

She stays silent. Watches me. Urges me to continue with a level, unyielding gaze.

'And other things. Painted toenails. Ankle chains. Bare feet. Tights. Stockings. Seams. Shoes with high heels. Beautiful shoes. Feet. Walking. Sitting. Climbing.

5

Lying down. Running. White skin. Tanned skin. Crossing legs. Toes. Soles.' I can't stop, but feel unable to embellish. I just spill my voice into the room. Fill it with absurd-sounding words, unsupported by excuses, reasons, explanations. 'Nylons. Especially real nylons. The sight, sound, smell and taste of legs. Nice legs and feet. Tall, short, plump, but mainly long legs these days.' I breathe out. Look at the floor. Wipe my forehead and face with a clean white handkerchief. 'I'm sorry.'

'Don't be. Please continue.'

'You see, I have a broken heart because of it. I'm pathetic. I found perfection. I mean the holy grail of a leg and foot fetish. What I'd wanted and dreamt about my whole life. But it wasn't just an aesthetic or sexual thing this time. It was more. Became more. I loved her. She was like me. Not identical, but very close. We had a connection. On every level: physically, mentally, emotionally. You have no idea how hard that is to find. It's what every fetishist desires. Fantasises about. The ideal mate. Not someone who just goes along with it to make you happy, though that is good if you can get it. But someone who fundamentally shares the obsession and is the ultimate object of desire. And she's gone. I feel one of life's great opportunities has been missed. The kind you get two or three times in an entire life, if you're lucky. And I'm sure that was my last chance. And I can't go back to how I was. Manipulating my whole life so I can look up skirts. Observe legs. Study them. Collect them. I know it's the only reason I wake up, or leave the flat. The only thing I look for in books, newspapers, television, films. The only thing I really see in a woman. Even you. Today. The most interesting thing I find about you . . . No, the reason I find you so interesting is because . . .' We both look at her legs.

Doctor Kim nods. She does nothing else. Doesn't fidget, blush, cough, speak, wince or pull her skirt further down. She doesn't ask me to leave, call the police or have me committed. She just nods and looks at me; her handsome slender face is soft, her eyes alert but consoling and not condemning. 'That's good,' she finally says. 'Well done.'

'Really?'

'Yes. We have begun a dialogue. But are you wanting to be cured?'

'God no,' I say quickly. 'I mean, I doubt it's possible.'

'I see. But perhaps you want help to manage your interest? You don't want to lose the pleasure, but you want to control it?'

'Maybe. I guess so. Yes.'

I reach for my glass of water from the black coffee table. Drain it. The glass feels clean and wholesome. The room is spotless. Polished. Comfortable. I realise it's a room where you might want to spend a great deal of time.

'Perhaps you'd better tell me more specifically how you feel your interest is controlling you.'

'I like that. A sense of being controlled by something inside yourself. Something that becomes more interesting and stimulating and exciting than anything else around you. Something that can be the cause of shame and remorse and a condemning sense of the ridiculous, but is just too good to leave alone. It makes me think of devout priests with white knuckles, clenching their fists and muttering prayers when confronted with temptation. Not something I could ever embark upon – that kind of abstinence. Though maybe I should have done just that. Less is more. I've indulged myself for so long. But I won't defer responsibility. No, I willingly give in to my impulses. My God, I almost have sympathy for men with more unacceptable compulsions.'

'But you feel your desires are unacceptable too?'

'Not exactly. It's no crime to admire a nice pair of ankles, or a woman with pretty feet and an excellent taste in high-heeled shoes.'

'But?'

'But it's not something you want to talk about freely. Or own up to. Unless you have the confidence of a fellow enthusiast. But it has led me astray. Seriously astray.'

'How? In a criminal sense?'

'No. No. Though I have taken things. Stolen things to support my habit.' I grin at the language of drug addiction I have automatically used. I suddenly feel dramatic, foolish again.

She stares at me, inquisitively. Another prompt.

'Well, garments. From drawers and laundry hampers.' I feel my face colour again and I look away. 'That's about the worst thing you do. And photographs. I have taken pictures of women who never had any idea they were being photographed. I guess I could be arrested for that. Though I'm no stalker. I just pretend to fiddle with my camera when a nice pair of legs walks by, or is sitting opposite me.' I sigh; I've started and this is confidential so I might as well give her the whole sorry story. That's why I'm here. 'And I have used a zoom lens. And telescope. A Japanese man once tried to sell me a walking stick with a hidden camera in the end. When women stop to cross roads, or pause to look in shop windows, or stand in front of you on an escalator, you just nonchalantly slip it forwards to take a picture up their skirts. I never bought it. I felt it was a step in the wrong direction. He had a website that was closed down. No surprise really. He took pictures around Tokyo. And anyway, I'm able to photograph women legitimately for a website. My website. Maybe you should look at it. Leg Lover.com. You'll see how far my obsession reaches. I'll give you a password. But in terms of voyeurism I would say I am capable of going to great lengths to get my fix. But not if it knowingly made a woman feel uncomfortable. Never. It's not a power thing. A vengeful pursuit. But more solitary. It's an inner compulsion to observe, to collect, to experience. While unobserved most of the time, unless you are with a consenting participant. But it's not a hobby. That would do me an injustice. To me it's always been a vocation.'

The doctor narrows her eyes and angles her head towards me, as if afraid she may miss part of my monologue.

'Even my professional life is all about legs. I once worked as a hosiery salesman who sold stock to buyers at department stores. I was very good. I had a passion for my product. But I was only doing it to be close to legs and the materials that cover them. As many legs as possible. Numbers were important. It was from my experience there that I began my business. The shop. I have a shop that sells hosiery, shoes, lingerie, nail polish. Anything to do with legs and feet. And I make my employees wear uniforms with stockings and high heels. And there is the adult fetish website too. I photograph strangers. Their legs and feet in more ways than you can imagine. When I'm not working I go online to see what's out there, or I work on my archive.'

For the first time since I arrived, the doctor shows a vague but discernible sign of uncontained curiosity. Not unease, I am pleased to say. But a vital, professional interest. Maybe she's always wanted a textbook case of extreme fetishism. I flatter myself by thinking I may be a more interesting case of post-historical dysfunction than another of her eating disorders or bi-polar cases.

'Freud would have maintained I am a sexual cripple. Someone who has failed to fully develop into a well-balanced adult. I looked myself up.'

She tries not to laugh.

'But in some ways he might be right. You can handicap yourself. With relationships. You see, I have

9

been unable to cure myself of a lifelong addiction to variety. My eyes are constantly lowered. Let me give you an example. I am at a party with a beautiful woman wearing sheer black stockings and spike-heeled sandals on her exquisite legs and feet. Which is just about the ultimate realisation of my fetish. Despite that, I'll still be checking out every other woman's legs in the room. I'll be wanting to touch and make love to those women too. Women less attractive than my date. But the Nylon Dahlia . . .' I pause.

Ice-cubes melt in my stomach. Even sitting down I feel unsteady. A lump forms in my throat. I then feel like I have indigestion. Dark inner clouds gather at the edge of my mind. That name alone prompts an extreme emotional response.

Curiously, there is no one else I can tell this to besides a complete stranger who is trained and paid to listen. Usually in a crisis, you would call a parent, a sibling, a best friend. I cannot. There are always sly smiles, or a sense of incomprehension bordering on discomfort when those closest to me ever have to comment on my retail business. Because it's so odd. I'm odd. And I have but one thing in common with my fellow enthusiasts met online and in adult clubs, our fetish. Nothing so intimate as an emotional upheaval could be discussed between us. No personal information is ever forthcoming. It wouldn't be right. We'd all feel awkward.

The sense of desolation, of a shrinking universe, of acute isolation briefly grips me in something I guess is akin to a loss of faith. Of course I am being dramatic. Like a jilted teenager, or heroine in a sentimental gothic novel who dies of a broken heart.

Time heals. It'll pass. I know the clichés. But feel there is no better time to tell these stories than now. Right now I have to tell the story. To someone. The doctor. Review my recent history to make sense of the complete history. At no other time will my recollections have such edge and resonance. I have to be irrational to go through with this. Unhinged. Desperate. Vulnerable. It has to come out. The Nylon Dahlia was the catalyst. Salvation turned nemesis. My heart is broken and through the breach must come my secrets. All of them.

'There, I've said it. There was a woman. Two women. A situation involving three of us. One of them broke the spell. I realised I had been bewitched my whole life. With one of them I was finally, briefly content. Don't ask me how I was so sure. But I knew it. At last I could rest. And I felt tired. So tired. Exhausted, but relieved. So worn out through over-stimulation. Decades of chronic indulgence seemed to have ended. At last, I could be in love. I could be content with one pair of legs and just two feet. I felt saved somehow.' I pause to gulp from my glass of water.

'But it was too late. You see, my fetish destroyed the very thing my fetish ultimately led me to. The thing it made me long for my entire life. And I don't think I can go back to the way things were the way before. This is why I am here. To tell it all while I'm less inclined to embellish or rewrite my own history. To let it out when I'm already open.'

The doctor nods. Studies me. Frowns. Crosses her legs. I have the grace to look away. But not before securing a glimpse along her thigh, so slick with a veneer of transparent nylon. She notices my momentary scrutiny, and a brief pall of discomfort settles in the room like a cloud of dust.

It is partially banished by the sound of her clearing her throat. 'I think we have made a good start, Al. And you are sure you want to see me on Friday as well?'

I nod. 'Definitely.' I asked for a block booking. Two afternoons until the tale was told. I would talk until I was all out of talking. The brief and intense story of my affair with the woman in possession of the most beautiful legs in the world is the conclusion of all my stories. Every other story was just preparation for the final one.

She checks her watch. 'This is a good time to pause. I'll see you the same time on Friday.'

Two

On Friday the doctor is wearing trousers. An elegant pinstripe trouser suit with flat-heeled shoes. But there is a chink in her armour: between the hem of her trouser leg and the top of her innocuous shoe, I catch a glimpse of her pale ankle coated in sheer grey nylon. Inwardly, I smile. Achilles heel. My eyes will find it. I once met a woman who wore hold-up stockings under her jeans. Through the denim at the top of her thigh, I still managed to detect the imprint of a band of elasticated lace. But how could the doctor know just how attuned my senses are to finding stimulus? She will find out before I'm done in here. In this cream-coloured sanctuary with blinds over the windows and deep leather chairs. A room at the back of her home, that has no intrusion of noise from any quarter. No cars or phones or creaks or bangs. Just us and the sound of our voices.

She waits for me to start. Today she is also wearing new glasses with chic black frames. They form perfect little rectangles around her discreetly made-up eyes and dark lashes. Am I transferring already?

She wants me to begin. Stares back at me, through my cursory appraisal.

'I think I'd better tell you about an afternoon a few weeks back. On the day I knew I had a good chance of meeting the Nylon Dahlia.'

'Whatever you like.'

'You see, that afternoon I was in your role. Your position. Giving and recording an interview for the leg library. I can tell you more about the leg library later, but suffice to say some of the material I gather at interviews goes on the website, but the majority is stored in my private collection. And I was talking to a young lady about her legs. She was telling stories, like I am now. Weirdly, I guess I always thought of it as a kind of analysis. But one that is designed to titillate and arouse. It's not unusual for me to do this. I have scores of these interviews with women and men. Mostly men. But the women, obviously, stick in my mind more. And on that day I was talking to Patricia, the wife of one of the fans of my website, who started his own site a few years ago featuring Patricia. She agreed to appear on Leg Lover. It's not uncommon for us devotees to swap and share willing models for photo-shoots and websites.

'And Patricia is an extraordinary young lady, who I was determined to meet and interview. She is very highly sexed and devoted to wearing stockings. She and her husband have an unusual relationship. His hosiery fetish has become hardwired into his cuckold fantasies that Patricia eagerly indulges. If you follow. So they are perfect for the leg library and the website. And if I start there, I can give you a better sense of just what my life is like. The normal course of a few weeks is often filled with meetings with fellow enthusiasts, photo-shoots and so forth. I use the word normal lightly. Because my everyday life and business is devoted to legs.'

The doctor lowers her face in assent, then smiles.

I take a gulp of chilled water. Water from a bottle she has then poured into an elegant jug that must have been designed in Denmark. I like this doctor; she chills Evian for her clients. And then I relax into my chair and find a place to stare above her head, near the thin steel rail at the top of the blinds, before I find the place in my mind to begin. I'll leave nothing out. As long as I don't look into the doctor's intelligent eyes, I'll be OK.

Strong sunlight fell through the sash windows in my study and lit up her legs. The golden light would be there for two hours, bright and penetrating, before moving over the roof of my apartment to leave the room in shadow.

I deliberately seated Patricia in that chair because the sun was strong and would guarantee a still life of exquisitely presented leg on show for a considerable duration. Out there in the world we leg men are most often reduced to furtive glimpses and suggestions, whispers of legs crossing nearby, quick asides with the eyes, or hasty glances taken in fear of discovery. Sometimes, if circumstances are in our favour, we get to look for longer, because we are unable to do otherwise as pretty legs strut down the street before us, scale stairs above us, cross on chairs on the far side of a room before a waiter or tablecloth obscures the view, or pass us slowly in a moving car we are afforded a view inside.

But that afternoon, I was able to feast and gorge my senses upon the leg beauty stretching from the Chester-field chair positioned no more than four feet away from my position. And whenever Patricia leant forwards to raise her wine glass or packet of cigarettes, my eyes fixed their gaze upon her legs and memorised what they saw; photographed them for future perusals in the greatest album of all – the mind.

'Well, stockings make me feel ... different. Good, you know. They always have done.' Patricia blushed. This approach and situation – a woman and a strange man and his peculiar line of enquiry – no matter how hard I attempt to relax my guests, it often makes us both self-conscious in the beginning. But once a start is made, I am rarely disappointed by where storytelling can lead.

Momentarily I was paralysed by a fear she might stand up, gather her things and leave my study. Muttering apologies as those shaped legs, skinned in flesh RHT nylons and black Ferragamo sandals, skipped away. For ever.

I was trying my best to put her at ease, to not stare at her legs, though she was used to that. Accustomed to her legs being the focus of male attention. But this contrived setting, at a private address, in the company of a man considered important in the leg-fetish community, made her feel marginally foolish.

The light turned the membrane of nylon on her knees and thighs into a see-through, sleek oil that I found most distracting too. Her nylons were so sheer as to be invisible to the untrained eye but, under closer scrutiny and powerful illumination, they shimmered. Appeared almost wet. Sparkles played within the pure nylon as if tiny crystals were trapped inside the fabric. But when she rotated her foot, and if I concentrated my stare at the bend of her knees, thin creases appeared. A shade darker than the fabric around the surface area of her leg proper.

Most men would be transfixed by the unusual beauty of her face for some time, and might not have the chance to look down and study her other assets. Eyes an aquamarine, or lapis lazuli – the colour of an iceberg just beneath the surface of a cold sea; a square bone structure, reminiscent of Scandinavian women, though without hard lines; skin tinted the colour of a thin honey; and blonde hair so soft but thick one was instantly startled by the lustre and sweep of such a golden torrent. But as an enthusiast of good legs, my eyes were drawn instantly and unequivocally further down.

She tapped a cigarette from the white and green carton on the coffee table. The cigarette was completely white; the red varnish on her fingernails contrasted in a pleasing way against it. She wouldn't look me in the eye; could not, as if some gravity of guilt was applying pressure to her face, lowering the pretty features, oppressing her smooth brow, pulling in the crimson lips from their natural pout.

In theory, the fetishist longs for a chance to finally confess to a fellow enthusiast. To unburden the mind of that which has been kept secret for years. Decades of shame, self-discovery, resistance, addiction, and the pure, wordless euphoria of indulgence. But it takes much trust to cultivate a dialogue with another who knows and feels and shares the adoration for the object of desire. It's not the same as talking about a woman's body, or trading stories about sexual experiences, no matter how intimate the dialogue becomes. Both parties have to share the passion and be initiates, otherwise at best you can expect ridicule. And I believe it is doubly difficult for a woman to admit to such, especially to a man she has just met and knows only through correspondence with her husband.

I cleared my throat. Smiled. 'Patricia. Everything you tell me will be kept in the strictest confidence. For the library, your identity will be changed. And everything you say this afternoon is falling on the ears of one who understands every last detail of your hidden life and passion. As I have said, it is so unusual for me to speak or correspond with a woman. Our particular fetish, in my experience, is usually the preserve of men, which is what makes you so very, very special to me. Only a handful of times in a life dedicated to my – our – fetish have I come across a woman of your near-unique status. And most of those were gay or bisexual. So please go on. Relax. More wine? Enjoy the comfort and the confirmation of confession.'

17

I shut my eyes, closed my hands together and placed my fingertips on the top of my nose, as if in prayer. In a manner of speaking I was. Patricia, my sweet, sweet girl, do not disappoint me. Your contribution to my study, to my sweet, narcotic madness is priceless.

There was a long moment of silence, ending in an exhalation of smoke and the clink of lacquered nails against a wine glass. She swallowed. 'OK. It's just, you know, difficult.' She giggled, nervous, feeling silly. 'Having sex and being filmed is actually much easier. I mean where do I start? I've had this . . . fetish for, like, my whole life. Well, since my teens anyway.'

I nodded, adopting the posture and manner of a sage. 'I find it's best if an individual starts to recall certain key experiences, no matter how ordinary, in which you can remember your fetish being particularly strong. From then, we have chapter titles into which the remaining subject matter writes itself.'

She giggled again, amused at the unusual way I expressed myself, as if I was an academic, or scientist gathering raw data. But then, in a manner of speaking, I was.

Patricia spoke, more quietly than before. Her short sentences broken by anxious sips of chilled wine. 'You know those times when you were young. When you get, like, a whole house to yourself. You're trusted to be on your own. You're old enough. But of course, you're not to be trusted at all. And there's that feeling. That urge to misbehave. To find secret spaces. To rummage around. Open drawers. Look under beds. Read stuff you're not supposed to. Touch personal items from another person's life. Try things on.' She deeply inhaled the smoke from her cigarette. Last drag. Stubbed it out forcefully so the ashtray slid along the table-top. She flicked her hair back from her face, smiled, crossed her legs. A rasp of nylon as the back of one thigh caressed the polished curve of the other filled the room, and my ears.

I breathed slowly. The nape of my neck tingled. Excitement rose through me at the merest hint of this girl misbehaving alone.

She allowed a thick curl of smoke to leave her scarlet lips. 'I'd always liked black and white films. Loved the way women dressed. You know, little hats, veils, spiky shoes, make-up, tight pencil skirts, those dark seams down the back of their legs. Well, I had a relative like that. A great aunt who lived in Bournemouth. Mo Mo we called her. And she was always old when I knew her. But if you had seen the photos of her when she was younger. She looked like a star from a black and white film. So elegant. Beautiful in a kind of serious, scary way. Even when she was older she looked immaculate. Always. Every day. She never married. But loved kids. Especially my brother and I. And for one week, in every summer holiday, we'd stay at Mo Mo's. Eat strange dinners on real china plates. Read weird books. Get told amazing stories about the war. Go on trips with her. Get spoilt. Eat lots of rich cakes. I loved it. Especially her house. Always smelled of flowers and old wood. Everything was antique. And it was so silent. So quiet, with sharp strips of sunlight streaking through old curtains. Which made the rest of the space shadowy and cool. Bit scary when you were on your own. But a nice fear. One that you wanted to feel over and over again.

'I remember one afternoon after lunch, when she'd taken my brother out in the afternoon, so he could swim in the sea, but I'd got a bit sunburned the day before, and Mo Mo thought it was better if I stayed indoors. I didn't mind. In fact, I was so pleased when she suggested it. I was too old that summer for messing around in the sand with my brother every day. I wanted to stay in her house and mooch around.

'She was always letting me dress up in her furs and old dresses and shoes when I was a girl. Covering me with jewellery and letting me wear nail polish and perfume, which my parents refused to allow until I was about eighteen. Can you believe that? Eighteen? But the dressing up was always harmless – a little girl pretending she was a lady or princess. But that summer, I was sixteen and everything actually fitted me. Even her shoes, without them looking like big boats flopping around on my tiny feet. And I had this really powerful urge to wear make-up that day. To look gorgeous like a movie star from the fifties. I wanted to look really sexy. It was more like desire than anything else. Like wanting sex.'

Patricia stopped talking. Lit another cigarette. Shook the match, about to put out the flame. Her pretty hands trembled.

'I was as bad as a boy for masturbating back then. Had been for years. Could spend all afternoon with my hand between my legs, just dreaming away. And so many of my fantasies involved me all dressed up like Doris Day or something. You know, in my head I was a femme fatale, seducing the guys I liked at school. And a few teachers too. Anyone who took my fancy.

'And I was really excited that afternoon. I was aroused but didn't know it straight away. It was the start of arousal. Mental but on the verge of becoming physical. And I was so excited at the thought of this private adventure I was going to have in the big, old, dark house. My tummy was tingling. My breath went all short and gaspy at the thought of being all dressed up. Alone except for the ghosts. The ghost men I would dream up to stand and bow and adore me.

'I took some of Mo Mo's cigarettes from her box on the mantelpiece in the day room. That was the day I actually started smoking. I just associated the smell of smoke with being excited and naughty from then on.

'Well, I laid the black dress I always liked best on her huge bed. It was backless – the dress, not the bed. And shimmery and tight all the way down to my knees. I shut the curtains. Turned on the lights. Lit a cigarette. Got out of my shorts and T-shirt and knickers. Put the ashtray on the dresser and just plastered my face with make-up. I love make-up, always have. And back then I used lots of it whenever I could. Hid it in my room so my mum wouldn't find it and just plastered it on. Pots and pots of it and big drag-queen eyes. Loved it.

'So I got all dolled up in Mo Mo's make-up. Even gave myself a beauty spot and these big wet red lips. Used false eyelashes too. Tied my hair up with pins and just let a few strands fall down and tickle my naked shoulders. And then I touched myself.

'Looking at my face in the mirror I thought I looked great. Real sexy. Like a posh tart. And that's when it became sexual. I rubbed my clit with a fingertip and pinched my nipples hard. Just standing there, adoring myself in the mirror and wanking on my Aunt Mo Mo's cushioned stool. And when I was close to coming, I made myself stop. I wanted to really climax on something hard. My hairbrush handle. I used it all the time. You know, outside and inside my sex, under the bedclothes in my room at home. And I wanted to be all dressed up in nice undies and stockings and high heels when I came on Mo Mo's big bed. Dressed in all the things I never had at home, that I used to fantasise about wearing when I was with imaginary guys. I never had any nice undies of my own at that time, but plain cotton knickers and thickish tights and crappy flat shoes.

'So I went into Mo Mo's top drawer. It smelled so good. Kind of like an old wood mixed with nice perfume, and this other smell that only comes from lingerie when it's all folded up together. And the drawer was full of underwear she must have had for, like, ages.

Years and years. Old-fashioned and squarish, but real sexy. Lacy suspender belts with waistbands that were see-through. Panty girdles, they called them. And she had all these silky bras that were so beautifully made. They were so stiff on my chest and made my breasts look like rockets. Real hard and pointy. And the bras weren't comfortable at all. But it was a nice kind of discomfort. It matched or got tied into the arousal I was feeling. My legs went to water when I was touching the stuff. Picking it up, but remembering exactly how it went so I could put it back without being found out.

'I was so excited. I had to wipe my pussy with a tissue so I didn't get any goo on her things. Couldn't keep my fingers still either. They were trembling and I could feel my heart beat in my throat and between my ears. I even had to sit down for a bit and smoke some more.

'In the second big top drawer in the dresser was the most enormous collection of nylons. Most of them still in the packets that went back to the 1940s and 1950s. They had these beautiful drawings on the packages. And lovely names. I remember a pair being called "Night Shade", and another was called "Kitty's Delight". I didn't open those packets. Just held them up and rustled the packaging and sniffed them, thinking of old movies. And the other half of the drawer was filled with nylons she had worn. Carefully folded together. This big smoky sea of weightless nylon. Lots of subtle shades and colours with lovely silky welts and thin seams. They even had little white signatures of the manufacturers on the stocking tops. So beautiful. You know, really expertly made. And so delicate. I held them so carefully so my nails didn't catch and make runs in them. Held them up before the light so the bedroom looked all misty and sexy through the fine material.

'I just had to get a pair on. My chest was all red and

blushing over this crazy black bra I'd got on. And that only ever happened when I was really aroused.

'And I knew exactly which ones I wanted to wear. Black seamed stockings. Just looking at them made me feel bad, but older and sophisticated at the same time. Ladylike but powerful simultaneously. So I shook them out to their full length and laid them on the bedclothes. One next to the other. Then chose a black garter belt so I'd be all matching under the dress.

'I'd never worn stockings before. Never ever. So it was such a thrill. I always loved to look at pictures of ladies' legs in stockings and high heels. I mean, aesthetically, it always hit a chord with me. I liked the colours and glassy textures and contrasts to the skin. I mean there's nothing to them, but they transform a woman's legs and I wanted mine to be that sexy and different-looking. Transformed.

'So like I did with tights, I rolled the stockings into hoops and pointed my toes down and into the middle. Then slowly, ever so slowly, rolled them up my foot and around my ankle, then up my calves. And just watched my leg change colour. My girly, innocent legs were just going all dark and silky right up to my thighs. Maybe my aunt's legs were longer than mine when she was younger, because the stockings went right up to where my thighs joined my pelvis.

'I twisted about and got the seams straight at the back. Then spent ages trying to hook them on to the steel suspender clips. I was getting really annoyed with my fumbling fingers. The stockings just kept pinging off the clips. I'd get three fastened, then it would go down to two. Then up to four, and I'd think at last, but one would snap off and I'd have only three attached again. I nearly gave up. But was glad I didn't. Especially when I looked at myself in the big oval mirror Mo Mo had on a stand beside the window.

'Just couldn't believe it was me in the reflection. Hair pinned up and face totally disguised and made to look older and glamorous in that make-up. I was glamorous. I was gorgeous. Black brassiere making my tits look huge. Just pushing them out. The girdle tight on my flat little belly. Silver suspender clips tugging the stockings to the top of my thighs. And my legs all shiny and shimmery in black nylon. Thought I was going to faint. I mean, it was like my reflection was actually turning me on. I was feeling real lust for myself. How conceited is that?

'And then the high heels. Black suede shoes with a peep toe and sling-back strap around my heel. I could hardly walk. It was like being on stilts and I thought I was going to fall forwards, on to my face. But God, what they did to my legs. Made them look so much longer and more shapely. They defined every single muscle and tendon in my legs and feet. And inside the shoes my feet felt really nice – silky and lubricated by the tight nylon.

'For ages, I just walked around and around in front of that mirror. Smoking. Looking sultry. Pouting my lips. Stroking my silky legs. Playing with my pussy. Then sitting on the end of the bed and crossing and uncrossing my legs. Then opening my legs and licking my shiny red lips, like I was in porno and looking at a camera lens.

'I never even got the dress on.

'I sat in front of the mirror and had a wank with the hairbrush handle. Had to sit on a hand towel because my pussy was so wet. I simply admired myself in the mirror and rubbed away. When I felt dizzy and was getting really carried away, I had to lie sideways on the bed and get the brush inside me.

'I really, really wanted a cock. Wanted a man. Was more desperate than ever to be penetrated by a real cock. A hundred faces and bodies and words whirled about my head as I fucked myself with that brush handle. I lifted my legs in the air and pretended my high heels were on some guy at school's shoulders while he screwed me. Screwed me while I was in black seamed stockings and loads of make-up. I just got so carried away and thought of things that convinced me later that I was a maniac. That I would end up a prostitute or in a mental home. But I really used that brush hard inside myself, fantasising about two guys having me, then three, then a whole bunch of boys on a field-trip just taking turns to do me in a hostel bedroom. Because I'd dressed up in stockings and slutty underwear and make-up. And they just had to have me.

'Terrible. Terrible. I used to have that dream all the time. And from then on, whenever I thought about sex, about having sex, in my mind I was always wearing stockings. Especially seamed stockings.'

Patricia looked at her empty wine glass, then at me. Her eyes were shining. 'May I?' I leant forwards and seized the bottle. Splashed wine into her glass. Droplets hit the table. My hand was unsteady.

'So, so . . .' I said, then coughed to loosen my throat. 'They became a part of your erotic life.'

'Oh, yeah. Most definitely.' She drank a long draught. 'But I kept it secret for a long time. With my allowance I started buying really nice tights and stockings. I wore them all the time. I tried to wear out the attraction. Make it ordinary. But it never happened. It just got worse. I mean, I was wearing them to bed and under my jeans and under the woolly tights of my school uniform. Except on the day we had P.E. because the other girls would have found out I was a pervert.

'I just loved the feel of that other skin. That second skin of really fine nylon on my legs and feet, under everything else. In class, I'd sit and rub my legs together and have fantasies. I loved the sensation of my legs sliding against each other. And whenever I got home from school, I'd always go straight to my room. Before I ate biscuits or did homework or anything, I'd get my shoes and woolly school tights off and get under the covers. And have a wank. It was so lovely. Better than sex with most guys. Rubbing my legs together while I fingered myself. Getting all hot and a bit sweaty under the duvet while I was wearing a garter belt and black stockings. Always black ones for ages. And you know, just really riding that hairbrush. That is until I bought a toy. From Soho on a sixth-form trip to London. We went to the British Museum for A-level history, but had a few hours' free time, so me and some friends went into Soho to drink and just generally get up to no good. You know how it is.

'So I bought this crazy big pink thing. This cock. No batteries or anything. It wasn't a vibrator. It was just like a big erection made from latex or something. But, my God, I had to hide it well. Just in case my parents or brother were ever in my room. I actually used to hide it inside the bed frame. But every afternoon and every night for like two years, I used that thing. It was the cock to represent all of the guys I had crushes on.' Patricia hung her head back and laughed. Touched the tears away from the corner of her eyes. Sniffed. 'Sorry. Oh, I'm so sorry. But I never thought I'd ever be telling anyone this besides my husband. God, it's exhausting talking about this. But nice. Nice.

'So, yeah, anyway, I was having a fantasy about Edward Sutton, this guy in the sixth form. He had a girlfriend, but I had a huge crush on him. Couldn't even speak to him or look at him if he was talking to me. God, if only he knew what he could have done to me. I had all of these elaborate fantasies about school trips overseas, and about what he said to me after class which led to us going to his bedroom, or my place, or to the woods, or something. For years he fucked me, at least in my head, at least five times a week. God, I'm such a stalker!'

Patricia laughed some more. 'Oh, God, my make-up's running.'

I smiled. My voice sounded thin. I felt small and baffled in the same space as her. 'So, in these fantasies, with your toy, you were always wearing stockings?' I can barely finish the sentence.

'Oh, yeah. I mean the fantasies weren't anything special. Every girl has them at that age. But the difference with mine was that I was always dressed up like a tart. And I know now how submissive I was. Am. My dreams were all about getting dressed up like a slut and being really aggressively used by men. Old men, young men, all kinds. It's a wonder I ever got through my exams and went to university. I just thought about sex all the time. I mean, I even used to read my brother's porno mags. Loved them. Once I found a bag in a park bin with three magazines inside. A *Razzle*, a *Fiesta* and something called *Escort*. And I was a really nice, polite, well-brought-up middle-class girl. It was scandalous. Oh, if my parents ever knew. Or their friends. I'd never ever be able to go home for Christmas again.' We both laughed.

I joined her and poured myself a glass of wine. Not too much; I didn't want to disgrace myself. She was only here because she trusted me. But I needed to take the edge off my nerves. While I had the bottle, I sloshed another generous measure into Patricia's glass. Her lovely face was flushed now and I could see she was excited and enjoying the exchange.

'So, the magazines actually had an influence on your sexuality?'

'Oh God, yeah. Definitely. I read stuff in there that was a total surprise. Shocking to start with, but then exciting when it sunk in. I mean, to get inside men's heads like that. You learn so much. And I always fantasised about being one of those porn-mag women. Dressed like the girls in the pictures and acting like the women in the stories and letters. I mean, I never really knew if those letters were true or not. It was like I'd broken into this secret club of perverts and sluts and nymphomaniacs. A place I should never have been. None of my friends would have looked at them. But I've always had a strong masculine side while being a feminine woman. I think it's that combination that has made my sexuality so weird. I get on much better with men than women.'

'So, these fantasies? I mean –'

'Oh, really crude stuff. Predictable though. But probably not for a girl of my background and education. You know, I'd be all dressed up in stockings and high heels. Loads of make-up. Skimpy lingerie. And I'd be with a guy in my room. Some boy from school, a neighbour, whoever I'd lured up there. And I would take off my ordinary clothes, like jeans, or my school uniform, and the guy would be totally shocked, but turned on, because I was wearing seamed stockings and a see-through bra or something like that underneath. And they'd be all confused but aggressive with me. Just not able to control themselves because I was a slut. And in would go that dildo, under the sheets, and I would be imagining boys from school calling me a slut while they fucked me, and stuffed their cocks into my mouth. Real deep into my throat. Just covering me with jizz, or filling me with it. And I'd be writhing away in my bed, wearing black stockings and a suspender belt, and riding that huge cock I bought in Soho. I mean I could get it right in. Really stretch myself with it. And yet I was a virgin. A total virgin.' Patricia paused to gulp at her wine and lit another cigarette.

'What kind of stockings did you buy during this period?'

28

'Whatever I could afford. I had a Saturday job in Boots and got some money from my parents too. But along with records and clothes and the make-up I was buying, money was always in short supply. But I always made sure I had enough to buy stockings. I would go into town to the department store and just spend ages looking at all the brands and packages. The women that worked in the hosiery and underwear departments of all those stores even got to know me by name. I'd get my fingers in all the samples and stretch them so I could see how sheer they'd be. The best ones were always in the flat, square packets. Charnos, Elbeo, Aristoc. I must have worn every brand going. I even still have a collection of the empty packets in a box.'

A collector. I was tempted to get down on one knee.

'Those would be really sheer and expensive. I just fell in love with Aristoc Harmony Points. Grey, flesh, navy blue, black. I had them all. Real nylons with seams and reinforced heels. So slippery on your legs. Like Mo Mo's. They were the best ones to sleep in. They were like my pyjamas. It got so I couldn't get to sleep without a really good wank first while wearing real seamed nylons. And I always had my dirtiest fantasies wearing them. I mean really filthy stuff that used to make me feel so guilty and shocked afterwards. I'd be like, where the hell did that come from?'

I didn't dare speak. Was afraid to distract her from this discourse. I just smiled and nodded encouragement.

'I mean, other than in Anais Nin's stories, I'd never even heard of anal sex. I knew gay men did it, but women? It was too much to comprehend. But I would get so carried away, thinking about my English teacher fucking me in his storeroom at lunchtime. You know, after I'd flirted with him and simulated sucking a cock with a pen while he was trying to teach us Shakespeare or something. And he asked me to stay behind and we ended up in the storeroom. That sort of scenario, but it used to drive me crazy. He took the place of Edward Sutton as fantasy man number one. Because, in the storeroom, I'd take off my skirt and navy-blue woolly tights and he'd see that I was wearing black seamed stockings and a suspender belt. Of course he'd just have to have me. I mean really just lose control and fuck me dizzy. Stroking and kissing my legs and feet while my ankles were on his shoulders, and he was deep inside me. And in time this fantasy would develop into him stuffing his cock into my arse while he called me names, like you dirty slut, you cock-sucking slut, you teasing slut. It was crazy. A crazy fantasy. And with Vaseline, it wasn't long before my plastic friend from Soho was giving me anal sex.

'I was actually scared of myself. My fantasies were so wild and getting more and more extreme, I was worried about what I'd actually do with a real guy when I got a chance. Would I get pregnant? Would they tell everyone I knew that I was dirty and a nympho? I was terrified of going the whole way because of my fantasies.'

'So you stayed a virgin until you went to university?'

'Nearly. Didn't lose my cherry until I was eighteen. I mean, at house parties, I would snog boys, sometimes. And I loved to feel their erections grow into my tummy. But I was discreet. Never gave out my phone number. Never saw them again. Chose guys that went to other colleges. I was just too scared of my dad. He was so strict. I just couldn't go wild until I'd left home. So it just built up and up, over the years. Fourteen to seventeen was hell in some ways. And when I did go official with boyfriends – I had about three before I went to university – I always picked quite effeminate men. Shy guys. Nice boys that wouldn't worry my parents too much. One of them was even gay. He never even kissed me. He was like a girlfriend. I couldn't even give him an erection. And the other two are probably scarred for life.'

'Why?'

'I had crushes on them and imagined that under the nice exterior they were real lions. And by the time my infatuation had worn off, they would be in love with me. Just sick with love. I mean, the second one was one of the reasons I went to university in Scotland. To get away from him. He was killing himself. I still feel bad. I used them. Used them for experience. I fucked them both and ended up fucking them both over.

'With Jamie, it started with kissing and stuff. But progressed to blow jobs whenever we could be alone. And I sucked his cock in some unusual places. Mostly outdoors. But he wasn't that crazy about my fetish. He loved my tits. Could spend hours just looking at them and feeling them up. And he always wanted to come over my tits once I'd sucked him. But he never paid any attention to the lovely stockings I would be wearing under my jeans or a long skirt and boots. When I finally slept with him, he actually took them off before we got into bed. Can you believe that? So the very first time I had sex, I wasn't wearing stockings. It was quite a disappointment. And the relationship didn't last long, but he wouldn't leave me alone. I mean, my dad even had to speak to him when he was staking out our house.

'But Hector was even worse, when it came to obsession. You see, he was a leg man. And when he discovered what I was wearing at school, under my uniform, and at weekends under my normal clothes, he just went crazy for me. I liked him. I never loved him. Though I was never sure at the time. But he was a nice guy. But simply too terrified of upsetting me and getting dumped. A real puppy dog. Totally doting. Spent all of his money on me. Watched me all day at school with this drained face. He was in real physical pain if I even spoke to another boy. And I was no flirt. I was a good girl. Really square. A female nerd until I got to university. Which is where I went to get away from him. I ended up hating the sight of him, but it was my fault. I treated him terribly. I loved the power I had over him. Loved to tease him and enslave him with my legs. Tell him what I was wearing under my jeans and boring tights. Rub his erection with my foot at school, in the study rooms. Make him come in his trousers. Let him touch the lumps my suspenders made under my skirts. And if we ever got a chance to have sex, I'd wear seamed stockings for him.

'They just drove him wild. Black Aristoc Harmony Points. He bought me them all the time. In fact, I never needed to buy stockings when I was with Hector, and that was one of the reasons I stayed with him. What a bitch.'

'But you met a leg man. Is this not what you always wanted?'

'Yes, but not Hector. He was very submissive. Not at all assertive with me. Didn't know how to handle me. Was terrified of hurting me or upsetting me or being a chauvinist. God, I feel sorry for guys who went through that whole soft liberal upbringing. He just couldn't even make a pass at me, or even say he wanted to fuck me. He would just give me this look instead – this pleading, pained expression. Wanted me to say I loved him. All the time. Wanted to keep analysing our relationship. So desperate and needy for reassurance all the time. And he spoilt it. So I treated him terribly. I was foul. Just used him for presents and for sex when I could get it, which wasn't very often, or very good when I got it.'

'Why?'

'He came too quickly. Like straight away. Premature ejaculation every time. I couldn't blame him. He loved my legs. Loved my feet. Loved stockings. Would kiss and lick them and suck my toes through my nylons. He even used to steal my socks and laddered stockings. Would get them out the bin and sneak them into his bag or pockets. But all that devotion made me want a fuck. A really hard, slut fuck. Like in my fantasies. Real porno sex. I was getting more confident. More demanding. I started to be bitchy and petulant, while being a real prick-tease at the same time. Hoping he would get mad with me and just fuck me. But he'd cry instead.

'I mean it wasn't a disaster. I loved the way he used to come on my legs and feet. He liked it if I wore my stockings all day under opaque tights and in my little, sixth-form court shoes. He loved to smell and taste my hot feet in a free period in the afternoon. Or we'd go back to his place for an hour or so, and he'd take my navy trousers, or pleated skirt and woolly tights off. In his bedroom. And then I'd lie on the bed and let him eat my hot nylon feet and rub my legs. I'd get so turned on. I would just, like, say, "Now. Take me now. Now." But as soon as he got between my thighs and put his cock anywhere near my pussy, he'd come.

'In the end we just gave up, and he'd wank off over my legs. Or I would give him a foot job. Wearing black nylons with red toenails. Just shuffle and stroke and wrap them all around his cock and he'd shoot all over my feet and ankles. He had a nice cock and was a really heavy comer. I'd always had my porno fantasies about eating come and things, and being made to eat come, so at least I got to do a bit of that with Hector. He'd fuck my thighs while my legs were in the air, or with me standing up and bent over in front of the mirror, and when he said, "Now", I'd spin around and get a mouthful, or have him pump it over my lips and chin. I loved it. At least, until it went cold. But the sex never lasted long enough. A few minutes every time. It wasn't just his fault. We lived with our parents. It was so difficult to meet and be naughty and he was too shy to do it outdoors.

'I bet he still thinks about me.'

'I think you are right.'

Patricia giggled. She was drunk. Had consumed about three-quarters of the bottle. I smiled. Reassured her. Told her not to feel so much guilt. At that age, none of us knew what we were doing. She agreed with me.

'Of course, it was different at university,' she said, through a mouthful of white smoke. 'I met men there. Men with experience. Men who were only too willing to give me what I craved. What I'd fantasised about for years. So those years at university were different. I had so much freedom. And I used it. When I went home in the holidays, for Christmas and stuff, I was the old Patricia. Older but still sweet and well behaved. But at uni, I was terrible. I was a slut.'

'Did the fetish remain as strong?'

She nodded, enthusiastically. Inhaled smoke deep. Raised her chin and blew a plume at the ceiling, where it gathered, then dispersed like a miniature atomic cloud. 'Yes. But I was still a bit restricted as to what I could wear.'

'Why?' I couldn't resist the question, which sounded more like an outburst.

'It was the late eighties and it was not cool to be girly if you were a student. Bloody woolly tights again. Clumpy Doc Marten boots. No make-up. Everyone was alternative. I kind of got round that at weekends, in the evenings at heavy-rock clubs. I mean, we used to dress like Hollywood hookers, but that was strictly off-campus. During the day, at lectures, in the canteen, library and halls of residence, it was dress-down time. A really powerful and political status quo. Women with careers could power dress. They were lucky. But in Thatcher's day, if you were a student, you only got to get all dolled up at a ball. So my fetish was back underground and under my other clothes. I wore suspenders and black stockings every day in my first year, but only my lovers and boyfriends ever knew.

'But I went crazy. I mean, really crazy. I was a very bad girl. Some weeks, I would fuck three different men. Older guys who were cool about one-night stands and buddy-fuck arrangements. I really got into musicians with long hair who played in bands. You know, that whole Whitesnake, Guns'n'Roses thing. That was my scene. So I would go to gigs and clubs in thigh boots. Patent thigh boots with Aristoc Harmony Point nylons underneath. Leather miniskirts. Big hair. Big make-up. Busty tops. And I made up for all of those wasted, frustrating years at home.

'I had a few long-term boyfriends. Two lasted for about a year. But before that, in my eighteenth year – and between those relationships, and after for about three years – I was what you could honestly have called a slut. I was really, really promiscuous. Doing a degree, well-spoken, nice middle-class girl, but a real slut. And I loved it. In some ways, it's set a pattern for life. You know, you just get addicted to the excitement of meeting strangers, of experiencing new bodies, new cocks. And my fetish drives it. Every single one of my lovers got to fuck a pretty girl wearing stockings and suspenders. And I always tried to go for the leg guys. The ones who checked out my legs when they were chatting me up. Or made flattering but naughty comments about them. Then I knew I might be meeting a like mind. Someone who wouldn't question the fact that I would sleep in my stockings all night. Even if they were shredded or covered in dry spunk.'

I swallowed the lump in my throat. Could hardly believe the strength and detail of her confessions. The absolute quality of her narration. One in a million. And she was telling me the truth. She needed to tell me. She gained nothing from this beside the benefits of a talking cure. 'And you managed to satisfy your submissive side, while wearing nylons?'

'Oh yeah. But Aristoc stopped making Harmony Points around this time. It was years before I could get real nylons again. Unless I found them in a charity shop and they fitted. Which was very rare because my legs and feet are so long. But I used Pretty Polly Nylons a lot. I liked the shine and tight fit. And always chose stockings with a high sheen that were also very sheer. Didn't really go for the matt ones. They were too functional. I liked special-occasion stockings. Flat packets again. And they made me more submissive. Nude sex was all about love and bonding for me. I'd tried it. Liked it if I was in love. But sex in stockings was about something else. About being the slut of my teenage dreams. The femme fatale. The seductress. The bad girl. And those fantasies were about variety. About fucking different men. I'm not very maternal and it's really hard for me to fall in love. So I guess I was a bit like a horny guy more than a typical girl. Somehow I just loved being ultra-feminine, but I had a sex drive like a man. Weird. In some ways I felt alone. I never met another girl like me until much later in life. Totally girly on the outside, but as promiscuous as a gay bottom underneath. And this period was all about variety. Numbers. Submitting. Penetration. The fetish scene came much later when I ended up working in London. But at uni, and for a while after, in the early nineties, my sexuality was all about fucking. You know, really hard sex with strangers and some regular lovers. I have so many stories.'

I opened a second bottle of wine. Even gave it to her in an ice bucket I kept in the kitchen. After I lit her cigarette, I made myself comfortable in my chair again.

'I met guys in bands who were real sluts. Men I could never take home. Crazy, but I was still terrified of my dad. My parents thought I was so reserved. I never seemed to have boyfriends. But I was meeting guys touring in bands and those metal clubs were so promiscuous. I could get laid every Thursday through Saturday if I liked. And sometimes I liked.

'I even sucked cocks in toilet stalls. Loved to do it on the back seat if he had a car. You know, high-heeled thigh boots spiking the ceiling, like in those magazine stories. And some guy between my thighs fucking me, or fucking my mouth. Apparently, I give amazing head. So I've been told. But I don't go in for silly techniques they teach in night school. As long as you suck with real enthusiasm. If it shows that you really love it a guy thinks you're great. They can tell.

'Not much action in my student digs, because I didn't want some of these guys to know where I lived, and people talk too. Especially girls. So I tended to go back with a man, which was a real thrill in itself. Kind of dangerous. And I loved that. A new lover from a club taking me home just for sex. And I'd be all submissive and girly. Play it a bit innocent. Make them feel all macho and strong. Make them want to really take me. Handle me. Rough me up a bit if they liked. And I loved mirrors. Loved to see a guy holding a fist full of my hair while he banged me from behind. I was slim and very pale, and it was so sexy to see a hard, muscular male body thrusting away at a pretty girl wearing too much make-up. With glossy stockings on her legs and her high heels still on like some actress in a porn movie. Men didn't even need to ask me to leave them on. I never took my shoes or stockings off, ever, unless they got carried away and wanted to lick the soles of my feet, or suck my toes naked.

'And I started to meet a lot of men with a real thing for legs. You know, they would take time to caress my legs. Lick them. Rub their erections against them. And just hold my ankles up in the air and stare at my shiny legs while they were fucking me. Like they couldn't believe their luck.

'Once or twice I went back with men who my mother would have preferred were behind bars. You know, rough trade. It was hard to get these guys to wear condoms. That took some doing. But the idea of some rough chap doing this girly, posh tart they've met in a biker bar just drove me crazy. And the reality was just as intense as the fantasy. Smell of sweat and a lot of black hair on my soft, white skin. And watching a big raw, red beasty cock just thrusting me around a bed or dirty floor. I had some real werewolves. It's how I got into spanking. One guy just got so carried away. I'd been teasing him with stocking tops all night. Giving him glimpses of dark welts on my white thighs. And he loved to see a woman's feet in stockings too. So I kept slipping a hot foot out of a shoe in the club so he could see my red toenails under the sheer black nylon.

'We both got so hot, we were in a cab before ten thirty, on our way back to his house. He was like thirty-six and I was only twenty-one. And he got so turned on with me bent over in front of his wardrobe. You know, legs apart and a posh, tarty face whispering encouragement. Very sheer black stockings on. And he'd told me to take my shoes off so he could look down at my feet while he was fucking me. And really hard too, so I kept losing my balance. But he held me upright with one hand. And unlooped his belt from his jeans at the same time as thrusting. It was the first time I was spanked. He really gave me his belt hard. Doubled over. Pulled out of me and just starting lashing my buttocks. I squealed like crazy, but it only made him do it harder. I loved it and saw him for like half a year. To get into this hardcore submission. To explore it. He started pissing on me and all kinds of things. He loved wet stockings, so we used to have sex in the shower all the time. He used to say that they were even more see-through when they were wet. Like they were really an extra layer of my skin. Clingy and wet. So I was happy to lie in the bath and get a golden shower before he fucked me.'

Patricia laughed. 'So it will come as no surprise for you to know that I now sometimes take a bath in the evening, wearing a pair of stockings I've worn all day at work. I've met men with some really interesting angles on their fetish. And it always added to mine. I saw an older guy for ages when I was twenty-three, who really got off if a woman was wearing a pair of sheer stockings over a pair of sheer tights. And it looks great. I do it all the time now. Especially if it's cold and I want to wear a skirt. Your legs look so shiny. Another guy liked to put my head in a stocking and lick my face. He was extreme, but I liked not being able to breathe properly with my face all squashed inside a stocking, while he fucked me.'

She paused. Checked her watch. Her face was flushed with drink and the excitement of recollecting her experiences. And, if I was not mistaken, she had also enjoyed my surprise and obvious rapture.

'I'm worn out. Sorry, am I making sense any more? I just started and it all came out.' She giggled. 'I'm a bit squiffy too.'

'I can't thank you enough. So many wonderful stories. I don't think I'll ever forget them. The development of your fetish, and how your accessories have become an essential part of your sex life, is just extraordinary. I'm amazed. I'm worn out too.'

She laughed, clearly thrilled by my praise. 'At least you don't think I'm a weirdo.'

'If I was a woman, I'm sure I would have been the same, though with other girls of course. But do you have to go so soon?'

'I better not be too long. But I want to see your library before I go. I've heard it's impressive.'

I nodded. 'It would be an honour to share it with one so beautiful, so honest and so damn rare.'

Patricia threw her head back and laughed. 'They broke the mould with me. They really did.' Then, from the corner of her eye, she caught me peeking again, at her legs. The sun was higher and I was dismayed to see it go, to see the sheen on her nylons slowly fade.

Patricia smiled. 'You like these, don't you?' She rotated her foot and bounced the top leg up and down.

'You know what I am, my dear.'

She nodded. 'I bet you even know what brand they are.'

'RHT nylons. Desert sand. From J. H. Anderson's Cocktail series. 1964.'

She smiled. 'That is so amazing. My husband bought them from a collector in America. They are so rare, but he insisted I wear them today. He's a huge fan of your shop and website.'

'Thank him. Thank him, Patricia, from the bottom of my heart. I envy and admire him. To share one's treasure with another hunter. Well, I'm touched. I think he might be the luckiest man alive.'

Patricia giggled. 'I know I said this was strictly a confessional. And that I'm faithful to John, unless we agree on letting me play for the website. But he doesn't mind me teasing a guy weak for my legs. He likes it. I can't fuck you. You know that. Even though I think you're cute. But John likes to hear my stories about me turning guys on with my legs and feet. So you can look closer if you like. You can even touch my legs before I go. As long as you promise not to get carried away. I trust you. You have kind eyes.' She laughed. 'You're a gentleman, I can see that. And I'm sure you're not short of sexy women who wear stockings that you can fuck. Especially in that shop you have.'

40

I hold my hands up, to deflect the suggestion. 'I'm flattered. And if you are sure, I mean really sure, how could I refuse the invitation to touch so perfect a pair of legs?'

Patricia stopped smiling. Her eyes widened and her lips parted. And I knew, in an instant, that many men had seen this face some time before they enjoyed intimate relations with her. Perhaps the most memorable sex of their lives. For a moment their ghosts and voices surrounded us in the room. I could almost hear the loud nightclub music and smell the alcohol, sweat, perfume and the cigarette fumes of her old hunting grounds. I knew it would take me a great deal of time to fully process and reimagine all that Patricia confessed that afternoon. As it should be. She was extraordinary. I was still overwhelmed by what she had narrated, irrespective of the sight of her legs. 'I can trust you, can't I? Not to get carried away?'

I nodded reassuringly.

'Go on, then. Be quick. Worship them. It'll be nice to tell John that one of the biggest leg men in the world was on his knees before my heels.'

I knelt before her, and accepted the offered foot. Cupped her heel in my left hand, placed my right hand on her calf muscle and stroked the slick leg. Then pressed my nose and lips against the top of her foot. Planted one kiss. And then a second on her toes. For the briefest moment, I allowed my tongue to flick across the nylon and thin leather strap of her shoe. Inhaled a faint trace of nail-polish ether, leather, nylon and her skin's mild musk. Closed my eyes to savour the bouquet. Thanked her again.

Patricia stood up before her chair, parted her legs and looked down at me. Sliding my open palms up and down the back of her legs, I looked up at her. She winked. Firm and yet soft. Toned muscle and pampered, shaven girl skin, covered by the thinnest, most slippery glove of barely coloured nylon. I felt my desire expand through my mind and body, making the former dizzy with lust and the latter tremble.

'I'd better stop,' I muttered.

She gave me a sweet smile. 'You better. For both our sakes.'

Reluctantly, I removed my hands from the warm area behind her knees and regained my feet. My knees crunched.

'Sounds like you have spent far too much time on your knees,' she said, laughing.

'And it hasn't been spent in church, I can assure you.'

'No. It's been spent in worship of something else, you naughty boy.' Her breath, so rich with cigarettes, wine and lipstick, I found intoxicating. Sluttish. Would have given anything to have been one of her lovers. Patricia, I will never forget you, I thought. Poor Hector. What hells has he walked through to find you, in other women?

'Come,' I said. 'Take my arm and I will show you what so few have seen.'

'The library?'

'The library.'

Of course, I could never reveal everything to her. There are parts of the collection that even a woman as imaginative as Patricia might find distasteful, though I am sure she would understand the fascination behind their inclusion in the library.

In my spare bedroom, which I keep locked, Patricia paused and glanced around in surprise, wonder, possibly disbelief. She ran a painted fingernail along the spines of nearly every motion picture released in the 1940s and 1950s that I have been able to acquire on VHS and DVD. She shook her head, saying, 'Incredible. You've seen them all.'

I nodded. 'But it's hard to keep up with so many new releases.'

'And women wear nylons in every single one?'

'That's why they belong here.' Each film meticulously logged with time-code and a synopsis, cross-referenced on database, microfiche and index-card systems, but I didn't need to bore her with the details of their storage and cataloguing. 'There is strong evidence of seamed or seam-free nylons on the legs of female characters in each and every one. In some of the films, they even put them on and take them off.'

But her fascination at my film collection was exceeded by her astonishment at the library. An archived library of periodicals, magazines, journals and books fill three shelving units on three walls; and all neatly presented in rows rising from the floor to my high Victorian ceilings. Some of the older magazines I archive in dust-free treasury boxes, and the silver blinds are always drawn to protect the paper from direct sunlight. 'It's not even all porn,' she said.

I laughed and shook my head. 'You may be surprised at what I collect for the library. I find advertisements for nylons in *Women's Journal* from the 1950s of equal interest and fascination as a sexually explicit photograph of a woman displaying her legs in *Leg Show* magazine.'

'Crazy.'

I smiled. 'You're probably thinking something along the lines of men and their hobbies?'

'Something like that. But what are they doing here?' She walks across to a bookcase and then frowns. '*The Handmaid's Tale*? Margaret Atwood?'

I smiled. 'A novel with one of the best descriptions of sheer pantyhose I have ever read.'

She shook her head again. 'And *Human Croquet* by Kate Atkinson? I've read that.'

'It contains many detailed and poetic descriptions of seamed nylons.'

'Graham Greene, John Updike, Denis Johnson, Kate Adie, John Fowles, Bernard Schlink, Richard Ford, Alena Reyes, Alan Warner – *Morvern Callar*? No way. I've read that too. They can't be fetishists?'

'I doubt it. But you can trust skilled writers to produce fresh and evocative descriptions of anything they observe. When authors turn their descriptive talents to legs and sheer hosiery, my readers alert me.'

'Readers?'

'An eclectic group of fellow devotees who happen to be inveterate readers, and collectors too.'

'What's next? I'm all out of surprise, but I bet you're not all out of surprises.'

'Well, this is the written and visual history. The artefacts are next. But before we leave, your taped interview will go over there.'

'With all the others. You've got hundreds.'

'But less than a dozen are from women and I've interviewed three hundred enthusiasts. I only keep the genuine. Which, inevitably, are the most interesting and well-articulated stories. Same for the written matter. I have many letters too.'

'Is that a fridge?' She nodded towards the metal cabinet, the size of a double wardrobe.

I led her to what I affectionately call the cryogenic unit. It is a stainless-steel cabinet with deep metal drawers that slide out from specially designed cabinets fixed closely together. 'It's chilly in here.'

'Temperature controlled. Dust free.' I pointed to the thermostat just inside the door. In the way some men collect cigars, or wine, I collect hosiery, and the preservation and order of the packages and their contents is of paramount importance. Most of the packages have never been opened. At night I often dream of sparking wires behind the skirting boards, and wake sweating.

Patricia pulled an aluminium drawer out of its interior wall unit. 'Wow. You must have everything. Everything.'

'Unfortunately, I can only dream of a complete collection. Though it is my intention to acquire an unopened packet of every single pair of sheer stockings and tights ever produced.'

Astonished, she turned her pretty face towards me, blinked, then shook her head and smiled. 'How many do you have?'

'I began collecting in 1984, so I have a complete collection of every manufacturer's brand and each series produced within that brand from that date. There have been so many in Europe alone, I have to store the majority of them in those packing cases over there. In the large box to your left you will find the Aristoc collection. Pretty Polly, Charnos, Dior, La Perla are all stored in there too, and so on. It is fortunate that sealed hosiery is easy to store. But acquisition is another matter. Before 1984, the collection is patchy and getting harder to complete as each year passes. But still, this may be the best collection of hosiery in the world.'

'Why not have an exhibition?'

I smiled. 'I am shy. Can you believe I still worry about what people will think of me?' But going public is something I am considering. And, I believe, historically, the collection will serve some purpose in the interest of fashion, of the development and marketing of female accessories over the last fifty years. So an exhibition may justify itself. Though, of course, it will also be a testament to one man's private sexual mania. And it is that interpretation that makes me cautious.

'But you have the shop. And the Internet site. And you did the coffee-table book. People already know.'

'No they don't. I am a very private man. My likeness has never been fully revealed in connection with any of my business ventures or products. I am merely a shadow who flits behind the scenes. My employees at Sheer Delight don't even know of the Leg Lover website and in the galleries there, my face is obscured.'

'You'd make a good villain in a superhero movie. Nylon Man.'

I laughed. 'What would I do?'

'I don't know. Tie women up? Cocoon their entire bodies in nylon?'

'Now, there's an idea.' Patricia was probably ignorant of the Nylon Binders, led by a gentleman in Hamburg and another in Ohio who had been doing just that for years. And only now had their craft begun to surface in online circles of fellow enthusiasts. And I was sure the Binders would have loved to work with her. But it is probably better that most people do not know of them; their work is to be studied and admired by the absolute connoisseur, not to be gaped at by the merely inquisitive. They have probably mapped the furthest extreme of legal leg worship.

'Where are the real nylons? John told me you have the most incredible collection. He's seen pictures on the Net. Are they in the fridge?' We turned our attention back to the cryogenic unit.

Raising one eyebrow, I peered down at Patricia's legs. I had much to thank John for; it was an honour to have made contact with such an enthusiast. I smiled at Patricia and bent down to open one of the bottom drawers. 'They are indeed. This holds my most prized collection: the original nylons. From the 1940s to the 1960s, and beyond in some cases. Some of the earlier ones may be the very last of their kind. Please be careful.'

Patricia slid the drawer all the way out. Tense, I watched her carefully, and knew I would only fully relax once the drawer was shut again and my rarest, most diaphanous treasures were sealed from the light.

'My God,' she said. 'Oh, they are so beautiful. Look at the packets!' She began to free them from their secure berths. I would have much straightening to do once she'd gone. 'And the names! Godiva. English Rose. Hi Jinks. Sheer Mischief. Miss Brettle. Park Lane. Tiara. Minion. Morley. You've got them all. Even Gloriana. Oh look, Caprice, Arizona, Fay. I wish they were mine. I'd love to wear them all.'

I moved closer, unable to blink as she rifled the packets and pried them loose to get a better look at the artwork under the lights. I delighted at her enthusiasm, but feared it also. I didn't like them being handled. The irony did not escape me, but I am what I am.

'They are works of art. I mean, some of them are in the old boxes. They're ancient. Where did you get them from?'

'Everywhere. Old warehouses, second-hand shops, auctions, other collectors, factory closures. Some are even donations.'

'You have to show them off.'

I smiled, and encouraged her to close the drawer. 'There's more, that only a handful of enthusiasts have ever seen. But, in return for your own wonderful contribution to the archive, it would be an honour to share them with you.' I felt myself blush. 'Though, don't be too hard on me.'

'Why would I be?'

I shrugged. 'Maybe you'll think I've gone too far. I'll show you. But you will have to wear gloves if you handle anything.'

'Gloves?' she asked. 'How rare are they?'

'You'll see.' I closed the cryogenic unit with the usual sense of relief, and led her out of the archive and back to the living room. I removed the original signed print of an Elmer Batters photograph from the wall to reveal the steel door of a safe, flush with the plaster. I twirled the combination dial.

'In a safe? Do they have real diamond seams or something?'

I laughed. 'No, it's not a case of what they are made of, or even how they are made. And few of them are even in their original packets. They are all standard, one hundred per cent nylon, or bri-nylon stockings like the others you've just seen. The value of these stems from who wore them, or at least who owned them.'

'No.' She stared at me in genuine amazement. Sucked in her breath. 'But how do you know they're authentic?'

'Put these on.' I handed her a pair of white cotton gloves. Then removed four of the twelve flat boxes from the neat stack inside my safe. We looked each other in the eye. Her face was full of a curious excitement, perhaps the same emotion that transfixed her beautiful young features in Aunt Mo Mo's bedroom when she was a teenage girl.

'We will begin with Marlene Dietrich.'

'No.'

'Yes.'

'No.'

'Yes. Look. But please, please be gentle with them. I don't want the runs to get any worse.' I removed the lid of the box and then gently raised a pair of grey nylon stockings from the rustling white tissue paper. 'Put out your hands. Palm upwards.' Then I draped the smoky fabric across Patricia's hands. 'I acquired them years ago from a curator in Berlin. When Dietrich died many of her effects were donated to the cinema museum. Clothing, letters, cosmetics, that sort of thing. And through an intermediary, I acquired some of her actual nylons from the estate. Three pairs.'

Patricia stared at the stockings in her hands. Then looked at me. 'Who else you got in there?'

'Grace Kelly.'

'No.'

I nodded. 'Judy Garland. Monroe. Doris Day.'

'How can you be sure they are genuine?'

'You'd be amazed what lovers take as keepsakes. Or the jilted, or their servants, obsessive fans, hotel porters. Anything the famous touch has value for someone.' I took the nylons back from her and returned them to their silent, dust-free nest of tissue.

'That's kind of spooky though.'

I nodded. 'It is. But don't find it too spooky. You may tell John, but please, do be discreet.'

She nodded. 'Yes, of course. And you've got plenty on me after our little chat. God, I can't believe I said so much. I think you have a talent for finding things out about ladies and their stockings.'

I smiled and was thoroughly flattered by such a compliment; she'd identified a skill I'd been nurturing for most of my adult life. 'I certainly hope so. And it would seem so.'

I led Patricia away to the kitchen – she wanted water and then coffee. A very satisfying afternoon and viewing, though I must admit to being a trifle disappointed that she found my celebrity hosiery 'spooky'. Did her ex-boyfriend not pilfer her underwear? And I'm surprised she could underestimate male obsession. I was relieved I had not exposed her to the royal collection – particularly the Diana set. With such wonderful legs and an immaculate taste in hosiery, combined with the relentless betrayals that hounded her life, they were actually the easiest celebrity hose to acquire. And as for the television-presenter album, it would have been unwise to open a collection of artefacts culled from the still living and famous. So the extensive set of hosiery pilfered from a variety of news-readers, television presenters and actresses would remain a secret. It cost me dearly to acquire such, but every work-experience researcher and wardrobe assistant in theatre and television I have approached has had their price.

As I closed the safe, Patricia must have been looking more closely at my collection of art. 'Who is that? She looks familiar.' I turned and saw that she was pointing at the predominantly black and white photographs arranged at regular intervals around the pale walls. 'I'm sure I know her. But from where?' she asked.

Even though I look at that photograph each and every day I am at home, it never fails to affect me. Never more so than when a female guest, filling my living space with her perfume and graces, as Patricia did that late spring afternoon, draws my attention to the photograph. Then, the power of the picture seems to intensify to the point that I actually experience a momentary, sharp but exhilarating ache in my gut – the very seat of obsession. I think the heart overrated as an organ when it comes to adoration.

The girl in the portrait Patricia referred to is sitting on a simple wooden chair and the background is as stark and white and featureless as the end of existence. Stretched out nonchalantly, her long and perfect legs are coated in shiny nylon. Taut in black, fully fashioned stockings – the true goddesses of hosiery and the greatest pinnacle of achievement in both man-made fabric production and female fashion design. In my opinion, no other garment has so transformed natural female beauty as the sheer nylon stocking.

The model's feet are long and exquisitely formed. Painted toenails just visible beneath the reinforced toes of her hose. Her feet are mounted on black sandals, in turn elevated by pencil-thin heels, and manacled in place by two spaghetti straps of patent leather – one across the bridge of her toes, the other circling her dark ankle like the finest bracelet.

The model appears to feel bashful at the very beauty and exposure of her divine legs – as if they have genuinely astonished her and provoked more attention than she can cope with. It's as if the haunting quality of her own legs overwhelms her. It must have been one of the very first times she modelled. Because in time she learned to use those legs: walked more confidently in commercials and along catwalks, exposed them in photo-shoots and on film sets, and manipulated their presentation more than any other part of her long, elegant and beautiful body. Oh yes, in time she grew to be less reticent. Even cruel, I have been led to believe. Which, I must confess, charges my fascination with an even greater electricity. Had she married and had children, I would have felt a swift and profound loss, that would have turned into a tremendous relief. Knowing her legs belonged to another would be a blessing. Though such beauty can never be the preserve of one man, especially when the beauty is empowered by so much adoration. It is a beauty that will endure and astonish whenever a visual record of it is observed.

She works under the name of Nylon Dahlia and she creates awe in me.

In the photograph, I feel her large eyes have a sad beauty, but I cannot read the smile. Is it dismissive? For it suggests a playful indifference to the onlooker. Her hairstyle has changed several times but always returns to the blue-black bob with a straight fringe she wore in that picture, referencing the fifties and their styles, which she adores. I have seen her photographed or filmed in little else beside pencil skirts, nylons and high-heeled shoes. And she is a great fan of hats – chic, elegant haber-dashery with veils to give the innate mystery of her stare a supernatural quality I struggle to look too long into.

She represents the reason I have never married. She is my Holy Grail. An archetype and icon that suggests the most intense pleasure on earth. The familiarity and routine of conventional relationships will always be thrown into a particularly unflattering light for as long as I look at the Nylon Dahlia in my private gallery here. Twelve photographs of her feet, her legs, or her form in its entirety. She is a vision that transports me out of this world.

When I finish, the doctor's face has not changed. There is not a suggestion of shock, or outrage, or pity in those cool eyes. If anything, I suspect an eagerness to hear more. A sense of suspense is almost tangible in this room when we meet. And of course she would be able to tell if I was lying by the merest inflections of movement in my posture and eyes.

She can handle her depravity, this doctor. I like that. And it's a very effective tool of discouraging self-censorship in her client. An effective means of encouraging me to continue.

I exhale loudly, dramatically. This talking cure is exhausting. It leaves me feeling curiously drained, but uplifted.

'Thank you, Al. Again I feel we are making excellent progress.'

'You do?'

'You sound surprised. What were you expecting?'

'I don't know. Maybe a bit of input about what a sick, crazy pervert I am.'

She smiles, but doesn't answer directly. She won't be led, this one. I should know better. 'What you think and what you feel is important. At this stage, I just want to listen. But maybe you feel you are not getting value for money.'

She's saying this in good humour, but I leap to her defence. 'No. Nothing like that. This is doing me the world of good, I think. I like coming here. I look forward to it.' Though I don't tell her that during my journey here on the bus, I had a fantasy that when she opened the front door, I immediately saw, beneath the hem of her trousers, that her long, pale feet had been freshly pedicured, the nails glossy with a new coat of scarlet polish. I chided myself, and once within the sanctum, these thoughts I managed to banish. This is one place my fetish should not interfere.

'Next time, though, I wonder if we could digress before you tell me about what followed your meeting with Patricia. Maybe you could tell me about the first few times you realised you were so attracted to women's legs and their coverings.'

Coverings. I like the way she said that. With tact. Coverings. A *neutral* word. Practical. Not a word I would have used to describe the accessories that have a narcotic effect upon me. But a choice of diction effective in maintaining her professional, detached tone.

So I will have to dig deep, and vary the chronology of my narrative with subplots from my past. I tingle with excitement at the thought. Yes, there are things I have told no one. Defining experiences, no matter how subtle, that I have never revealed. Dreams and encounters I kept to myself for fear of ridicule, and perhaps to also maintain the edge of the illicit, and to sharpen the very poignancy of my desires.

Secrets. Hoards and collections and hidden photographs and private liaisons: these are the things that keep a fetish alive and fresh; that cultivate its evolution and prolong its lifespan. Resistance to them is always futile but it is partly through resistance that these secrets are made.

Three

Her face composed in a studied openness, that suggests her interest in me and the sense that she actually cares, I am immediately struck by an understanding of how therapy can become addictive. It's the attention, the sympathy, the lack of hostility, the opportunity to hog the mic. As for its benefits, despite the relief of unburdening, I will reserve my judgement.

Today, the doctor once again wears a trouser suit. Simple and black with a white blouse beneath the jacket. On her feet, she wears low-heeled but elegant shoes and opaque black tights that are slightly glossy under the sunlight that streams through the blind behind her head. Today she is safe from my transference and voyeuristic scrutiny: hosiery without transparency has no erotic value for me. But then leg men form a subculture of much diversity. Of course, we are all leg and foot bigots in that we believe our own peccadilloes and special interests are superior to all others. I would suggest that half of the fetishists I have come across prefer the leg and foot bare. The other half tend to prefer adornments and accessories. Of course leg and foot shape and the exact nature of the accessory create endless additional strata of preference and taste within the general subject. Some men are obsessed by shoes and feet alone, others cannot bear an unshod foot, some can only desire a woman in a particular type of hosiery and footwear, while many more need the object of desire to be engaged in some activity, like trampling or squashing. For me, an appreciation of the bare leg and foot developed later. Not until my late thirties did I ever show much interest in the unclothed lower limbs of women. And in my teens and twenties, I was only interested in dark or black stockings. Flesh tones in hosiery were too innocuous. But by my late twenties, I began to enjoy the sight of them as much as the darker shades. We change; our fetishes evolve. Sexuality is fluid. Now, in my forties, I can appreciate legs and feet bare or clothed, but prefer the latter. But, curiously, fishnets, patterned hosiery and opaque hosiery, no matter how expensive or exquisitely produced, leave me cold. Sheepishly, I've often hinted to new girlfriends about my preference for hosiery without giving too much away, only for them to show up for a date in fishnets and high heels. It's been hard to contain my disappointment. I've met other attractive women who quickly confess to hating heels and 'girly stuff'. I know from the start the relationship will go nowhere. Others, who may not be considered particularly attractive by the brutal canon of popular taste, have met me wearing good sheer hosiery and high-heeled shoes or boots without a single hint or prompt from me, and my fascination in them has been more intense and lengthy than in women considered traditionally beautiful.

But as for the pop sock, it actually makes me experience a sense of repulsion.

'Can you remember the first time you felt an attraction to legs?' Doctor Kim talks slowly, softly, as if coaxing a shy animal out from its den. She wants to win its trust, lure it forwards and not send it scampering back into the undergrowth; particularly at this point when the most sensitive and precious stories are called for. An adult mind is better at dealing with its attractions and dislikes, no matter how strange, but a developing consciousness can recoil and experience a greater sense of anguish at its sense of difference.

'As far as I am aware, it was always there. Even in my earliest memories I was particularly aware of the legs of adult women. Neighbours, friends of my parents, even relatives. And on television. Especially commercials for hosiery. Catalogues too. Pictures in magazines. Illustrations in books. I used to look up the skirts of dolls to see the legs.

'And when young, before I had anything but an ephemeral understanding of sex, I experienced the same dream for years. It was very strange.'

I notice a perceptible narrowing of her eyes at this mention of a dream. Dreams seem to hold tremendous weight with analysts. Though I would never underestimate the conscious act of will, and would perhaps put more of an emphasis on it. Dreams are too intangible to me, though this one is specific and telling.

'Hovering, but gradually descending from a tremendous height, I found myself above a wriggling forest of legs. There was no space between each pair of vertical thighs. This was a strange land in which the living ground was made up entirely of upside-down female legs with their toes pointing at the domed sky. Moving slowly like the feelers of anemones in a rock pool, each shapely leg was either stirred by a breeze or existed purely to drift through the warm air of the dream world. Each leg was transformed by a thin film of hosiery. To the distant reaches of my eyesight, there were hundreds of thousands of attractive legs and feet clad in sheer tights. But no two shades of leg were ever the same. An infinite variety of coloured nylon stretched into eternity.

'I would awake flushed and tingling with a longing I could not satisfy, but with a sense that the future held a great deal of promise. It was the main reason I wanted to grow up. To get my hands on these legs. I could not will the dream to occur, but often during sleep I would return to the leg forest. And I would descend to the point of being able to look at the pale toes through the sheer tights, but was never able to touch. I would wake up whenever I reached out.'

Doctor Kim nods, thoughtful, before her intelligent features momentarily stiffen in a pensive frown. 'You clearly remember being attracted to legs at such a young age?'

I nod. 'Absolutely. And particularly my teachers when I was at school. Come to think of it, I was always fascinated by older women. Irrespective of whether they were kind or stern, liked me or found me a nuisance, if they wore high heels, boots and sheer hosiery, I was instantly infatuated. At school I was invariably the teacher's pet if she was older and well heeled. And they never knew why I was so attentive. I can also remember my first touch.'

'Touch?'

'Of a woman's leg. A grown woman's leg. They always enchanted me when presented in fine hosiery. Something I could just stare at and admire. I'd be pacified by them, but almost unable to speak for shyness. But it wasn't long before I managed, perhaps even manipulated, my first caress.'

Always difficult to make a start, but once you begin, the talking cure really becomes euphoric. A tremendous release that can leave you mentally, emotionally and physically exhausted but relieved as if some great pressure has been removed from one's shoulders and head. This dialogue with Doctor Kim contains all the dangerous pleasure of sharing a secret. And the longer it has been kept and locked away, the greater the satisfaction of sharing. Though after sharing, I have begun to feel a sense of loss.

But, bound by discretionary clauses, she is forbidden to share my revelations or reveal my identity. Or to outwardly judge me. She may be getting paid for her time, but I fancy I am better off at the end of our hour.

You see, I'd already regressed my memory of my own volition. Such is the inevitability of self-absorption and grotesque self-interest of which I am guilty. Though it is one thing to remember and replay a memory – which is always partly false, because I always see myself from a fly-on-the-wall perspective as opposed to reliving the moment through my own young eyes – and something else to actually describe and articulate an experience.

But I would do my best with my story of Penny, the babysitter.

For about a year, my mother would go out and pick my brother up from school, which meant I must have been four years old. It was one of my first years of living memory and I spent the day at home with mother, waiting for my elder sibling's return. With my father at work, I was sent next door to be looked after by one half of a younger, childless couple – the Martins – while my mother was collecting my brother. And Penny Martin I remember distinctly. She reminded me of the actress from *Carry On Screaming*. Attractive, with long black hair and very pale skin, who I can remember only wearing short dresses and sheer black tights. It was the late sixties and tights had all but replaced nylons and the relevant scaffolding required as undergarments to hold stockings in place.

Penny used to both entertain me and feed me fish fingers and baked beans, or faggots and peas with mashed potato, for about an hour. Dessert would always be served in a glass bowl: Angel Delight with chocolate sprinkles from a little plastic dispenser she kept on the spice rack. My mother cooked exactly the same thing with the same ingredients, though their food tasted different. I remember that clearly. I also remember they had a dark-brown corduroy suite in the living room and weird wooden African masks on the walls. The ones with black hair attached gave me nightmares until my early teens. But that was the only downside. A few bad dreams was nothing compared to the powerful and enduring resonance of my first and completely free leg show.

Before she fed me tea, Penny would amuse me. She liked having a kid around, and by the time my family moved out of Walmer Road, she'd had two of her own. Even back then, I can remember peering at her legs for the hour or so I remained in her care. They were longer than my entire body. And she was the first woman I can remember painting her toenails. Usually purple. And to what I suspect was Neil Diamond or Elton John on her record player, Penny would place me on her slippery knee, so I was facing her. She would hold my hands and bounce me up and down as if I was riding a horse.

Straddling a wide adult female thigh and being ridden to market fascinated me. Sometimes, she would let go of my hands and see how long I could hold on. Both of us engulfed by paroxysms of laughter, we would play this game until she tired of it. Of course, I never did. I couldn't exhaust my interest in the game because of her legs and the transparent dark fabric covering them that I clutched at with my chubby fingers while in the nylon saddle. I remember her squealing and saying, 'Don't you ladder my tights, you little monkey.' I never did, but I groped handfuls and slid my tiny palms the length of her thighs. Peculiar boy.

And I remember another game I insisted we play, every time I was left under her supervision. Until school intervened, that great spoiler of fun, and my evenings were no longer spent with Penny next door. In the second game, I would roll about on the patterned, brown and orange carpet while she tickled me under the arms and on the tummy with her stockinged feet. She would sit on the couch, in her miniskirt, with her gigantic legs stretching down to me, and be genuinely delighted by the giggling, blond boy under her soles. Occasionally, if I managed to seize one of her feet in my snatching paws, she would rub the other large, slippery foot over my face until I released the captured foot.

I would then sit in the kitchen on a stool and watch her legs as she made my tea. Of course, she was my first love. The recipient of my first crush. And I admired but resented her husband Keith, who drove an MG while wearing leather gloves. I remember longing for adulthood until it hurt, so I could have my own Penny.

'And then there was Mrs Skinner. A teacher.'

The doctor nods. We have time for another tale. Something we'll need plenty of until I empty.

Mrs Skinner wore stockings every day, even during the hottest periods of the summer. And she liked to complement them with peep-toe high-heeled shoes. Sometimes with a small bow over the section of the upper that covered all but the top of three toes. My favourite pair were made from black suede with a gold trim on the open part of the upper, with a red inner, save for the little gold label printed in the inner sole.

We all thought her odd at school. Heavy make-up, a beauty spot, a white-blonde bob out of mainstream fashion since the thirties, but an absolutely classic hairstyle that has looked chic in any era since. Imperious of face, with a stern, handsome quality I have since been enthralled by. Short-tempered, frighteningly witty and very hard on the girls. But she did have her favourites, and I was one of them. She even hugged and kissed me on my last day of lower school.

Though even a teacher as strict and experienced and clever as Mrs Skinner could be fooled by my young and eager face during every form period and English lesson. She must have thought me motivated, well behaved, smart, and thrilled by her teaching methods. But, if anything, this period of my education was marred by a propensity to daydream at such length, I reached the age of eighteen still unable to complete even rudimentary long division. I calculate about four years in total of my schooling was lost to inner worlds, and of the lessons taken during that period I can remember nothing. But with Mrs Skinner, I did concentrate. Not on her lessons, but on her legs.

Utterly obedient, desperate to please, engrossed in her every reading and instruction, and infatuated into a trance-like state by her very presence, it was no wonder she told my mother during one parent–teacher evening that she wished she 'had a classroom full of Algernons'.

When reading Dahl, Tolkien, Kipling or C. S. Lewis to us, she liked to sit on her desk. Legs crossed, chin raised, glasses with thin black frames adding a slight magnification to her charcoal eye-shadow and clever green eyes, she would cast her voice over the terrified, bored, sullen or sleeping pupils arranged in rows before her desk. I sat in the left-hand, front corner of the room, directly before her desk. In fact, the ends of our desks touched.

And as she read, her shins and knees and feet would be no more than three feet from my face. If I could lean further forwards, resting on my elbows, I could get within two feet and directly inhale the musk she sprayed down her shins each morning and in the staffroom at midday. And whenever she was seated, I would spend every second of the lesson staring at her legs.

I was positioned close enough to see the actual knit of her stockings – myriad minuscule squares that form the net of transparent hosiery. When she changed her position and recrossed her legs, I would be ready, my eyes trained like a sniper's to peer up and into the shadowy up-skirt region. Ears full of the music of rustling slip and rasping nylon, I would get brief glimpses of long thighs slick with hosiery; pale thighs above the dark bands of her stocking tops; dark creases flexing behind her knees. She was old school, with a penchant for vintage glamour; she actually wore stockings. My first real glimpse of stocking tops in the field.

And she was also the first woman to confirm my love of shoe dangling. After the small raspy sound only a shoe can make when partially dropped from a female foot, she would bend her toes back and balance the weight of the high-heeled shoe from the bridge of her toes. Show off her tender sole, dark with damp nylon and the secret intimate interior of her shoe – the material showing signs of wear, the label faded by the friction of a warm heel, the instep broadened by the entry and removal of her long feet. Dangled before my transfixed stare, she would then bounce the foot up and down, gently, idly, absentmindedly. Then, with a faint *clumf* sound, it would be flicked back up and on to her heel. Sometimes she would press down on the floor with that leg and press the shoe more firmly in place around her foot. I remember all of the details. Memorised them. The thin wrinkles of black nylon at the base of her shin when she bent her toes back; the sheen of sunlight on the polished glass of her nylons at around two in the afternoon; the smack of her lips, the scent of her make-up and perfume about my head, like an intoxicating cloud of pollen; the faint lines about her eyes and mouth; the heavy bust in red cashmere; the exhilaration of her roar at a miscreant; the smoky laugh at one of my obsequious asides.

And she actually began my collection, with a pair of discarded dark-tan stockings. Laddered on a splinter at the front of a wooden chair, removed outside the classroom, then returned in her hand, bunched up and pushed down inside the metal bin beside her desk. I watched that bin as if it contained a bundle of used bank-notes that only I was aware of. Until the afternoon break, when she hurried to the staffroom, on her bare, pale legs, to smoke and drink coffee. My classmates rushed outside and I stayed behind, feigning a momentary distraction from something inside my desk, then went and rummaged in that bin like a bum with a taste for discarded hamburger.

I retrieved that silken ball of translucent magic, slipped it inside my pullover and then stashed it inside my school bag with the deftness of an illusionist with a stream of coloured handkerchiefs up his sleeve.

She made me bad. She made me be bad. And I liked to pretend she knew. Knew and enjoyed my fascination with her pretty legs.

And as she operated a system in which the most successful pupils were promoted gradually down the aisles to the front of the classroom, I made sure I stayed in first place, right next to her desk. For all the wrong reasons. But as most of my classmates were so terrified of her, I now believe they deliberately underperformed to stay as far away from her desk as possible, thus facilitating the illusion of my superior intelligence. That is, beside a few clever swot girls who had no interest in her legs but were naturally competitive.

But Mrs Skinner grew to like my company at the front, down by her sharp heels with the brass tips. Always ready with an answer, or a guess at best, to her questions, there would be no awkward silences with me beaming up at her. And if I'd been informed of some misdeed by another child, planned for lunchtime, or after school, she would always appear to foil the robbery or beating as if she were a beneficiary of telepathic powers. I was her odious little spy and, even to this day, I still cringe at the thought of selling out my classmates just to please the older woman who wore stockings and high heels. I was incorrigible and destined to get worse.

To my lasting shame, I even ratted on my best friend, Stephen Hartley.

Overweight, a constant figure of ridicule, excused from sports due to asthma, Stephen Hartley had few happy memories of his school days. But at least, in me, he had a friend. An inseparable companion for at least three years. Frighteningly clever for a thirteen-year-old, and very generous with his open exercise books and whispered answers, Stephen helped me to maintain academic standards high enough to remain close to Skinner's painted toenails and glossy calves. But I sold him out like a rat to please her. *Her*. Everything was about pleasing her when I was in her classroom. When she was pleased, her legs would cross and whisper within reach of my curious, greedy eyes.

And on one summer afternoon, during the lesson right after the lunch break when Mrs Skinner was called away by a messenger, the classroom erupted into a savage pencil-eraser battle, in which Selina Goodyear was hit painfully in the eye with one of the hard, gritty red erasers designed for removing ink from paper. An eraser from Stephen's wooden stationery case with the brass hinges. He was the only pupil likely to have such a sophisticated eraser. But the object had left my hand like a bullet targeted at some whooping acquaintance on the other side of the room. Poor Selina was merely caught in the crossfire.

Of course, Mrs Skinner was furious. Not so much at the shock of seeing Selina's red and weeping eye, but at the temerity of her class to noisily misbehave in her absence. Before her return, Mr Craven was forced to step in from the Geography room next door, which made it doubly embarrassing for her. Selina was sent to the nurse with two friends, one on either elbow like guide dogs. And the interrogation began. We would all be confined in the classroom after school until the culprit owned up and confessed his guilt. Stephen and I exchanged looks with our pale faces. But when the offending projectile was retrieved for Mrs Skinner, and the initials S. H. discovered on the flip-side of the object, her attention turned, as did every grinning face, to our little corner of the classroom.

Of course, I was never under suspicion. Not the favourite, never. In her cold and painted eyes I could do no wrong. But poor Hartley had no such defence.

Her demand that he stand was discharged like a cannon shell. It made every pupil in that classroom feel the peculiar sickness mixed with excitement that precedes punishment at school. Nothing feminine about her voice when enraged. Never failed to surprise me. And Stephen stood, light on his feet for a big lad, and even lighter at that moment as he couldn't feel his legs for fear and shame.

His face was trembling and ashen-white when it looked down at me and pleaded for help. Of course, he couldn't finger me publicly – no one liked a grass – but he must have expected I would confess, to save him, to see justice served. I looked away; couldn't meet his eye; stared at the peep-toe apertures in Mrs Skinner's shoes instead.

He was taken, though dragged is a more accurate description of his journey, to the front of the classroom, and turned to face the blackboard.

No one could breathe, or move, when Mrs Skinner's red nails clawed at her desk to retrieve the wooden metre rule. I cannot remember what she screamed at him, but I do remember her face colouring a bright red under her heavy foundation. And he began to cry before the first blow whumped across the grey seat of his school trousers. We all jumped. And winced. The second struck the back of his legs. The third broke the rule across his lower back.

In my throat, something the same size as a small apple refused to sink. But I cannot remember desiring Mrs Skinner more than at that moment. She was dangerous, all powerful, beautiful.

Hartley was sent to the back of the classroom, where he remained for the rest of the school year, and Janine Tima was moved up to his still-warm chair. I was never as sharp again in class after his removal from the favourites' row; Janine stubbornly refused to let me copy her answers and there were no more whispered answers to the teacher's questions from my sidekick.

To my shame, I never did own up to hurling the eraser like a flat stone cast to skim across a pond. To his credit, he never held it against me. Even though, for the next two years, he would be known as the 'Weeping Whale' by every child in the school.

But I learned early that I would stop at little to get my fix, to feast my eyes and fill my belly with a fetish that was gradually influencing the most important decisions in my life. If I am honest, the list is long: I pursued many unsuitable girlfriends with pretty legs who favoured the wearing of sheer hosiery, at the expense of opportunities with more compatible partners; I would only consider work in an environment in which women displayed their legs, especially in high heels and skirts – which accounted for years in menial positions in retail, legal administration and finally a brief stint as a cabin steward for an airline; I began the leg library and collection, and spent an increasing proportion of my time and money indulging my fetish. Simply, my sexuality became a vocation. A life's work. And Mrs Skinner was one of my first muses.

Four

Trousers again. They look new. Black and loose and made from a silky fabric. I was cramping the doctor's style. She clearly liked restrained elegance, but was more of a skirts and dresses girl. Especially with those slim legs. Old school. And yet I was coercing her to change her style by the very nature of my ailment. As if subjected to some Islamic scrutiny, she's also covered her feet with a charming pair of well-made ankle boots. I wonder how much thought she has to invest in her outfits before we meet.

Today, I decide to talk about that significant day when my fortunes changed. To continue from where I'd left off with my interview with Patricia. We'd had a Freudian digression, but I want to work through the course of events that led me to the doctor's couch in the first place. And the day I interviewed Patricia was a fair reflection of my life and preoccupations at the time, now somewhat subdued in light of what has happened, of what I have lost through my maniacal obsession with legs and feet.

So after Patricia left my flat, I needed fresh air and an opportunity to prolong my state of heightened arousal. Even after her confessions, I was left not so much dissatisfied as restless. Patricia's stories were not enough. Neither was her invitation to caress her legs. You may think I would have retired for an afternoon of gleeful self-pleasure, accompanied by the replaying of my recording of her confessed misdemeanours. But no. I launched myself into London on a bright day, with good visibility, in order to walk to Sheer Delight, my boutique in Kensington, and one of the few businesses yet to succumb to retail franchises in that part of West London.

Of course, when times were better, I did have opportunities to expand the store into a chain, but decided that one business and three employees was time-consuming enough, and I decided against diluting the concentration of quality and good leg karma I had achieved with one store. I had no desire to become the fetish equivalent of Sock Shop.

I would have enough time to get to the store before it closed at six, and would enquire as to whether any of the girls fancied a drink after work. You see I am a glutton. Always have been. This addict needed further stimulation, possibly even an overdose. And Sheer Delight is the only business in London where one could be certain of seeing the feet of the female staff shod in high heels, with legs reskinned in sheer hosiery every single day of the year, regardless of the temperature. Sure, Agent Provocateur has a dress code for the shop assistants, but the girls there sometimes wear fishnets or micro-nets, which I forbid. Tingling with excitement, I still longed to admire the legs of my handsome staff in something very fine and slightly shiny. Needed to would be a more accurate assessment of my yearning. But then, research is an essential component of fetishism.

Because a hoard offers one kind of pleasure to the collector: printed, visual and physical evidence to inspire private pleasures and musings; props to fire the imagination; mementos to relive past exploits; objects to be adored and examined and analysed. But there is also another kind of pleasure. Stronger delights are to be found of a far more accidental nature, whose relics exist solely in the mind. For ever.

For my particular weakness – some may say a shortcoming, and at times it is the most distracting burden – the street, the shop, public transport, the escalator, the waiting room, bar, club, or aisle seat on an aeroplane can offer infinitely superior thrills to those gained by leafing through photographs, watching old films or reading memoirs. Is it not better for an ornithologist to come across his desired object of feathery, singing delight in the wild, than to admire its plumage and ever silent pose behind glass at a natural history museum? I think so.

Of course, the pleasure of which I speak also costs nothing and is founded on pure chance. Not at all limited by the awkwardness involved in asking a recalcitrant lover or begrudging wife to wear the specific item of interest. But it is a free and unlimited supply of erotic stimulation existing, out there, in the everyday shop, street, train and office. Viewings costing you as much as the air you breathe. And strangers are always more fascinating than the familiar and the known. I often wonder how many of the women of our world are fully aware of the fetishist's narcotic, irrepressible scrutiny. Of the profound interest and desire that exists for their attractively presented legs and feet.

Which leg lover hasn't secretly admired the pretty office worker with her silky feet withdrawn from court shoes? Or the traveller sitting opposite in a train carriage or bus seat, her skirt raised as she sits, her shapely knees and slender legs crossed before us? Or the motorist alighting from a car seat, one foot in the road, the other in the foot well, her knees parted, her inner thighs revealed?

And during my stroll, I intended to take full advantage of the leg show London's girls offered that afternoon. For spring is the finest month for the leg voyeur of my persuasion. The bare leg and foot admirer prefers the summer for obvious reasons. But the hosiery and heel man prefers the cooler months when women are encouraged to layer their lower limbs with a second, attractive skin of see-through insulation. Too cold and wet, and the ladies opt for trousers and hide themselves away – though the tight leather knee boot has a particular allure unmatched by any other boot, in my eyes. One's vision is not only drawn to admire the aesthetics – the texture and shape of the booted leg, but compelled to dream of the pale, scented treasure within. But the spring and the autumn are the seasons I favour over all others. And for good reason. Evident immediately as I walk the length of Westbourne Grove.

Alighting from a Mini Cooper GT parked beside the post office is a striking blonde girl in her mid-twenties: suited in a black jacket and skirt, with a silky cream blouse open to the sternum of her chest; highlights in her shoulder-length blonde hair; heavy make-up, big red lips and a good athletic bust – small but firm and pronounced in a well-chosen bra. But my discreet stare does not linger long on her pretty face and outfit upstairs. Instead, it diverts – without a blink, lest I should miss even an instant of her accidental revelation – to her briefly parting legs as she clambers from the vehicle no more than four feet from my angled face. A moment earlier or later and the opportunity would have been missed. Sometimes the gods are kind.

Ultra-sheer, nude hold-up stockings with a faint shimmer in the late-afternoon sun are momentarily glimpsed all the way up her legs to their elasticated, golden tops. In less than a second before that silken valley of thigh is closed from me, for ever, my mind photographed and stored the image for future perusal. I remember a mole on the inside of her left thigh and the white satin strip of her panty flash as her black skirt slithered back to the top third of her thigh. It helped to cement the recollection.

Stocking tops: result. No need to wonder – though that is a pleasure all of its own – whether the subject is wearing tights or stockings. My curiosity was instantly gratified. Though my imagination was left wanting, and began an immediate visual narrative of the pretty young thing dipping her toes into a ruffle of nylon, rolling her stockings up her legs that morning, then zipping her shapely calves into the boots. Was a boyfriend present? And if so, did he notice her dressing ritual? I hated to think of it going to waste. As I followed her, falling into step behind the *click*, *clack*, *scrack* and *screek* of her tipped heels on the uneven paving slabs, my eyes fixed like a sniper's scope on to the back of her legs. And particularly on the split in her skirt. Each time her right leg flashed back at me, the aperture in the rear of her skirt extended to reveal the back of her hosed thigh, just glossy enough for the expert eye to know it wasn't naked. And I liked the way her hosed legs met the tight wrapping of her leather boots. Made me think of one membrane of warm natural skin, a second layer of nylon and the third skin of supple leather. When I pondered the heavenly fragrance of her legs when she later unzipped them off her hot, working-girl legs, I had to move the hem of my overcoat about my groin to hide my erection. I did it with one hand in a pocket.

When she turned from the pavement and skipped into an estate agent's office, my eyes moved to the left to catch the last of her legs before the closing door stole them from my gaze.

But fifty feet ahead, before I'd gathered my wits, I could already see the next object of my fascination.

Crossed beneath a table, shiny in black hose and patent court shoes, the legs and feet of another working girl. An older, more matronly specimen.

Pulled as if by a rip tide, I picked up my pace and marched towards the café where she drank a latte, alfresco. With the front of her body facing me, she was speaking into the mobile phone that she held in one hand, and idly twiddling a coffee spoon in a glass cup with the other hand. As she was facing me, I looked away and pretended to be fascinated by the trees on the other side of the street; I didn't want her to detect my ardent leer from so far away in case she glared at me or adjusted her position. But as I drew to within fifteen feet, and to a range where the details of her lovely, plumpish legs could be examined, I was pleased to see she had lowered her eyes to watch one of her scarlet fingernails pushing at crumbs on a saucer. Free show.

Slowing my pace, I squinted and absorbed the full curves of her calves, before her broad knees stretched the sheer fabric of her black stockings to a lighter tone. For a second – the round table was blessedly small and didn't completely conceal her lap – I was even able to concentrate my vision between her lightly parted knees. Casting my eyesight up and into the shadowy cave of thigh and skirt shadow, I implored the darkness for a sign of hosiery type: tights, stockings? Too dark, but two quality up-skirt glimpses in as many minutes? On the back of my liaison with Patricia, I wondered if I might suffer a stroke.

But no sooner had I strained my eyes, when I suddenly intuited the presence of her own scrutiny against my face. It made my face feel suddenly cold and vulnerable. I looked up. Stared for a fraction of a second into her frosty blue eyes and was smitten by the half-lidded disapproval and the tense line of her lips.

Clocked. Deterred, I looked away, my cheeks red and warm. She uncrossed her legs and pulled her knees together while I wished I was aboard the passing number 23 bus.

Too greedy, too careless; served me right. I glanced at her one final time as I passed her table. She had lost interest in me and was again listening to a voice inside that phone. I checked out her shoes. Formal but shiny. Nice. And a thin golden ankle-chain glittered under her hose. Slut. Compelling eye candy but don't look unless invited.

Have mercy on us.

The incident made me wonder how many thousand, perhaps tens of thousands of glimpses and observations I had stolen during the lifetime of my obsession. Sometimes after walking the length of Oxford Street during the lunch hour, I have to pause by Centre Point or Marble Arch and actually force myself to replay every sighting captured during the length of my journey. Those that stay with me are entered into a leg journal at the first opportunity. I have journals recalling and describing the most memorable of these brief sightings – location, time, date, and a concise description of the woman and her legs and feet – going back to my seventeenth year in the lower-sixth form. A largely futile but ingrained practice of refusing to let the beauty die.

After the disagreeable incident by the café on Westbourne Grove, I only managed to reach Bayswater tube station on Queensway before fresh stimulation took control of my conscious mind. Outside a business that sold mailing addresses to a local transient population, a female member of staff leant against the wall beside the front door and smoked a cigarette. One hand tucked under the opposing armpit; shoulders hunched against the cool breeze; a middle-aged face blessed with a character of heavily made-up haughtiness; pretty green eyes that struck me as playful, even coy; a tight black skirt over a shapely bottom and good, thick thighs;

glossy flesh-tinted stockings shimmered on her calves; one long foot was removed from its bronze shoe and idly stroked the shin of the other leg; the sheer toes of her stockings revealed a mouth-watering shade of Maroon Lustre nail varnish. I wanted to get down on my knees. If she'd been a prostitute I'd have run across the street to the cash machine.

As a result of her outfit, general demeanour, pose and legs, I failed to limit my eager stare at all. So much so I became embarrassed at my own ardour, but was unable to tear my eyes away from such a vision. It invited admiration. She caught me looking, but her face adopted a subtle, knowing smile. Not a come-on by any means, but an acknowledgement of my interest twinned with an amusement at my peculiar taste. It made me feel a little ridiculous. Yes, she knew she had good legs and sexy feet, but never failed to be amused by men who were weak for them.

Three of her fingers were heavy with white-gold rings, including a jewel-encrusted engagement ring and a thick gold wedding band. Her stockings were expensive and her feet pedicured, so it was quite possible her husband was a foot guy. Or she preferred to be well presented from head to toe at work. A woman concerned about her appearance whose wardrobe leaned towards glamour. Bless her. Old school – early forties, always in heels, working class, liked to smoke and drink, and enjoyed wearing nice things on her legs, every day.

I looked back twice. The second time she smiled to herself – one of those 'still got it' smiles. Maybe the male members of staff had been glancing down all morning – a visiting delivery man may have made a comment. I'm speculating, but she was conscious of having desirable legs and had presented them in an eye-catching style. Perhaps it did her self-esteem no end of good.

She made me a little dizzy. A really good find, but I deeply regretted having no access to her. Then out from the shouting mouth of Bayswater tube station, a pretty Japanese woman in a tan suede skirt and matching high-heeled sling-backs skipped on to the street and I found myself captivated all over again.

Busy girl. Face set with purpose and a hint of self-importance. Out of the underground station and straight away out comes the mobile phone. I crossed the road and fell into step behind her outside the casino, glancing down frequently. Beige La Perla hold-ups, I was certain. Great shine and gossamer fine and she'd found the perfect shade to match her boots and skirt, which meant she hadn't just yanked a pair of tights on that morning. On the contrary, she'd studied the packets and fingered the fabric before buying to get just the right tone and style to match a particular outfit. A ritual preceding purchase I adored watching a woman follow in my boutique. Women with exacting specifications for their accessories to match outfits; the female customer in no hurry, who would be thorough with the samples and hold the flimsy fabric up to the strong white lights in the ceiling. Stretch it wide between her parted fingernails. Examine the knit, while I struggled to breathe. Making sure they were exactly what she wanted to cling to her legs for the desired effect.

Merely the knowledge that an attractive woman thinks carefully about her hosiery has a singular thrill for me. It's why I began the boutique: to observe and to imagine. And this Asian vixen really confirmed both my salacious mood and my desire to reach Sheer Delight before it shut. To be among my unopened treasures. And to muse on their potential.

I picked up my pace, but the free street-floorshow had not concluded. I became dizzy. Great pair of high-heeled sandals with tight jeans outside the Chinese, followed by a pair of long legs in super-fine barely black tights on show in the window of Starbucks. The girls of spring were spoiling me. Three more pairs of black knee boots and practically invisible flesh tights on parade before I reached the iron railings of the park. I began to long for the shelter of the trees. Briefly, I became baffled, disoriented and fatigued by arousal. But I asked for it. It's why I went for a walk. And would I have had it any other way?

Shaven, moisturised, wrapped in see-through nylon and lycra, then packed into clinging leather shoes and boots, in homes, offices, shops, cars and pavements. There are moments when I long to see and touch, to inhale and taste every well-presented female leg in the world. I am insatiable. Depraved. Unreasonable. But of course, without an omnipotent power or supernatural psychic abilities, I am sentenced to rely on fate and chance in order to get my thrills. Unless, of course, I engineer a situation. Nothing wrong with that. But how many great legs am I missing each day by simply being in the wrong place, or the right place at the wrong time? Could I even comprehend what I am constantly missing in other places and times? The futility of my fetish rarely escapes me. I am damned. But, if I am honest, happy to be so.

In the post-historical world, we are forced to think of what we don't have and to crave it until we go mad with desire. My fetish is another form of consumption. Perhaps less is more, though it's a lesson I am unable to learn.

'Algernon. Didn't expect to see you,' Samantha cried out, hoping the other two naughty girls could hear her warning. Cecilia and Lucy were out back, in the office and storeroom. But as the music is louder than I prefer, I doubt if Samantha's voice carried.

'Are you disappointed?' I teased, while temporarily stunned by my manager's appearance. Full but carefully applied make-up enhanced a face already blessed with a girlish prettiness that never failed to fire an electrical charge through my colon. Dressed in her white dress coat, complemented by patent high heels and glossy black stockings, there was something instantly succulent about her. Part of me flung itself into the usual emotional infatuation, while my more primal instincts demanded an instant feast upon her soft flesh. Ever since I hired her to run my boutique, I had been an admirer of the rare hyper-feminine quality Samantha was in full possession of. In any space she occupied, no matter how briefly, a lasting, beguiling fragrance lingered. And any object her long white fingers and lacquered nails touched was additionally enchanted by a scent that made me shiver as desire and dream collided.

That day, her blonde hair was elegantly coiled into a chignon and her eyelashes were so long and black she appeared to have created a beauty more dollish than mortal. And I had never met a woman before or since with feet of such enduring beauty. So pale when naked as to startle the fortunate onlooker with their milky brightness, and with such flawless skin it took some considerable investigation to detect any visible sign to prove they had not been created in the heavens, by the design of an immortal.

She would also laugh at even my weakest jokes – a flash of perfect teeth behind lips red and glossy wet – and every man likes to be indulged with even an illusion of significance by an attractive woman. 'Come to check up on us?'

'If you were all out back playing cards and smoking cigars, I wouldn't be angry. You're too pretty to incur my wrath.'

She giggled. 'Charmer. So what brings you in?'

Again, I felt she wanted to add. Maybe I was making too many visits, but since Cecilia had started work the month before, I could not keep away. Our new girl had coltish legs and long, slender feet and favoured stilettos with an open toe on the shop floor. They made a lovely cracking sound on the marble tiles. Changed out of her boots with the spike heels each morning, then slipped her feet into peep-toe sling-backs. I know this for a fact, and have the evidence on tape in full colour. Cecilia was a girl, I suspected, with an empathy and real enthusiasm for my dress code and concept: hosiery consultants with stunning legs dressed in luxurious stockings from our current stock, to promote our products in-store. Well, that's the professional justification. But I am always generous with my staff. They each receive six new pairs of stockings each week to wear at work. I heavily subsidise their footwear – no low heels; I pay for a monthly pedicure, paraffin wrap and leg wax at the local beautician; and provide two new uniforms every six months. With a salary higher than counter staff in most department stores, medical plan, pension scheme and corporate gym membership, I offer attractive opportunities for the right girl at Sheer Delight. Even at the expense of an attractive profit, never my main concern. Here, I was making art. Leg art.

For half of the year, I broke even; for the remainder I made a small profit that was immediately ploughed back into a new feature in the store's design – like my floor mirrors. But Sheer Delight was only ever conceived to make me rich in other ways. So many other ways.

'Post. I'm expecting a few things. Mmm, you smell good. What is that?'

Samantha blushed. 'Chanel. Lush isn't it?'

'It's lovely. Great lipstick too.'

'So that's why you came in, to check me out.'

'Oh dear, rumbled again. But can you blame me?'

'I don't mind,' she said, quietly, but not too quietly. And though that comment made my stomach turn over,

I reminded myself to be careful. Samantha and I no longer had a strictly professional relationship. I had crossed a line three months earlier, and continued to cross the border at every opportunity. Up until the first time we had sex in the office, she'd had a boyfriend and I'd been content to admire her. But things change. The time was ripe for us to be together, only I couldn't accept it.

'Place looks great,' I said, and glanced about the shop. Each tier and table was neat and well stocked with glossy packages and shiny shoes. The plinths were dust free and upon them our latex legs were beautifully presented in hose and heels. I turned and smiled at Samantha. 'How's business?' Through the long counter, made entirely from glass, where the real nylons and vintage hosiery were stored, you could also see all of the consultants' legs. A display case with a dual purpose. And as the girls wore tight white dress-coats with a high collar, full make-up and high heels, it was a view you'd thank me for. Several fetish publications had given us favourable notices, and there had been four features of the store in the style sections of Sunday broadsheets in the two years since we opened. Samantha had managed the store expertly from day one of her eighteen-month period as manager. Bookkeeping, stock control, customer service, staff training, occasional lover: she was an angel.

'Slow today, Al. Weather's getting warmer. But them sun-tan sheen tights are doing well. And the fancy stockings for evening-wear are going steady. Lady came in today and bought six pairs of the Fogal and a pair of seamed stockings.'

'Oh,' I said, looking far too interested for my own good. But a lady with expensive tastes and particularly one who made a purchase from the locked cabinet was always cause for scrutiny.

'Too old for you,' she said, with a naughty smile.
'How old?'

Samantha wrinkled her snub nose and looked up at
the ceiling as she recalled the customer. ''Bout sixty.
Very sniffy. But nice clothes. Big fur coat and you'd
have liked her shoes. Amazed she could walk.'

I wanted to know more. Every last detail. Having a
strong affinity for the mature dame with classic lines and
style. But I restrained myself. Too close an interrogation
and I would have made Samantha jealous. Possibly
alienated a manager who, I suspected, had recently
developed stronger feelings for me. I was also very fond
of her, but at that time was too spoilt by opportunity to
pay such feelings much attention. With so much stimulation about, I didn't have the head-space. Never had
the time for commitment. Every fresh glimpse out there
in the world seemed to reinforce my natural disinclina-
tion to settle down.

But when the girls had gone home, I could always
play the security tape back and at least get an approxi-
mate idea of what my mature buyer of fully fashioned
nylons looked like. Real nylons are more expensive than
other styles and, without the benefit of lycra, they
require a great deal of maintenance from the wearer,
especially if they are seamed. So we sold fewer pairs
than the cheaper, more user-friendly varieties in stock.
But when a customer bought nylons, I insisted on a few
select details from the girl who made the sale. As they
made a commission on every pair sold, the consultants
were usually forthcoming without too much prompting.

Of course they all thought it odd at first, that a man
should own a hosiery and lingerie retail business. And
all must have suspected me for the pervert I am,
especially as company policy insisted on a uniform
which included the wearing of black high heels and
sheer stockings every day in my employ. Though

Samantha handled the finer details of staff presentation after the successful applicant's interview; much better coming from a woman, I found. And once an employee became accustomed to my occasional, genial visits, I found their anxieties were soon dispelled. No consultant had ever been made to feel uncomfortable by my enthusiasms. I would have hated that. Loathed myself. Instead, I operated with discretion. You would never catch me strolling into Sheer Delight to blatantly slobber over the girls' legs – though the devil knows I was tempted. I had standards. In fact, I only ever admired my staff with tact. It was an art practised from youth, and perfected like a craft thereafter. Of course observation is made much easier in Sheer Delight because the walls are all mirrored to waist height. An excellent ploy to get a customer to examine their own plain legs and to admire the beautiful, shimmering pins of my staff as they browsed. Though they did serve another purpose. I'd had the mirrors installed for my own indulgence and insisted they were kept highly polished to catch reflections from every angle of the customers' legs and feet as they tried on shoes.

My main weakness with my consultants had always been my inability to restrain myself from flattering them. Every girl in my employ always dressed to my own peculiar specifications, and had been selected by me at interview primarily because I liked their legs. I baited the trap myself, and although careful where I put my feet, I had been known to slip. So to speak, there were occasions when I'd been caught with my fingers in the till.

Samantha, in particular, had begun to watch me closely. I feared our relationships, both professional and personal, were becoming confused. And I could only hold myself accountable. We had enjoyed a long flirtation that progressed into an easy-going physical association, and, as a result of frequent intimacy, feelings had become involved: hers apparent, mine unacknowledged. *Flirtation*? *Physical association*? *Frequent intimacy*? I even have trouble using the word *relationship*. But that is what it was.

'Is it safe to go in?' I pointed at the door to the staff area.

'Yeah. Lucy's getting changed. She's got to go early and catch the opticians before they close. And it's slow today, so I thought it'd be OK.'

'Sure. Sammy, no need to explain. There'd have been a "Closing Down Sale" sign on that door twelve months ago if you weren't at the helm of this crazy ship.'

Her pretty smile is full of pride. 'Just don't want you to think we're taking the piss.'

'Perish the thought.' Though I needed one, so would have to get backstage and into the staff toilet.

In the office – desk, computer, filing cabinets – which also served as a staff room – kitchen, microwave, fridge, Ikea table, three chairs – Cecilia was engrossed in massaging Lucy's feet.

'No. No, carry on. Don't mind me,' I said hurriedly, flustered at chancing upon such a wonderful scene of female innocence and intimacy. 'It's my fault for making you wear such high heels.'

The girls exchanged a loaded glance, then giggled. 'New shoes,' Lucy said, and kicked at a pair of idle black stilettos on the marble tiles with one foot, before returning the other foot to Cecilia's lap. Whereupon Cecilia's long fingers went back to work, rubbing at the ball of Lucy's foot with a supple pressing action I found hypnotising. 'Been killing me all day,' Lucy added.

'Well, they're very pretty instruments of torture,' I said.

The girls laughed at that. Which settled my nerves as I still pondered on that glance they'd exchanged when I first appeared.

Through the sheer tan fabric of Lucy's Couture hold-ups, I could clearly see the red lines her new shoes had embossed on her skin: over her toes, at the back of her heel and down one side of her feet. 'Mmm, Ce', you got magic hands,' Lucy said.

I hovered beside the in-tray on the desk, then made myself comfortable slouching against the kitchen counter, the position with the best view. My bladder could hold off for a few more minutes; I couldn't risk missing a moment of Lucy's lovely foot show. 'Can I get you girls a coffee?'

'No ta,' Lucy said. 'I got to go in a tick. Sam said it was OK.'

I smiled. 'Then it's OK with me.'

'I know. You're really cool about it. But I had that day off for the doctor's last week too. I'm such a slacker.'

'You know you girls don't have to worry about things like that. As long as someone's here, it's OK.'

They looked at each other again. Clever smiles on dark red lips passed back and forth. I liked them to take advantage of me. To dress for me every day and to take little favours without permission. For some reason I had not fully examined, the thought of their misbehaviour, no matter how slight, increased their value to me. Not as employees, of course, but as the objects of my desire. And Lucy had been coming in late, according to Sam. While Cecilia, the minx, took longer than an hour for her lunch. And my manageress wanted me to say something. The other two, it appeared, had formed a coven. A fragrant, painted, tight-waisted, shiny-legged conspiracy against Samantha. But I couldn't step in. I was helpless before the pointed toes of their new shoes. Weak near the flutters the delicate extensions of their false eyelashes made. And reduced by the clack of their heels all over the hard floor of my boutique and the soft tissue of my heart.

Under the white glare of the spotlights on the ceiling rail – so characteristic of the interior design of my bright, clean, marble and mirror leg-world – both of the girls' pins were dazzling. Glossy and liquescent as they both preferred to wear the high-impact shiny stockings we kept in stock. The split in Cecilia's dress-coat showed me most of the inner thigh of one leg. I leaned back but couldn't catch the dark suggestion of a stocking top. Tights. Yes, sheer to the waist. No indentation of a suspender clip on the front of her thighs where the tight material of her uniform pressed her thighs together and made her take short steps in my private peep show. Tights for sure. Against company policy, but I'd let it go. She mesmerised me in tights. And amidst the scents of their perfume and hair conditioner, and the dead synthetic blandness that office furniture and stationery adds to any environment, there was just a mild musk of Lucy's hot feet in the air. She pulled her toes right back when Cecilia kneaded her knuckles into the arch of Lucy's foot. 'Don't, Ce'. It tickles.'

'Keep still, you.' She slapped Lucy's calf muscle.

'So how are things with you two?' I said, in a breathless voice.

'Good.'

'Great.'

'Lucy's got a new man,' Cecilia said.

'Really. Good for you,' I said, my teeth almost clenched. No, I did not like sharing. Though I liked to torment myself with thoughts of the impact their legs had on others.

'A customer,' Cecilia added.

'Shush, you! There's no rule against that. Is there, Al?'

'No,' I said, quickly, while privately wishing I had made one. Some degenerate leg-licker had been in here then. Drawn in, his throat tight with excitement, by the beautiful uniformed girls, their polished legs and spiked feet.

'A guy?'

'Of course, I'm not a lezzy, you know!'

Yes, there was just a flicker of disappointment on Cecilia's face when Lucy said that. Her topaz eyes darkened – irises pretty as the clear marbles you could lose yourself inside as a child. Cecilia was single. There had been no mention of a boyfriend at all during all the shop talk since her arrival. She was too busy, she'd said, with her evening courses in aromatherapy. Made me wonder. Couldn't help myself. A gay girl, perhaps, who was drawn to the kind of fetishishtic ultra-glamour that Sheer Delight peddled, and was aroused by the sight of such on the curvaceous bodies of other girls, like our Lucy? I held the large tin of Nescafé over my crotch – my trousers were far too thin to conceal so much as a paper clip in a pocket, let alone something approaching the density of a rolling pin.

'So how did you pull a male customer?' I asked.

'Pull! I was pulled.'

'When he was in here buying a Valentine's present for his girlfriend,' Cecilia added, without looking up, just content to caress the slippery, hot feet within her long fingers.

Valentine's gift? That old chestnut. I used it a score of times as a teenager while dabbling in hosiery departments. My face blushed and a prickling of sweat broke out on my forehead as I recalled, then quickly suppressed, past shames and deep humiliations as a youth in lingerie departments.

Lucy smiled. 'Anyway, he's really sweet.'

'Spends a fortune on her, Al,' Cecilia added, a hint of playful sarcasm in her voice.

Lucy blushed, but looked pleased with herself. 'So?'

'But he don't need to buy her any stockings, does he? Which is what he likes.'

'Bitch!' Lucy slapped the back of Cecilia's hand.

Bastard. A fellow devotee has come in under the wire and burgled me. Irrational, I seethed. 'Does he now?'

'Damn right he does. He makes –'

Lucy withdrew her foot from Cecilia's lap and launched herself at her friend, quickly smothering her mouth with one of her pretty manicured hands that must now, I tormented myself, be wrapping itself about some hose-freak's rigid pole in their after-work liaisons. A degenerate who was probably ruining my poor Lucy while still dressed in her uniform, heels and stockings. Though I was only guessing at Cecilia's unfinished sentence, I could not prevent my imagination from twisting an inexorable hot poker in my envious gut.

Unfortunately, my arrival and subsequent nosing brought the foot play to an abrupt end. Lucy slipped her glossy feet into a pair of white trainers in order to walk to the tube. Then reached for her coat. 'This boyfriend isn't an optician?' I remarked, unable to keep the brittle edge from my tone.

'No. I'll show you my appointment card if you don't believe me,' Lucy cried out.

And I felt like a heel. 'Don't bother. I'm only kidding. Because I'm jealous.' This made the little blonde beam. Oh, she loved attention, our Lucy. Especially from the boss, who had a thing going on with Samantha, the manager. And she and Sam weren't getting on. Not anymore.

'Jealous of what? Who?' Samantha said, as her wonderful long lines in blinding white cotton and black nylons suddenly made the doorway look more appealing than I could ever remember it being before.

I laughed. Cleared my throat. 'We were just fooling around.'

'I can hear that. What a racket. Customers must have thought there was an orgy back here.'

Odd choice of word – 'orgy'. Samantha didn't like me flirting with the girls. She felt it undermined her authority. I began to wonder if it was undermining something else too.

'Cecilia, can you watch the shop?' Sam asked.

'Sure.' Cecilia was out of the chair and teetering to the door without hesitation, apprehension in her priceless topaz eyes. Naughty girls, but they knew who was boss. Not me of course. We'd be flogging tights from a market stall if I managed the shop. And the mere thought of Sam disciplining her mischievous assistants kept me up at nights.

'Lucy, get off now. You were supposed to be gone ten minutes ago.'

'I know, I know. I'm gonna be late.' Before she pranced out of the staff area, she flashed her eyes at me and poked me in the stomach. 'Al's fault.'

I blushed, delighted with the contact of a single painted fingernail. But quickly straightened my face on seeing the cold disapproval in Samantha's eyes. On occasion, she would lose her temper with me. And I can never remember wanting her more than at those times.

'She told you about her new boyfriend?'

I shrugged. 'No harm done.'

'You hope. But there are too many men in the shop and it makes the women uncomfortable. When you're buying undies and stuff, you don't want men watching you. And he comes in every day.'

'Any excuse,' I said without thinking.

Samantha laughed, derisively. 'Another perv on your patch. Thought you wouldn't like that.'

'Shush! Cecilia will hear.' I pointed at the door.

Samantha rolled her eyes. 'Like they don't know your game.'

'Aye?'

'And what do you expect? You can't keep us all to yourself, you know.'

'As long as you remain mine I'm happy.'

'Don't count yer chickens, mate.'

'Oh. Something I should know?' I felt wounded. So much so, I surprised myself. Maybe I had become more attached to Sam than I'd thought – which is the very problem with unexamined feelings while being preoccupied by something else. But I also knew this kind of conversation was no good for business.

'No. No one special. But maybe it's best to keep business and pleasure separate.'

I swallowed the lump in my throat. Felt a bit dizzy. The thought of losing my monopoly on Samantha's perfect legs and feet – of the end of our special relationship – caused a disappointment so intense it produced a physical pain. A perfect afternoon was immediately threatened with extermination.

I checked to make sure Cecilia was occupied behind the counter, and was pleased to see her ringing up a sale to a customer. But one I couldn't, infuriatingly, see. I am incorrigible.

Sam walked to the desk and opened a ring binder.

'You're annoyed with me.' I stood behind her and gently kissed the back of her neck, where the almost invisible golden hairs grew – those not long enough to fit inside her chignon. She shivered. Closed her eyes.

'S'nice,' she whispered.

I filled my head with her scent. Admired the way the curves of her hips and thighs looked compact in the tight uniform. I leaned back to see the sleek and aerodynamic shape of her calves and ankles in black stockings.

'We need to talk,' she said.

'Sure. What's on your mind?'

'Not now. Ce' could come in.'

I felt light-headed, weak in the limbs, as if my entire skeleton had changed its consistency to that of milk, while the alchemy of my attraction to Sam also transformed my cock from liquid to stone. I wanted her. Suddenly, really wanted her. Blinded myself with need. 'She'll be finishing in a minute,' I whispered.

My head was swimming with echoes of Patricia's voice; images of her legs; the recent memory of Lucy's feet in Cecilia's hands; the woman seated outside the café; the tarty blonde outside the mail company – one shoe off, the foot pawing the other leg; pairs of leather knee boots marching; a blonde unfolding and opening her legs from the driver's seat of a Mini. I had reached the point of mental saturation and desperately needed a release.

'That's not what I meant,' she said, her voice clipped with petulance. 'Better we don't discuss it here.'

'I came in today to take you out to dinner. If you were available.' I lied like a cheap watch. But this was no time for a conscience. Arousal had seized control of my every thought and motive in a swift coup d'état.

To my immeasurable relief, her posture softened perceptibly, and even though she stood with her back to me, I knew the pretty smile had returned to her eyes. 'Liar.'

'I'm not. I missed you.'

She turned around. One eyebrow raised. 'Your nose is getting longer.'

'Not my nose. Something else.'

Squealing, she slapped my shoulder. 'You're terrible.'

'Can I kiss you. I want you.'

'No!'

'Please. Don't make me beg.'

'Do what you like. The answer's still no.'

'Even on my knees?'

Laughing, she pushed me aside and tottered expertly into the small store beside the staff toilet. 'These came today, from Finesse. Thought you might like to see them.'

'Oh, the new range.' My enthusiasm was genuine, but the weightless treasures in the cardboard box in Sam's lovely hands could wait. 'So, dinner? Without begging? At a table with us both in chairs, and me not under it, on my knees.'

'For a change, you dirty sod.'

'What do you think I am?'

'Exactly what you are.'

'So, can I take you to Cicada? I fancy some crispy salt squid and a few cocktails.'

'We'll see. If you behave and counter-sign those forms from the accountant. He's coming in tomorrow.'

'Well, he better not stay too long. He's got a soft spot for you. I shall be banning men from this shop shortly.'

'Yourself included I hope.'

We helped Cecilia close up and then returned to the staff area to check the Finesse delivery. Just watching Samantha sort through the packets and place them over the desk for my approval increased my arousal. I had to sit down and flex my toes to keep the blood circulating.

'You all right, Al? Look like you're having a funny turn or something.'

'You've no idea how close I am to a seizure.'

'Ooh, these champagne ones look nice,' she said, peering at the fabric through the little plastic window of a packet of hold-ups.

'Try them on.'

'How did I know you were going to say that.'

'I need to see how they look.'

'Do you now,' she said, giggling, her painted finger-nails already busy with the flap on the flat, square packet. The cover was pink with a great pair of legs crossed, shoes off. My mouth filled with saliva.

Samantha unbuttoned her dress-coat. I leaned close to see every detail. The slim belly circled by a thin black suspender belt; white skin, so soft it never failed to surprise my fingers when I was lucky enough to touch it; her bust hammocked in a see-through Calvin Klein bra; trimmed little pelt under matching panties; and, of course, those slender legs in positively glistening Pretty Polly Nylons.

Nodding at my lap, she said, 'Go on then, you pervert. Get that belt undone.' Her pupils were wide with a familiar excitement. No doubt about it, Samantha loved to misbehave on company premises with company property. One of the things I adored about her: she genuinely enjoyed wearing the new stock and had become an expert on every brand. She also loved the effect her legs had on me, though was becoming less keen on the effect the other consultants' legs were also impressing upon me.

It was even possible for me to speculate that her sexuality was developing a strong association with the wearing of sheer hosiery and high heels. We had only ever had sex under the pretence of her wearing new products. 'Road-testing it,' she would say. 'Well, they are all about screwing, aren't they. They turn men on and women feel sexy.' I had never forgotten that, and often quoted her to extract more of her simple wisdom. Which was rarely forthcoming, but of high impact when it was shared. She always held something back. Never fully indulged me. Always left me infinitely curious about what else she hid from me, and how far she would go to please and enslave me further. Of course, I never gave her enough incentive, having long taken an oath against monogamy. With my condition, I couldn't see the point of making promises I would be unable to keep. But still, I couldn't bear the thought of her not being mine.

'As you wish, nurse. I'm in a lot of pain.'

'You will be, my love, if I catch you sniffing round Lucy again. She's a tart.'

'I have my hands full with you, my dear.'

'Lying bastard.' She nodded at my freed erection and raised an eyebrow. 'That was hard before I came back here.' She sat on the desk and looked down at me, unbelted in the office chair.

On either side of my cock, she placed both high-heeled feet. Then closed them, so I could feel the hard leather of her insteps against the side of my shaft. The spear points of her heels passed under my balls and grazed the base of my buttocks. 'Bloody hell, Al. It's so hard.'

'It may not be for long. You've turned me on so much, Sammy love.'

'You've done it to yourself, you dirty bastard.' Her eyes seemed to narrow with an aggressive need – jealousy, frustration, desire. Samantha had a filthy mouth when she was aroused, which I found to be nothing but an incentive to reveal my own keenness for verbal excess. Up and down my length she slowly worked that patent leather gripping her long, sweet feet. I watched the mirrored toes and heels. Clutched the underside of the chair with my fingernails. Began to shuffle my buttocks about, to gently pump myself between her leathered feet. Found it hard to talk, but wanted her to tease me with her lovely red mouth.

'Toenails?'

'Same colour as these,' she said, knowing the routine and holding up both hands so I could see fingertips the pink of Pacific coral.

'No.'

'Take me shoes off then.'

Slipping my cupped hand behind her heels, I levered the shoes from her feet. The action produced a hiss and her warm nylon-covered feet were released. Immediately, they began to move. Stretched like cats in sunlight. Toes bent back to show me the tender pink flesh underneath her digits. I raised her shoe to my mouth, inhaled the perfume of leather, nylon, nail polish and her thick, savoury foot musk. Then licked the inside of the sole until it was damp, while staring between her parted knees. 'God, you drive me crazy,' I muttered, while breathing out. 'I want you so much.'

She smiled, then her face hardened. 'I want to be fucked tonight. Really good and hard. You hear me? While you lick my feet.'

'Sam, don't. I'll come.'

'It's all right. I'll put some of them Finesse hold-ups on for dinner.'

'Will you leave the uniform on?'

'Maybe. If you're really nice to me.'

'I will be. I'll do anything.'

'You would as well, with my feet on your big fat cock.' Rolling and sliding her slippery feet in my lap, she tugged my erection back and forth, producing a single grey tear of pre-come at the tip. Then pressed my length against my belly and rubbed it up and down with the firm ball of her foot. I felt faint. Gripped her legs. Stroked her slick calves up to the back of her knees where the nylon was warm.

'God, your legs . . .'

'Had them waxed last night. They feel lovely in these stockings.'

'Don't. I'll come.'

'Mmm. Can I have it?'

'Where?'

She stuck out her tongue and placed one glossy fingernail on its surface while looking inside my wretched soul with lidded doll eyes. 'All of it.'

'You slut.'

'Better believe it.' She slipped two painted fingernails inside her transparent panties and began to circle the pads of her fingertips on her clit, as if she were polishing a rare penny. The first time we were intimate together, in the storeroom, she did that without a glimmer of shame. Just rubbed herself to climax while I thrust into her from behind.

'Oh, Al. I'm really wet. And me nipples are so tender. Will you give 'em a good seeing to tonight?'

'I – I promise.'

As the speed of her busy fingers increased behind the gossamer shield of her panties, so did the pushing of her silky foot against the underside of my cock. I clenched all the muscles of my groin to hold back, just for a moment longer, to prolong the euphoria of watching my manager masturbate while pumping me with her shiny feet.

When her shoulders began to make little jerks and her eyes rolled to white, I knew she was lost and oxygen deprived while up her own peak. Never took Sam long to come. She was curiously unencumbered by reticence – was comfortable with me from the very beginning and, for such a pretty feminine creature, ate like a glutton and slept like a drunken princess.

Her foot pressed my erection hard against my belly, as if she were flooring an accelerator on the carpeted floor of a sports car. Then folded her toes over the head of my cock as her head dropped back and she began to call me a bastard – over and over again. I loved that. We were good for each other. We were bad together. Always.

Sliding my hands up the back of her legs, I stood up between her thighs. 'Now. Get me in your mouth.' I cupped the back of her head, sunk my fingers into her chignon.

Swivelling her silky bottom about on the desktop, she stretched her long body behind her and lay tummy down in one smooth motion. Sam liked to call me names and swear, but she liked to be given orders too.

'Mmm,' she moaned, and opened her mouth wide to take me inside. Deep inside, as if she just adored having me inside her warm mouth. Her pretty face began a frantic sucking motion into my groin, and her mouth emitted a series of squelching sounds I found delightful.

Bending her knees, she showed me the soles of her feet, pink and crinkly through the fine mesh of her stockings. Rubbed them together. Made them hiss. That did it. As I've reminded myself, so many times: it's all in the details. My fingers tightened in her hair. 'All of it, slut. All of it, you gorgeous slut.' I began to push at her mouth and her eyes opened wide. 'Now,' I said with a grunt, and for a second I replayed every intoxicating image of the day across the inner screen of my imagination. And listened to the gulping sounds she made, down there, in my lap.

And the excitement of that day seemed reluctant to end. I was belted away and Sam was reapplying lipstick, but I still had dinner with her to look forward to and, had decided impulsively, to take her home to my place for the first time, to show her my apartment and part of the collection before further vocal depravity in my big white bed. For three months we'd had sex at work, or in her flat in Fulham; her not seeing my place was becoming an issue. While Samantha distracted me by changing into her new Finesse stockings, my enthusiasm for the evening increased immeasurably after opening the post.

Incredibly, it appeared the Holy Grail had come to me. Despite the endless invitations for her to appear as a model on my website, to model hosiery for my salon (for a not inconsiderable sum), and a miscellany of imaginative but utterly desperate ploys to meet her, the Nylon Dahlia was to appear, in person, for Pin-up Pussycat retro lingerie, at a London launch of their new range. And I was invited to intend by their sales team.

As I was an inveterate stockist of all their imitation nylons and corsetry, it was the least they could do. Black-tie affair and she would be performing one of her famous burlesque routines at the launch. I would get to actually see her. Maybe meet her. Two emails from my contacts on the London leg scene registered the same news. The second from Seam Straightener, a fellow devotee of real nylons and a graphic designer for a Soho facilities house, who had actually seen her on Dean Street wearing an animal-print coat, pill-box hat, pencil skirt and black fully fashioned stockings:

> Maybe I'm going crazy and hallucinating but I'm sure I saw the Nylon Dahlia today. I was out fetching a sandwich and I just came to a standstill when this vision of utter loveliness walked out of Paradiso on the other side of the road and stepped into a cab. I saw her for no more than three seconds, but am sure it was the Dahlia.
>
> SS

I remember feeling my pulse up between my ears. Heard the rush and roar of blood inside my head while my stomach flopped over and then vanished without a trace. I could barely swallow, let alone speak when Samantha announced, 'Cab's here. You ready? I'm bloody starving.'

Spoilt, depraved, greedy, I thought of the Nylon Dahlia all through dinner. Composed opening lines. Imagined the outfit I should wear to the launch party. Calculated business propositions to draw her into my orbit. And all these desperate machinations, despite the fact that Samantha pumped my erection with her silky feet throughout the time we waited for our first course to arrive.

97

At the same time, in that cosy leather booth, she sucked an olive with her big red lips and batted her doll eyes at me. Like a degenerate king indulged by concubines on his fetish throne, I wore my mind out thinking back to Patricia's confessions, musing about Lucy's love life, Cecilia's sexual persuasion, their legs, their feet, the Polish waitress in shiny flesh tights bending over the next table. I was blessed, had acquired a fetish that was on offer on every city street in the developed world. Could seek it on a zillion websites and hoard every periodical that took my fancy, find its innocuous strands in vintage films and in contemporary advertising. I was delightfully and willingly hobbled. And here I am, I thought, with my trunk being lathered by the slippery, insistent feet of a hosiery shop manageress. I wanted to live for ever. Could not cope with thoughts of it ever ending. There would never be enough time in which to relentlessly bombard myself with the infinite stimulation on offer. And despite having all of this, what else was I missing? Elsewhere.

Such appetite. And one I tried to placate – to blunt the edge of – with Samantha back at my flat. Regardless of the risk I was running with our involvement beyond the boutique. Sharing my sanctum seemed like the next step for Sam and I. A progression I wanted and rejected simultaneously, in the same spurt of thought. And I had not ruled out the potential for her horror at my collection. It was impossible to keep any visitor ignorant of my obsession. Even without access to the film, periodical, sound or book libraries, the hosiery museum, or pre-worn artefacts captured by my agents out there in the wild, the framed prints of beautiful legs that graced every plain white wall of the lounge – images detailing the history of the Dahlia's career that turned the room into a shrine – gave the game away to the casual visitor. My home was gallery space. And there was also the collection of designer shoes, exquisitely mounted on tiny individual dais, filling a cabinet in the hall; another presented an array of nail-polish bottles, arranged in a startling spectrum from rose pink to Gothic black. Even my china in the kitchen was decorated with images of Betty Page and Luke Morgan shoes.

But Samantha, despite her initial fascination with the true extent of my pathology, never commented much about any of it. She appeared to have no trouble accepting it instantly as a feature of my character. Beside the odd murmur of appreciation at a particular display or print, she felt immediately comfortable in my unconventional surroundings and flopped into the cushioned glove of my leather sofa as if it were her own.

'Do me feet, Al,' she said. 'Been on these heels all day.'

'Thought you liked them,' I said, falling to my knees and barely restraining myself from licking the pale leather of her street-worn soles.

'Mmm. I love them. What they do to my legs. But I must have had them on for about fourteen hours in total.'

Her feet were hot again and the shoes had fastened tight to her feet. Took some coaxing to remove. And after a moment's pause to admire her pretty feet in champagne stockings, I sank my face on to her damp soles. Tongued the salt and shivered with delight at the way the fabric of her hose moved over her tight, sensitive foot skin. Flesh with a satin texture all of its own, doubly empowered by another skin: a fine mesh of lycra and nylon. While inhaling the strong but pleasant musk under her toes, that had been so tightly bound in the pointed prow of her shoes for most of the day and evening, I vigorously stroked her calves and shins, creating tiny dark ripples in her stockings, then smoothing them flat with the downward sweep of my palms.

'Oh that's nice.' She watched me for a while, her pupils dilating as her eyelids narrowed. Her excitement matched mine. The greater my eagerness for her, the quicker she lost her inhibitions. It was never long before she craved penetration if she watched me lose control with her legs and feet. Kissing my way up her legs, I never once broke eye contact. Her lips parted and she called me a 'bastard' when I reached her polished knees.

'Let me taste you,' I said. 'I want to eat you through those panties.'

'Dirty bastard,' she whispered, and closed her eyes. Unbuttoned her uniform to her waist and opened her thighs. One leg across the back of the sofa, the foot of the other placed on the floor, Samantha opened herself to my mouth, my hunger, my teeth, lips and tongue. Up and down the sopping black fabric, thin as her stockings, I lapped that crotch the way a cat laps a kitten's fur. Intense, furious, committed, I tasted her until my mouth and throat were saturated with the meaty bitterness of her intimacy. Until I could taste her no more. Then I peeled her saturated briefs from her drenched sex, and slipped one, two, three fingers inside her. Tickled her slick walls with my fingertips, until she called me a 'fucker'.

Cheeks flushed and face hot, she made a croaking sound. Bit the side of her hand. Frowned. Began to cry. Stopped. Opened her mouth as if to yawn. Then wrapped her thighs around my neck and pulled my face down to her again. Held me there with her silky legs until she had juddered and trembled all over my oily face.

Desperate, as if my jeans, shirt and underwear were on fire, I tore and tugged at my clothes to become naked. Tossed my garments like rags about the wooden floor, and then fell upon her. Raised her legs into the air. Kept them straight so her pink toenails pointed at the ceiling. Pressed her knees and ankles together and then slipped myself between her glossy thighs. Slightly rough, the texture of her stockings grated gently against my phallus until I was through and poking between the front of her thighs. Holding her trim ankles tight, I then slipped back and forth between her legs, while looking down at her red wanton face and sluttish smeared mouth.

'Oh, that's good. Fuck my stockings. Fuck my legs. Then put it inside me,' she muttered to me, while I worked myself faster and faster between her thighs.

'I want to come on them.'

She closed her eyes at the mention of my impending ejaculation. Samantha liked to see it come out. Liked it splashed over her, before fingering it into her mouth. Better still, she liked to pull a draught of it deep into her throat and down into her little belly from source.

'Fuck me first. Then chuck it all over.'

'Your legs.'

'Yes. Fuck it all over my legs and feet, you dirty bastard.'

Something began to pound at the front of my skull. I felt so excited, my brain tissue appeared to have expanded to the point of rubbing against bone. My vision coloured a dark red and a powerful shudder ran down my neck and into the spinal cable between my shoulders. 'God, you turn me on.'

'Cos I'm a slut,' she goaded, and rubbed her clit up and down with the pads of four fingertips. 'Come on. Fuck her. Fuck your slut. Fuck the slut hard.'

With a whimper, I withdrew from between her glossy, hosed thighs and sank inside her in one quick, deep motion, taking her breath away. She dropped her head back. Clenched her eyelids shut. Rubbed her clit frenziedly to add friction to a wet surface, to short circuit again into a powerful climax that made her moan from the bottom of her tummy, like she was giving birth. Her moan of excitement then warbled, from the force of my thrusts into her. I held her ankles down, on either side of her head, which raised her buttocks to meet my pounding. We slapped and slithered together. Shouted and swore. Until I said, 'Now,' in a hoarse voice, and pulled out to shoot all over her belly. Four long streamers to splash on her stomach and breasts, liquid pearls across the white chocolate of her flesh. I'd wanted to come on her new stockings but the position wasn't right.

She moaned again at the sight of the mess I'd made on her. Then began to dip her pink nails into the cream, before spooning it between her sucking lips. Oyster eater. Sugar dabber. Cream licker. I leant forwards and kissed her moist forehead. Lapped some of the thick red rouge off her cheekbones. Then, using my own fingers, I helped her to feed herself from what remained on her breasts.

When I woke, late the next day, Samantha had gone. Left to go to work, for me, at Sheer Delight. Vaguely, I remember the alarm on her phone beeping, followed by an assortment of shuffling sounds as she stealthily showered and dressed before kissing me goodbye. I never heard the front door close. But her essence remained behind. Beside the bed I found a cup of cold tea, a slice of toast cut cleverly into a heart shape and spread with raspberry jam, and the empty packet of Touchable RHT nylons I had given her the night before from my private stash in the flat, hoping to watch her slide them up her legs in the morning before I ruined her make-up for the third time in about fourteen hours. But I'd slept through it.

I felt touched by the toast – pleased to be reassured about her feelings for me, but also horribly indecisive about what to do next. With the Nylon Dahlia in town, to my lasting shame, Sam would not be my priority. So I attempted to put the manageress of Sheer Delight out of my mind and to try and replace her very real presence with the long-familiar ghost of the Dahlia. In my imagination and dreams I had elevated the model into a deity. Living a thousand explicit scenes and lives with her since my infatuation began some four years earlier. And I justified my treachery by deciding I owed it to myself to at least meet her when an opportunity presented itself.

And at the thought of the Pin-up Pussycat launch the following week, I couldn't face breakfast. Not even a nibble of Sam's little heart. Instead I paced the kitchen wrapped in a towel, chain-smoking and throwing down pots of tea until I felt ill.

Deciding to avoid the lounge where her image and her mysterious smile gazed at me from every wall, I entered my study to throw myself into work. It was already midday and nothing irritates me more than a wasted day. And as this one was approaching the write-off stage, I forced myself to sit down and update the website.

LegLover.com was still getting six-figure hits every month and I had a queue of both professional and amateur models waiting to have their legs and feet photographed in clinical detail. The weekend coming I planned to shoot two girls together who were beginning to be a hit in fetish publications. So I wrote and fired off a confirmation of the details for our shoot and then tried to answer the requests and suggestions and queries that filled Leg Lover's mail service. I valued my customers, but just responding to overnight emails could take all day. While I acknowledged an email from a gentleman foot fetishist in Wisconsin who wanted to see a model's bare feet completely covering a male face, and who asked if it was possible to have more galleries featuring attractive younger women willingly feasting on the toes of older women, the phone rang.

'Al. Someone's just been in looking for you.'

It was Lucy. And the moment she said that my skin turned to goose-bumps. Instinctively, I knew who. It was like my restless period of longing that morning had either drawn her to my boutique, or I had experienced the anxiety as a result of her close proximity.

I swallowed to regain, at best, a thin voice. 'Oh?'

'Really beautiful girl. Looked like a movie star from one of them black and white films we play on the store telly.'

'Nylon Dahlia?'

'How did you know?'

'Oh, she's in town. I want to use her for a promotion.'

'OK. Well, she's like really weird. Walked around the shop and looked at everything. Wanted me to get out all these nylons from under the counter. She knew all the names and everything.'

Of course she did; she was the woman I was destined to be with. No suggestions or instructions required to educate her to my needs: she was the world's most extraordinary leg model, and as I had long suspected, she was a real, living female with a leg fetish. It was the way she stroked her legs on shoots, the genuine delight in her eyes as she adored her very own legs in photographs, the fact that she confessed in a *Leg Universe* interview that she wore real vintage nylons every single day, and had done since the age of twenty-one – the Nylon Dahlia was a woman with an endless fascination for female legs.

I tried to slow my pulse, to get words to form in my mouth. 'What did she say?'

'Not much. Just asked if you were around. And looked at the stockings. Bit cold if you ask me. Up herself, you know. I thought she was a bit scary.'

I cut Lucy off; didn't want to hear a word spoken against the empress of seams. 'Sure, sure. But is she coming back? Did she say when? A card? Did you give her my number at home?'

'Steady on. You're a bit keen.'

'No. No I'm not. But it's really important I see . . . meet her. For the business. I mean, what did she say about me?'

I heard her laughing. 'Nothing. I said you weren't in and she just nodded.'

I gulped back the thickening of shame in my throat. 'What was she wearing?'

'A really tight skirt that made her walk with baby steps. And, erm, yeah, she had a corset on under the jacket. Very pretty.'

'And?'

Lucy giggled. 'What else?'

Yes! I wanted to roar. Her legs! 'Heels?'

'Mmm. Strappy sandals and them seamed nylons you like. Black they was.'

I wanted to admonish Lucy for not giving her my direct number at home, but then realised the Nylon Dahlia must have it anyway if she knew of the shop. She must have read my correspondence then. Though she had never replied to any of my emails to her website, or letters sent care of her management, she must be aware of me. I mean, to visit the shop looking for me? I suddenly became insanely jealous and resentful of every other man in London who had the audacity to look at her, admire her, maybe try and speak to her. From my contacts among fetish photographers and in the adult magazines she'd appeared in, no one ever mentioned her having a boyfriend. They just said she was very professional, but rarely said much. Was cold. I had heard that before. But maybe she had never met anyone with a complete understanding of her interests. Someone who shared her enthusiasms.

'Al. You still there?'

'Yeah. Sorry. Was thinking.'

'You always got your head in the clouds. Must drive Sam crazy.'

'What do you mean?'

'Well, I thought you two was an item.'

'Oh?' I couldn't say anything else for a while, but Lucy filled the silence with a cheeky laugh. 'Did Sam meet the Nylon Dahlia?' I eventually ventured.

'Nah. You're all right there, mate. She never saw the competition. She was working in the office with the accountant.'

Once again, I thought how satisfying it would be to put Lucy over my knee and to take a wooden-handled hairbrush to her tight-skirted backside. Or even better, to see Cecilia do it, while in the fiery back-draught of some lesbian rage after forcibly stripping Lucy down to her flimsies. Lucy's sluttishness was matched only by her garrulous mouth and I longed to see the two combine preceding some non-consensual punishment ritual. A desire made stronger by my suspicion she would be thrilled by it. Slut.

I rang off and walked through to the lounge. Lit a cigarette and sat on the floor. Reduced to the boards in my own home, I remained still for a long time and tried to fathom the significance of the Nylon Dahlia's visit to Sheer Delight, while simultaneously torturing myself with Lucy's description of her outfit. I was still there when the sun went down.

Five

'Last time we were talking about your preoccupation with the legs of strangers, with women in the street, but mainly about your relationship with Sam.'

Somehow I knew the doctor would dwell on this. Call it male intuition. 'Yes. Though I didn't see it as a relationship at the time.'

Her face does its best to refrain from reflecting the disapproval I am sure simmers beneath the handsome exterior.

I glance down at her trousered legs: pinstriped trousers with a matching jacket and black leather boots that rise to her knee inside the trouser legs, but are hidden from my prying eyes.

'I took her interest in me for granted. Like I always did. Was greedy. Stuck in my ways for sure. I feigned indifference for the remainder of that week, as if the evening at my flat was no big deal, but went into the salon every day. In case the Nylon Dahlia came back. My casual attitude hurt Sam. She tried to be intimate with me when Lucy and Cecilia weren't around. I evaded it. Even avoided being alone with her. She'd spent a night with me and we'd taken things another step towards a commitment of sorts. I knew it. But the Nylon Dahlia was all I could think about. It felt like I'd waited my whole life to meet her.' I pause to get my breath and to swallow the cold lump of guilt that seems to have lodged at the back of my throat. I haven't been sleeping well, nor eating much, and I feel the familiar exhaustion and nervous worry intrude through my stomach.

'And it gets worse.'

The doctor frowns. 'Worse? What do you mean?'

'At the end of the week I met two models for a Leg Lover shoot. I'd been wanting to photograph them for ages and this was my chance. So I met them in a hotel, the Hilton in Park Lane, to do a girl–girl foot-fetish scene for the website. Things got out of hand.'

'I see.'

'Maybe you do. Despite my infatuation with the Dahlia and my indecision over Sam, I still managed to misbehave with other suitably attired women. Now you probably have a better idea of why I am here. Why I came to see you. My fetish is out of control.'

'That's it, Angela. But put your legs higher. Get your toes level with Jenna's mouth. Perfect. Hold it right there.' I knelt down to get the shot from the side of the bed. Angela and Jenna were giggling again. Jenna was kneeling by the pillows; Angela lay on her back, propped up by her elbows, her head near the end of the bed.

'Now, Jenna, can you make that great face I've seen you do. As if you're really aroused. In a swoon. Pretend Angela's sexy little feet are just the most desirable and adorable things you've ever had so close to your face.'

'Maybe they are,' Angela said, laughing. Short and busty and tanned, Angela was a pretty glamour girl and adult model with a growing profile online and in the red-top magazines. Though her feet were petite, they were exquisitely shaped. Pretty little toes extending from the sweet unblemished feet at the end of her small curvaceous legs. Through her suntan-sheen pantyhose her silver toe rings and Raspberry Ice toenail polish caught my eye, and held it.

I took half a dozen shots from three angles as Jenna and Angela held their first pose. Jenna kneeling, dressed in a startling white cotton bra and sheer-to-the-waist white tights, through which the dark patch of her sex was clearly visible behind the see-through gusset; and Angela lying on her back on my pink satin sheets, topless and bereft of panties in a pair of Pretty Polly suntan-sheen tights which made her compact legs look wet.

'Pull your toes back, Angela. Jenna, put your nose close to the underside of Angela's toes.'

Angela laughed. 'Don't make her. They might be really horrible. I've been wearing boots all morning.'

For a few seconds I breathed deep to let my own dizziness pass as I watched Jenna place the tip of her thin nose against Angela's feet. 'Mmm,' she purred. 'They smell nice.' She pulled a face expressing such a convincing longing for Angela's pretty tootsies that Angela stopped laughing. 'Don't you get me going again, Jen.'

My digital camera clicked and processed at maximum speed. I zoomed in, I zoomed out. Without any prompting from me, the tall and slender Jenna extended her tongue and drew it up the silky sole of Angela's foot.

Angela's eyes hooded. Her big red lips broke into a wide smile. Jenna licked again at the nylon lollipop held firm in her right hand. Dragged her long pink tongue from Angela's heel to the tip of her toes.

'Ooh. That's making me a bit wet,' Angela said – not to me, but to Jenna. They were notorious for playing together during shoots. Jenna was gay and Angela was bisexual. Genuinely enamoured with each other, as well as being best friends. The queue of photographers waiting to work with them was long. I'd waited three months to get them together for a day, in a hotel bed, and was paying each of them five hundred pounds plus expenses. A fee they would earn to the last penny, before appearing on the Leg Lover site in a new May gallery my loyal members were anxious to view.

I'd told the girls to bring every pair of high-heeled shoes and boots they could get inside a taxi. I knew their shoe sizes, so I would provide the hosiery. In the corner of the double room at the Hilton, beside the small table containing the champagne bottle and glasses, each of the girl's carry cases were stacked – filled to busting with garter belts, lingerie and shoes for the shoot.

Slowly, I moved nearer to the bed to close right on to Jenna's open mouth and Angela's damp foot. Knelt on the mattress and took six snaps at close range. Every detail of Angela's feet was captured – the sheen and sparkle of her tights, the fine web between the ends of her toes, the little wrinkles of skin over the joints of her metatarsals, the odd freckle on the brown flesh of her ankle.

Hoarse with excitement, I didn't recognise my own voice. 'Can you take the bra off, Jenna. And Angela, will you rub your feet against Jenna's nipples.'

'Not a problem,' she said, smiling up at Jenna, who quickly unhooked her bra, plucked it from her breasts and dropped it on the bed. Angela's little feet immediately covered Jenna's milky bosom and pink nipples. And started to slowly run up and down, and then whirl in circles like she'd done it before. Jenna's pupils grew as large as black olives and she stared down at Angela with a mixture of desire and what looked like annoyance at being so weak for the busty creature wriggling below.

'Jenna,' I said, with a rasp, then cleared my throat. 'Jenna, can you stroke Angela's legs –' But she'd already begun to do just that. Stroking her long white fingers up and down her partner's polished shins and calves. Strong white spotlights arranged around the sides of the room created a lustre on their hosed legs, making them reflective like polished glass against the more metallic refraction of the ruffled satin sheets I'd dressed the bed with before they arrived.

Viewfinder ablaze with a nylon glister, I crept around the bed; moved in; drew back; stalked the perfumed, glossy beauties in my stage-managed fantasy life. I was an auteur in these situations. I indulged my own vision first, exactingly. And somehow the results of my passion and enthusiasm, and my attention to detail, appealed to my fans. Though they were never short of suggestions to indulge their own obsessions.

'Hold it. Right there,' I instructed, while trying to change the card with trembling fingers. Before me, the girls were staring into each other's eyes. Pupils wide as owls'. Desire was growing. Jenna lavished her palms all over Angela's hose-slick legs, while her smaller partner flicked and rubbed Jenna's nipples into pink pellets. The nylon on the soles of her slippery feet must have been causing considerable friction.

'OK. Just a few more.' I took another six of Jenna's bright-red fingernails against Angela's gauzy leg flesh.

'That's it. Let's have a little change of position.' Remembering a popular request from my website members, I had Angela kneel on the bed, buttocks upwards, chest leaning forwards, face turned to the side my camera would cover. Then asked Jenna to stretch from the floor up to Angela's smooth, hyaline arse cheeks. And to make it appear as if she was about to eat Angela's anus and sex through her pantyhose. 'Can you poke your tongue –'

Again, there was no need to finish the instruction: Jenna knew exactly what I wanted.

111

Angela released a little sigh and slipped two fingers into her mouth, as Jenna's long, pointed tongue swept against the tight, pellucid film covering the brown button of her anus. As she pushed back at Jenna's mouth to increase the contact, to make it firmer, I got in closer with the camera. 'Jenna, just pull your hair back. That's it. Beautiful. I can die now. I am the happiest man alive.'

The girls laughed but never broke position. Jenna's tongue moved down. Followed the barely invisible seam between Angela's bulbous cheeks, before she angled her face to get her tongue on the smaller model's pussy, wet beneath a transparent film of fine nylon.

'Bum up a bit, Angela,' I said, nuzzling in close to Jenna to get a close-up of her mouth working against the taut glaze over Angela's trimmed pelt. As her saliva soaked into the fabric of Angela's crotch, and as Angela's sex leaked its own salted lubricant, the filmy gauze of her tights became completely see-through. Jenna suddenly made a sucking noise and, for a moment, I noticed how wide her eyes were – trying to devour as much of Angela's quim as my lens. Each side of her nose then briefly thinned as she inhaled and savoured the scent of her lover's excited sex.

'Can I rip through these fucking things?' she said to me, over her shoulder.

I tried to say 'sure', but my vocal chords were dry and I made a pitiful fluting sound in response. But Jenna got the message. Digging two sharp fingernails into the crotch of Angela's tights, she made a hole and then ripped the sheer fabric along the seam. Broad ladders spread across Angela's buttocks, but her tights were so sheer and saturated with moisture, it was hard for me to see where the nylon ended and the flesh began. A tuft of mousey floss, dark with damp, poked through the rend in her tights. And Jenna's tongue dabbed up and in. Lapped quickly, pumped in and out of Angela's brown lips.

Creased with pleasure, open-mouthed, Angela raised her face and frowned at the ceiling. Then dropped her head between her shoulders and peered through her open thighs, mesmerised at the sight of Jenna's long, feline body gently swaying as her pretty face ate between her thighs. Angela made little crying noises. Then coughed like a cat with a fur-ball in its throat as she came. Jenna began to rub her whole mouth and chin into Angela's sex like she was licking a bowl clean. Her hands gripped Angela's translucent thighs, then rubbed them, up and down, up and down, making her hose hiss. A multi-sensory experience. I could smell Angela's sex too and, like a male beast, I felt a strong desire to mate with these felines in my pride.

Unable to move with ease or comfort on account of the thick and dewy erection poling out my jeans, I clicked and zoomed, clicked, clicked, zoomed. Only stopping to change yet another card. Failing to do so because my hands were shaking, I snatched at my spare digital camera. Already down to the back-up. I needed to pace myself.

Eventually, Jenna sat back smiling and breathing hard. Red lipstick was smudged a pinky colour up to her nose and down her chin. 'God, she's wet,' Jenna said to me. 'But she tastes so good.'

I got busy over by the refreshment table to hide my red face and obvious erection. I poured more champagne and filled three glasses with iced Evian, before taking a silver tray across to the bed to serve my girls. 'Time for a costume change, ladies.'

'Sure. What you want us in next?' Jenna asked.

Sleepy-eyed and flushed, Angela lay on her back and rolled her tights down her legs. Immediately, I saw a magnificent shot. 'Hold it there, Angela!' I moved into position and took several pictures that I would arrange like still-frame animation in the gallery, as Angela's petite fingers pushed a roll of tan flimsiness over her ankles and down her feet until they were bare. Pantyhose guys love every detail.

'Thanks, babe. Men love your feet. You don't know how much. Nylons next. Jenna in black fully fashioned stockings and Angela in the same, but in chocolate please. Can you both start with strappy sandals and get fully dressed too. Then, I'll take some detailed close-ups of you both individually, then together, followed by you stripping each other. Real slow.'

'You sure this is for your website, or for you, Al?' Jenna asked, her eyes smiling.

'We are indivisible.'

On my knees I then sat before each girl's legs as they slowly removed the long ribbons of transparent nylon from the square packaging. Filmed them rolling the stockings into ruffles in which to dip their painted toenails. Recorded for all time, the images of them drawing the dark roll up their shaven flesh until the roll diminished into the dark welt of a stocking top at the top of their thighs.

To my delight, I captured the genuine excitement on each girl's face as they performed this innocent but powerful ritual. I can think of no other practice that defines women at their most vulnerable and feminine than the process of putting on stockings. It is magic.

'If she don't ruin them, can I keep them, Al? They're lush,' Angela said.

'I'll give you both a new pair after the shoot. Those already belong to the winner of the March Leg Lover competition.'

The girls giggled and wrinkled their noses in feigned distaste, as I took pictures of the dark material of Jenna's reinforced instep and dark toes; the glassine shimmer of Angela's calves under the bright canopy of illumination; the delightful creases around each girl's ankles and behind their knees; the smooth planes of diaphanous thigh; the long ink-black seam running up the back of Jenna's long limbs, the pale skin luminescent beneath the smoke-screen of black nylon; the tug of each silver suspender clasp on the shiny stocking tops. I anticipated over two hundred pictures in this fully fashioned gallery alone.

'They're all so slippy and silky,' Angela said. It was her first time in real nylons. 'But I can't keep the seam straight. They go baggy every time I move.' I was glad I'd put a microphone under the head of the bed. Her dialogue was priceless for one so in thrall to his fascination.

My arousal heightened as they buckled their feet into black strappy sandals. I felt light-headed. Fatigued by desire. If I was to rush to the bathroom and spend more than a few minutes in there, my purpose would be obvious. No, I wanted to prolong my arousal until it actually hurt.

'Look at you both. Beautiful,' I muttered, unable to blink, my eyeballs dry and hot and stinging from over-stimulation.

'So what do you want us to do now?' Jenna asked.

Dozens of thoughts crammed themselves into the doorway of cognition in my mind, until I was mentally paralysed and unable to speak.

'How about this?' Jenna wrapped her long legs around Angela's waist, to make the smaller model effectively sit in her lap. Immediately, Angela's small hands began to explore the shiny length of her friend's thighs.

'Ooh, don't they feel nice.' Her pretty brown eyes were alight with a genuine fascination and excitement.

'You're getting me going again, you little slut,' Jenna muttered to Angela. I wasn't sure whether I was supposed to hear but was glad I had.

Pressing into each other, squirming about, their nylons creased and whispered against shaven flesh, roaming hands, the smooth sheets. They began to kiss. Rolled on to their sides. Ground their groins together, until Jenna looped a long leg over Angela and began to rub her pussy against Angela's hip. Pushing herself back and forth towards her climax. 'How's this, Al? Mmm? Perverts like this? Will they get off watching me in stockings wank myself on another girl's body?'

I nodded. Took pictures. Felt my body shake as Jenna's dark sexuality gravitated into the bedroom. And filled it.

Smiling, Angela kicked her feet into the air and wriggled under Jenna's rubbing sex. Leaning forwards, I took a set of pictures of Angela's feet, the dark reinforced soles and toes visible through the black spaghetti straps of her high-heeled sandals.

Jenna began to moan and shake. Her eyes began to close and her long toes locked inside the manacles of her strappy sandals.

'Her leg, Jenna. Can't you fuck Angela's leg?'

Moving backwards from Angela's hip, without pausing in her frantic humping of Angela's pelvic bone, Jenna slid her sex on to Angela's stockinged thigh. And squealed. 'That's nice. That's good. So good,' she muttered to herself and worked glossy smears all over the nylon lubricity of her lover's stocking. She used Angela as a toy, a pretty, voluptuous doll. Pushed and ground her long sex against the smaller girl's shiny leg. I was damp with perspiration, but shivered.

Jenna came quickly, with a cry and a few final quick humps of Angela's leg. Angela's eyes grew black with excitement at the sight of her friend in such rapture.

'Sixty-nine each other.' I couldn't help it. Their desire for each other and tipsy abandon was now directing this shoot; I was but a spectator throwing in the odd suggestion from the sidelines of the studio. 'Eat each other. Stroke each other's legs while you're doing it. I want to see those seams moving and nylons creasing under your fingers.'

Before I'd finished giving the instruction, the girls had writhed into position. Eyeliner running, lips glazed and smudgy, they gripped each other's thighs and sank their beautiful mouths on to each other's damp trimmed fur.

Fingers shaking, I checked the battery level. If I missed this, I told myself, I'll pitch my body through the window. Battery was nearly dead, but no time to change it, so I switched back to the first camera, changing the card with the proficiency of a professional soldier un-jamming his weapon under fire.

Getting in tight with the girls, I began to snap the action: the dabbing and stroking tongues; the little pink mouths of their open slits; the pressing of wet quims, soapy with cum, against the hard bones of each other's faces; the grasping red nails against loosening, twisting nylon stockings; the thin, black creases of nylon rubbed loose above their soft flesh; the pointing and bending and flexing of long toes inside dark silkiness. I captured as much as was humanly possible.

Straightening my back, I hurriedly checked the camera and levels again, terrified of a technical glitch. And as I ran a quick preview, to make sure the pictures weren't too dark, I felt a pressure against my groin.

I looked down. And saw the sole of Angela's patent sandal pushing at the tumescence in my jeans. I looked at her face. Saw half a face, half a smile obscured by Jenna's thigh, the milky skin a background for a suspender strap. Angela's one visible eye winked. So I pushed against the shoe. Rubbed my mound against the sole and spiked heel. Grabbed her ankle and then photographed her foot against my swollen crotch.

I had not foreseen this. Couldn't have hoped for it. But on more than one occasion, a model of mine had seduced me into the frame. But Angela and Jenna? Never. Surely not. They were famous.

Angela's face disappeared back between Jenna's thighs, but an invitation had been delivered to join the party. I hung the camera around my neck. Unbuckled Angela's shoe. Slipped it off her foot. Unzipped myself. Pulled my wood-meat into the warm air. Then pressed it into the wrinkled instep of Angela's petite foot. It responded by closing – a warm, black nyloned hand – around my shaft. Gripped it between her bent toes. Worked it. Made me gasp. As her excitement grew from the lapping of Jenna's big tongue on her pussy, her little foot increased its pressure against my cock. Unbuckling, I pushed my jeans down. My boxers followed. Holding her silky calf, I guided it between my thighs. Slippery and ticklish, her sleek foot twisted between my bare thighs. I shivered as a field of ice crystals grew up my back and then melted at the nape of my neck. Angela then rubbed her foot against my sac. Pulled it up and out so my cock poled up against my stomach.

On the bed, Angela started to moan and gulp at the air as she climaxed. I held her foot steady and fucked myself against it. Pumped at the creasing nylon, the webbing folds, the soft pads of her toes. Seized the camera from where it hung about my neck and recorded my cock against her foot.

Jenna writhed on the sheets, and began a hoarse coughing noise as she too came from the insistent, relentless administration of Angela's full lips and little square teeth on her intimacy. They held each other. Kissed each other's flesh. The foot was withdrawn. I was still excited but began to feel self-conscious, standing beside the bed with my trousers down.

Jenna saw me, as if sensing my humiliation. Frowned, then smiled. 'I wondered how long it would be until you had to have a wank, mister.'

'No. Angela. She . . .'

'I rubbed his prick,' Angela said, looking at me with glazed eyes. 'It looked huge. He must have been in pain.'

I shrugged. 'I volunteered for this. I can't complain.'

As I bent over to pull my jeans back up, Jenna said, 'Why don't you foot fuck him, Angela, while I take photos. Bet your members will love that.'

I smiled at Jenna. 'Not as much as the site owner, but I applaud your improvisational skills. Where do you want me?'

Angela glanced about the room, then at the foot of the bed. 'Sit on the end of the bed. Let me get the other shoe off.'

After kicking off my trousers and underwear, I surrendered the camera to Jenna's long, ghostly hands and then assumed a position with my feet on the floor and my upper body propped up on my elbows on the mattress. Under the sudden scrutiny of Jenna's big eyes, and in all the commotion, my cock had begun to soften. But Angela soon reversed the decline by shuffling her bottom closer to me, and extending her legs so her feet reached my groin.

Jenna stood over us and peered down, squinting through the camera viewfinder. 'She's got sweet little feet, which makes your cock look bigger.'

'Cheers.'

'Don't mention it.'

Angela's feet grasped my shaft, so each instep was firm on either side of my rigidity. Then, slowly – her face frowning in concentration, lips parted – she began to rub her feet up and down, up and down. As they moved her nylons creased around her feet. I looked at her legs, varnished in chocolate nylon. Then looked at Jenna's long legs and slender feet, all glazed by a black hose-gloss. 'This won't take long,' I murmured.

'Good. Cos there's only ten pics left. I'll save one for when you come. And milk all over her sexy toes. Oops, too late.'

And it was. The soft caresses of Angela's feet combined with all I had seen that afternoon brought me to a swift climax. My head reeled. My short-term memory saturated with the sight of glassy nylon, beautiful girls, scarlet nails, spike heels, sucking mouths, I watched my own come shoot, plop, spill and run all over the tops of Angela's shiny feet.

'Last one,' Jenna said, leaning forwards with the camera to capture the messy feet. 'And it's a good one.'

Six

'And then I assume you met the Nylon Dahlia?'

I nod. Say, 'Yes,' with a sigh. A brief exhalation of air loaded with a longing that will never let me rest. A noise taut with genuine anguish, frustration, guilt. In the doctor's room, I suddenly have a clearer understanding of the Chinese businessmen who become eunuchs to concentrate on business. Post-historical man: remove the struggle for food, shelter, warmth, clean water and territory, and we fill our heads with the legs or breasts or backsides of women.

'Do you want to talk about her today?'

I nod again. It's probably the right time to tell her the next part of the story. To fill the room with my words again. While they are still unreconstructed. Before my imagination turns the narrative into something creative. Let the truth fall upon her understanding, patient ears.

But I wonder what the doctor thinks of at night, in bed. I'd like to know. Little is as fascinating to me as female sexuality. I never underestimate it. But if she understands the human condition so intimately can she just let herself feel and dream, or are her fantasies hampered by clinical theory as they unfold?

She has pretty legs. Even hidden inside those silky black trousers, you can still see their rangy, coltish shape. Her lovers must have been attracted to her legs.

She has a small bust. Or does she tantalise them by the strength of her mind alone? No wedding ring. I wonder.

'Well, I opened the box.'

She frowns.

'Some women achieve such a height of physical perfection, they transcend the real world. They go beyond the expectations of ordinary people and become mythical. Become living dolls sustained by male, and female, adoration. But should they ever be taken from the box, I wonder? Who is courageous enough, or foolish enough, to attempt such a thing?'

So long as to appear slightly unreal, her legs were the first I saw of the Nylon Dahlia in person. As it should be, I thought at the time.

Most of the couch and the sides of the small stage were in darkness. Her burlesque act began with the music – Sinatra. Then the round moon of spectral light appeared on the back of the couch.

Slender to the ankle and tapering into black Cuban-heeled shoes, her legs unfolded into the air. Feet first from behind the red leather sofa, centre stage. The single white spotlight picked them out: two shimmering silhouettes, sleek as wet eels.

She must have been lying on the sofa cushions with her legs tucked in. Then swivelled her upper body to ease her legs upwards into the air. Snakes with transparent black skins, hypnotising every man in the room. And they played, those legs. Slithered and writhed together. Kicked out to the music. Pointed at the ceiling, her muscles taut beneath her seamed nylons. Rotated from side to side, as if we were watching the legs of a synchronised swimmer: one bent, the white leather sole of a new shoe touching the knee of the other leg.

And then her hands appeared – thin, long, white hands. Ghostly fingers. Red clots of varnish on the nails. Reminded me of glazed cherries; of fingers dipped into an open heart. Up her legs they moved, smoothing the nylon against the shaven flesh beneath.

She pulled her legs together and back. Tensed her calves. Showed us the glossy contours of thigh to ankle, the thin black seams from heel to golden suspender clips, four to each black welt. Caressed her own legs with hands so beautiful and pale in the white light I thought them sinister and cruel in their beauty. Pinched the seam behind each knee, pulled it out. Tented the nylon over white skin. Released the cobweb of black gossamer. Danced those legs again, to the beat of the music. Had them smooch together, ever so slowly. Each leg began to take on a character of its own. They were her puppets; but then we were her puppets too.

Lips parted, mouth dry, I watched. Spellbound, until my eyes burned, I strained to see every swish and jig of right leg and left leg: the most beautiful legs in the world. Legs that crossed and strutted all over my living-room walls.

Then they suddenly parted. Hooked themselves over the back of the couch, in the same way they would grapple the back of a lover's thighs as he lurched and ground himself into her. Then up and over she came, in one swift movement. Must have pushed herself up from the floor in the same position as a gymnast performing a handstand. And she stood before us, smiling. Wet lips red as murder below the hem of a thin veil that fell across the biggest eyes and longest lashes. The audience erupted into applause. My own clapping deafened me.

An unfeasibly tight purple corset with transparent panels cinched her waist. A single strand of white pearls fell from her ballerina throat to the alabaster cleavage. She stood on one foot and bent the other leg so the toe of one shiny shoe touched the kneecap of the straight supporting leg. Then she kicked the bent leg up high, above her head so her outstretched hand caught it and held it up there, thigh flat against her chest, shin tight to her cheek. I had no idea she was this supple and was not prepared for her full height. For a while I stopped breathing.

And then she danced for us. Fanned two gigantic ostrich feathers about herself. Never killed that scarlet smile once; just petrified us with her dollish beauty. Nor did she seem to tire from the exertion as she pranced and pirouetted about the stage, never leaving the bright spotlight, as if she were a marionette only able to exist within the silvery glare of a moon. And how it made her stockings shine.

'Ooh, she's so good,' Sam repeated beside me. Even she was bewitched. To my shame, I regretted taking her. But all three of my girls at Sheer Delight had pouted at the thought of being left out. After all, Lucy said, 'She invited us too.' And she had done, leaving a small pile of invitations on the counter of Sheer Delight after stroking the packets of real nylons. Packages I had touched and stocked with care in the glass cabinet. But Sam and the girls did have their use; it was much better to be seen by the Nylon Dahlia in the middle of a group of attractive women. Especially my girls, dressed at my insistence in their pretty uniforms and each wearing a new pair of Gio RHT stockings on their shapely legs. And it was also the girls that drew the Nylon Dahlia to us. Later, after the show.

Across the club she strode towards us. Agile on dancer's legs. Sculpted face held imperiously high, her exquisite eye make-up still dramatic behind the black mist of her veil. Having changed into a rubber pencil skirt, leaving her upper body still manacled within the corset, spectral arms bare, she came to us. Me, I wanted to think. To me.

A champagne flute pinched between long fingers that alone were worthy of any fine artist's obsession, she smiled, but only when she stood close to us. 'How delightful your girls look. All co-ordinated. What a wonderful little shop you have,' she said to me while staring, in turn, deep into each of my assistants' eyes. 'Full of so many pretty things.' All of the girls blushed. They too reeled under the icy force of her personality and the glare from her snow-witch face. 'I must have one of these pretty dresses. I really must. For one of my routines. The airline stewardess.'

'You can. I will. I mean we don't have your size, but I'll get one made,' I jabbered, feeling uncomfortably hot in my dinner suit and bow tie. I felt Sam's eyes shift to me, narrow, and nick my cheek like a new razor.

This was not how I imagined our first meeting. We should have been alone. My head emptied of most of what I meant to say to her. What remained seemed trite and foolish.

'You were great,' Cecilia said.

'Yeah, really fab. You're so fit,' Lucy added.

I grinned; helpless, smitten, in pain and confused. The Nylon Dahlia subtly lowered her chin and fluttered her eyelids to acknowledge the praise. 'And you,' she said to Sam. 'Did you like the show?'

To her credit, Sam smiled sweetly, her eyes full of warm and genuine admiration. 'It was beautiful. So graceful. Like ballet.'

'Oh darling,' the Dahlia said, and leaned forwards to kiss Sam on the cheek. It made her giggle.

I felt stunned, baffled. She had yet to even look me in the eye. I suddenly felt ridiculous. Thought of the letters I had written to her, her booking agent, sponsors, manager, the emails to her website. A disappointment cold as grief filled me up. Something stoppered my throat. My enthusiasm had gotten the better of me: I had made her wary; become obsessed with an image; invested her with a character and life like a love-struck adolescent. Shame washed across my face like a flannel soaked in boiling water.

'Daaarling!' she said, turning on her heel, away from us, from me. Having caught the eye of another man I had been half conscious of during the exchange, hovering near us, beaming and irritating me. She embraced him. Kissed him on both cheeks. Held him around the waist. Allowed him to lead her away to mingle.

'Wow, she's a bit weird,' Lucy said.

'But so lovely,' Cecilia muttered to herself.

'What did you think of her, Al?' Sam asked me. 'You've been dying to meet her. Does she measure up? Looks even better than all those photos you got of her.'

Lucy and Cecilia exchanged knowing looks and fought to restrain their smiles. I took a mouthful of fizzy beer, swallowed hard, stuttered something, but couldn't conceal the wretchedness I was feeling at having been ignored. Spurned, it felt like.

As we too moved about the gathering, my mind was hardly present during any of the conversations with the distributors, manufacturers, journalists and general liggers you always get in attendance at these launches. I was too aware of her. In the room with me. Out there somewhere, talking to someone else. At times I caught glimpses of her among the heads in the dark confines of the club; a beauty it pained me to look upon. Always the centre of attention, her pale throat and astonishing eyes towering above anyone near her. How shabby I thought the other women looked. How conniving and mercenary the men about her. Then she would disappear and I would feel suddenly bereft. Choked with disappointment. Looking everywhere, excusing myself to go to the gents, I searched for her and she evaded me. Disappeared. Imagining her beside an admirer in a cab, speeding off to an apartment or hotel room, I mourned the end of what felt like the greatest opportunity missed and never to return. I despised myself for failing at such a crucial stage in my crusade to have her.

Finally, exhausted by a man with terrible breath who ranted drunkenly about the state of the purchasing trade, I slunk away from the crowd and slumped on to a couch in an empty corner. Leaving the girls with his oily corned-beef cheeks.

Dizzy from beer and champagne and disappointment, I tore my tie off and massaged my brow. She had gone. Without so much as a goodbye. She hadn't even looked me in the eye. I had to accept she found me unattractive, desperate and unappealing; a schoolboy with a crush, not a real man.

But at last, another part of my tortured mind cried out. At last it's over. You are released. The curse of an appalling, debilitating desire is lifted.

A warm, invigorating relief began to rise through me. My judgement had been impaired for too long. Such a fixation with a complete stranger was unhealthy. Unacceptable for a man of my age and experience. Sam adored me and I held her at arm's length with my cruel and shameful indifference. Angela and Jenna, Patricia and myriad other attractive women indulged me beyond the dreams of most men who shared my fascination for legs. How dare I be so ungrateful, so corpulent with greed and selfishness. I shook my head, ashamed, as if to knock the last of some demented sleep from my mind. And then she spoke.

'At last, an opportunity presents itself.'

I looked to my left, stunned, as the Nylon Dahlia took a seat beside me, legs whisking, one across the other. Cigarette in a holder held aloft between long fingers. Eyes half-lidded. A sly smile about her voluptuous mouth, she spoke to me. 'You're an interesting man, Algernon. And I don't meet many interesting men.'

I think I said, 'Thanks.' But at best it was nothing but a mumble.

'We are the same, I think. Have too much to say to each other and so make each other congested. Perhaps it is an unspoken attachment. Words come later. With familiarity.'

I wasn't sure I knew what she meant. But I knew I was back in that maddening place peopled with frustration, hope, false hope, desire. 'With familiarity': was that an invitation to something I had hitherto only dreamt about?

'You got my letters?' I said, my every word sounding uncouth in her presence.

She nodded. Smiled. Froze my gut and heart with a direct, penetrating stare that made me lower my eyes in deference. 'Every one. But I get many letters. From many persistent admirers.'

'I bet. I guess . . .'

'Go on.'

'I guess, I always hoped that you would realise we had an empathy.'

She frowned, a little uncomfortable. What was I doing with this talk of empathy? I wanted to boil my tongue in hot piss.

'I meant to say,' I continued, sitting up straight, 'I've always believed there are but a handful of women on this earth who not only understand but also share my interest. My passion.'

'And you think I am like you?'

'We have dedicated our adult lives to . . . well, to a certain look.'

'To these, darling.' Stretching out a leg to catch the distant shore of light that washed about our feet, she then rotated a long beautiful foot that I knew every inch of. Then tensed the cut of her feminine muscles under a veil of sheer black nylon. 'You are right. I am an unusual girl.'

'A muse for some.' Unable to help myself, I confessed so much in that one line. It was more the way I said it with my voice on the verge of breaking that made her look at me with a vulnerability in her expression I had only ever seen in certain photo-shoots. An expression that softened the angles of her face. Made her look youthful.

'Am I your muse?'

I nodded. 'You were never a girl who just put on sexy clothes to make money. I can tell. You actually invest yourself into your image, into your work. You've become art. It's not superficial. Not just on the surface. I can sense your imagination, your character in every pose.'

She smiled. Seemed almost ready to blush. Looked down at her hands, cupped about her polished knees. 'I liked your letters.'

'You never answered.'

'Would you, if a strange man on the other side of the world enthused about you, flattered you, desired you even?'

Clearing my throat still left me with nothing to say.

She laughed. Threw her head back.

'I never intended to make you feel uncomfortable. I just thought –'

'Just thought what? That you would possess me. Bring me to you with business deals? Feature on your website?'

Inside, my organs twisted, hot and uncomfortable. 'They were legitimate. I am a businessman and you do have the most beautiful legs in the world.'

'Of course, darling.' The aloof façade was back. I wanted to reach the tender part of her again. 'And you are disappointed in me now?'

'No.'

'You are. You expected more from me. You seem dejected.'

'Actually, I was just about to accept defeat. Admit you were unobtainable. Release myself from a ridiculous infatuation. I'm sorry.' I wouldn't have said any of this had I not been so intoxicated. To even get most of it past my lips I had to look away from her shiny legs – the glimpse of a dark seam, the triangular shadow of the reinforced heel of her stocking emerging from the patent curve of her shoe.

'Ha!' she cried out, and kicked a leg into the air, before crossing it tight over the other thigh with a whisper I felt in the marrow of my bones. 'Do you think I would release such devotion so easily?'

Betraying every volt of wonderment, hope and excitement that coursed through me, I turned my face to her but remained mute.

'Why did you think I came to your store today? Mmm? Of course it was to find you. Out of curiosity. I wanted to know who you really were.' Again, her voice softened. The challenge vanished from her eyes.

'Let's meet then. Be alone together. I mean, dinner. Somewhere quiet where we can talk. If nothing else, let me listen to you. To me you have always been perfection. I'm sorry. But I may never get the chance to say so again. You represent the furthest reach of my passion. Not just for certain things. But for the way they are worn. And used.' I no longer cared. My entire body tingled. My skin goosed. It was hard to keep my voice from shaking.

She turned towards me, one foot brushed my leg. I tensed. An erection struck me, took me by surprise. The hard muscle was afflicted with a tantalising attack of pins and needles at the very end. A pleasing numbness that seemed to anticipate a series of paralysing contractions. I had never experienced anything like this before. Not even as a teenager. Just the briefest touch of her leg, so smooth in stockings and exquisitely mounted on a pedestal of leather heel, made me ready to ejaculate. In public.

'Monday, then. I'll meet you at Sheer Delight. You can give me a gift.'

Suddenly my bad conscience opened for business and filled my mind with images of Lucy, Cecilia and, of course, Samantha. They would be there and I would be seen going out on a date with the Nylon Dahlia.

'You don't seem so sure? But I have engagements the rest of the time I am in London. It can only be Monday.'

'No, no. Monday is fine. Wonderful. Sevenish?' I said, thinking of dismissing the girls and waiting alone. 'Then you can have the store all to yourself. You can point at things and they will become yours.'

She laughed. 'Like a girl in a magical toy shop.' Placed a long hand on my thigh. At the top of my thigh. Brushed my shin with her shoe. Pulled her toes back so I could see a series of discreet wrinkles on her nylons about her ankle joint. I felt faint. Heavy-headed. Delirious from the pleasure of making her laugh. Of genuinely amusing her.

'And I can have you all to myself for once,' I said with sincere relief.

She smiled. 'Those pretty girls must be a handful. Pretty girls always are. They cast spells, you know.'

'I know.'

'And in those uniforms and nylons all day. Teetering about you like sweet, little hostesses, it must be hard to concentrate. And that pretty blonde with the angel mouth, she likes you. Many men would be enslaved by a smile from her. You and she? You are together?'

'Oh no, not at all.'

'Don't lie and say you only have eyes for the Dahlia. I've seen your website. So many naughty girls have taken your cock between their feet.'

She was teasing again. And I was momentarily crushed with humiliation. The kind of shame that presses the very air from your body. Caught masturbating by parents shame.

Her foot curled around my shin, then withdrew. 'But you must have lovers, of course you must. Enthusiasts like us are epic in our loving. We adore variety. The thrill of the hunt. The pride of capture. Yes, you and I are much the same.' Her teeth seemed to flash bright and large as she said this. Maybe it was my imagination, but I thought I detected a hint of spite in her words. She was smiling, but did she intend to wound?

'Maybe. Because maybe we are looking for a certain someone through others.'

'Oh. Good answer. The right answer. And I can see in your eyes that you meant it.'

Confidence and esteem restored, I exhaled. Terrified of losing this rare catch from the taut and straining line of my will, I forced myself to concentrate, to dispel the fog of alcohol mist, to reclaim control of my jaw.

'We're going now,' Lucy said from my right side.

I turned and smiled. 'No, so soon?'

'It's late. Some of us have to get up early for work, mate.'

'You tell him, girl,' the Dahlia said, laughing. Cecilia was already in her coat. Samantha wasn't with them.

'Where's Sam?' I asked.

'She's gone,' Cecilia said, without looking at me. But the wretchedness never returned. I felt a brief flicker of guilt, like a little blue flame inside my ribcage. But it was quickly doused by the exhilarating force of complete and renewed desire for the Dahlia. Only this time, there was nothing ethereal about my feelings for her. This was no crush. I had actually met her. Impressed her enough to be granted an audience. A second meeting. She was curious about me. I had made her laugh. I would not sleep, I knew that. And after the weekend I would be the happiest man in London.

But as I took a taxi home and replayed the episode over and over again in my mind, my euphoria was disturbed by an irritating suspicion that the Nylon Dahlia had been acting. She had an American accent but spoke like a countess in a Hollywood movie. Had she been in role?

Seven

'You were telling me about the Nylon Dahlia.' The doctor can barely say the name. It doesn't seem easy for her to shape such a name with her elegant mouth. It's a name that comes from a world I am sure she has only read about in textbooks, the adult world of pornography and strippers; or something she has only heard referred to by smitten, stricken wretches like me, who come to her looking for answers that will allow us to leave the labyrinth: the self-generated but endless mazes of our own obsessions, of stimulation and arousal.

Sorry, Doc, for dragging you down into my world.

Today she wears a nice pair of black trousers with a slight flare over her ankle boots. They look new. Perhaps she has gone shopping again in order to conceal herself as I reveal myself.

I want to tell her that I like her orchid-red lipstick, but know it would be inappropriate. Even here I am not safe from myself. In anticipation of my own funeral I resent the fact that I will be unable to see the legs of the female mourners in black stockings and formal shoes. Perhaps in my will I can insist on the wearing of trousers at my send-off.

But if I am to get the sequence right in this story of the Nylon Dahlia, then I must digress. Because the weekend before we had a date I had another visitor to my flat to contribute to the archive. Someone I had pursued for over a year, and eventually persuaded to make a recording of her extraordinary sexuality and its relationship to her legs and the worship of them.

My head was so full of the Nylon Dahlia, I wanted to postpone the meeting, but secretly felt this was a once in a lifetime opportunity. I dared not risk losing, for the sake of posterity, the story of Lillian.

Lillian is the kind of woman who would cause small seizures in men of my persuasion. To see her on the street, or seated nearby in a café, would cause paroxysms of excitement combined with a baffled yearning for what is painfully out of reach.

And in her presence, the leg man might very well experience an immediate urge to please and to obey. Such a surrendering of the will to an individual as handsome and powerful as Lillian could lead swiftly to servitude or, worse, enslavement. And during my interview with her for the archive and the website, my analysis proved correct. This is exactly the kind of effect she has always had on men.

Her appearance is incongruous in this day and age, but it reaches the height of elegance nonetheless. Classic, you could say. A small hat and veil, perched upon coils of blonde hair arranged in a glossy chignon, with rolling platinum curls for a fringe. An unusual, but not unattractive, streak of black follows the wave of the fringe. The face beneath the veil has the stern and handsome quality of the well-presented and mature matron or headmistress. A woman of intelligence and one accustomed to responsibility and authority. Both mother and tyrant in complementary measures. Conservative, formal, of impeccable reputation and exemplary manners – a lady of the old school. And it is this cast of face, with its discreet make-up and icy green eyes, that so suits the cut of her cloth. A smart pinstriped suit consisting of a tight-fitting pencil skirt and perfectly fitting jacket, complemented by a white blouse of silk, taut about her large bust, and some carefully chosen accessories exhibited elsewhere. A single strand of pearls lies tight to her soft throat. Leather gloves so close-fitting as to appear as the virtual flesh of her hands draw the eyes but swiftly deliver a short shock of mixed signals; despite the complete acceptability of such well-crafted and expensive items upon such a respectable lady's hands, there is something immediately erotic about the tight leather squeaking around her pale fingers. The ordinary becomes sexual. The subtext is discreet. But of course we dream of unwrapping those hands, or at least falling into them.

But it is her legs that transmit the most arresting charge and inspire the most intense fascination. There is something pleasingly solid and ample about the width of both her thighs, which are concealed, and her calves, which are exposed. Nothing slender or graceful about her legs. Not at all. But the very fact that the curve and length is so substantial is all of their magic. There is so much of them, and their natural feminine shape is beautifully sculpted by the height of her classic black court shoes. The kind of footwear a fashionable and powerful woman might wear to court, or to some poor soul's funeral. Her ankles are both delightfully feminine and stout at the same time. The same contradiction I have observed elsewhere in her broad but shapely figure. And her ample knees and wide shins are made as sleek and aerodynamic as the engineered alloys of aviation by a tight webbing of vintage nylon. Black and glassine beneath the bright wall lights of my living room. Elmer Batters would have loved this woman.

Had I encountered her as a teenager, or been blessed with such a woman as a neighbour or teacher, I wonder how sharp her image would have remained in my memory. And had she been a lover, I wonder how deeply, how irreparably my sexuality might have altered after such an erotic attachment. Would I have been rendered utterly submissive and not able to switch between the passive and assertive roles as I do now?

Fortunately for the archive, Lillian likes to talk. About herself. Has learned how special she is.

'I learned how to use my legs at seventeen. I clearly remember the incident. I was about to catch a train. Going to an interview. I forget for what. But I had dressed up. Which was uncharacteristic for me. I was never a beauty. Always leaned towards the plump side once my bottom and breasts filled out quite early. So I was surprised at the sight of myself in my bedroom mirror before I left for the station.

'I'd worn make-up and lots of it. A very fetching red lipstick, I remember. And my best suit. My only suit. With matching black shoes that had a high heel. Heels that high I had never worn before. And these were the last days of real nylons. I only had one pair. A gift I think from my mother. Her attempt to encourage me to be more feminine and to take more care of my appearance. And they were a dark-tan colour and seamed. And I wore them with a tight-fitting girdle. Which made me look very compact and curvaceous under my skirt. And I guess I wanted to impress – to at least do my best to look glamorous, as most girls do at that age.

'And I recall being immediately disconcerted by the looks I started to attract from men that morning. Soon as I left home it began. A car sounded its horn, which I immediately took as ironic. Derisory even. But then at the station three men in suits, all much older than me, kept looking at me. And particularly at my legs as I stood on the train platform.

'I remember inspecting myself. Peering down to see if I had a terrible ladder or had picked something up on my shoe. I was utterly unused to this kind of attention. Had never had a boyfriend. Nor could I remember so much as a single admiring glance from a boy at school. And the only compliment I can ever recall was from my grandmother, who told me I had good strong legs, one afternoon when I was sunbathing in the garden. I thought them fat, of course. Disliked my body. But, begrudgingly, had become used to it.

'I blushed terribly of course. At the station. Felt most uncomfortable. Was utterly confused as to why they were staring so hard at my bottom and legs. And again, when I was seated in a crowded carriage, the young man opposite me kept looking sideways, as surreptitiously as he was able, at my legs and feet. Holding my ankles together, my hands nervously fretting in my lap, I squirmed for the entire journey.

'Once in town, I sensed a few heads turning to watch me walk by. And one brazen chap even said, "Hello doll," or something like that. And I remember thinking, my God, I'm a woman now. I've dressed like a woman and entered a new world. Boys and men are actually admiring me.

'And my confidence started to grow. To grow in a direction it had never reached into before. By the time I had completed the interview, walked around town a little and made my way back home, I knew my life had changed. For the first time, I actually took pride in my body. I liked it. Felt as if I had passed some test. Though I did resent the fact that the attention of men made me feel this way. Perhaps this is why I became so hard on them. Later.

'But, of course, from then on, you couldn't get me out of seamed nylon stockings and high heels. I even affected a pretty wiggle in tight pencil skirts, and perfected my make-up, using Diana Dors for inspiration. What little money I had went on cosmetics, clothes, and especially hosiery and shiny high-heeled shoes. Though I was never tarty. Always formal. Elegant. Very feminine.

'The assertive attitude came naturally. I was always something of a bossy terror as a girl. And empowering myself with my clothes, and having what I now considered an advantage of size, the dominant streak in my character came to the fore.

'Increasingly, after I left school, I did well in administrative environments. Was very prompt and organised and reliable as an office worker. And so smartly dressed. I grew to love the doors held open for me, the chairs pulled out, the admiring looks and inviting smiles.

'I suppose when still in my teens, my more tomboyish and dowdy years, I had accepted that I would never attract men. So why bother playing the lady? But now, dressed like a proper little madam, with my forthright tone and quick temper, I tended to attract shy men. Sensitive men. Who could be very submissive. Adoring even. And I liked them. Liked being in control. Even went through a stage of being quite cruel. Manipulative. Perhaps even vengeful. Somehow, seeing their pained expressions at a harsh word from me pleased me. Even my fury at their clumsy passes at the cinema or during an escort home gave me a tremendous sense of control and power I had always lacked in my dealings with boys. I consciously dressed to be admired, but would never allow them to do more than stroke my knee or peck my cheek. It tormented so many of them, but drove them to subjugate themselves even more. I even received proposals from men who had never so much as kissed me.

'After several years of being watched closely by one dear old chap who I worked for, he eventually confessed to an infatuation with me. Never expected me to return his affection, nor expected any physical favours from me, considering the difference in our age. But asked if he could act as an escort. Take me out and about and show me things. Very cultured chap too. He seemed utterly harmless and my desire to be in control flexed. Deep inside, I found such an opportunity irresistible.

'So we would ramble around town in this big old Rover he owned and attend concerts and theatres and so forth. I learned a great deal from Malcolm and became extremely fond of him. He's not with us anymore, God rest his dear soul. But I did become close to him. Closer than I had ever been to any man before.

'And in time, of course, we became more intimate. But in a very unusual way. I was still a virgin, but sleeping with me was never his explicit aim. Gradually, he introduced me to what would now be called an alternative sexuality.

'In the beginning, he simply wished to stroke and kiss my feet at the end of an evening together, or after an outing. He spoilt me rotten, of course. Nylons and high heels and beautiful suits I never wanted for. Jewellery and watches too. So, though a little taken aback by his request, I agreed. And came to like it. A distinguished, well-dressed man on his knees before my legs which he adored. And I mean adored. Worshipped. Totally.

'He would kiss my shoes. Heel, sole, toes. While stroking my legs. And he was very thorough. He could spend half an hour kissing and caressing his way from my toes to my knees. And in time I even took my shoes off for him, so he could admire and worship my silky, pedicured feet. He insisted on my regular attendance at the best beauty salon in town. Ragfords.

'And this form of admiration developed, at the pace I set. I made him wait for the privilege of licking the soles of my feet. He liked the taste. And the sensation of nylon over my smooth skin against his tongue. He was quite the puppy at times.

'And I would walk for him as a treat. Fully dressed to begin with. Then stripped down to my nylons and foundation wear, wearing the highest heels, I would parade about before him, at his home. And eventually, I would walk upon him. His back. Trample him when sitting in high heels with him stretched out on the rug before me, or actually put my full weight upon him in stockinged feet. It was the first time I had seen a cock.

'In fact, the very first one I touched belonged to Malcolm and I touched it with my feet. Tentatively at first, and only if he'd done something to really please me, but then more vigorously. I liked to grasp it between my arches and rub it hard. Stroke it and watch it come with a fascination that was both horror and desire in equal measure. Malcolm learned to work hard for such treats. As did others.

'You see, dear Malcolm was not at all possessive. He not only allowed me to dominate two of his middle-aged friends, but actually encouraged me to enslave timid men. It was a form of betrayal his utter submission to me required. And these two men also became very attached to the young lady in heels and seams. A woman always immaculately dressed in the old style, despite what Mary Quant was doing in London.

'But these chaps were quite different to Malcolm. Both of them liked to be caned. Which I found very exciting. Both reprimanding a man with my mouth while marking the flesh of his buttocks at the same time. I punished them because they desired me. By doing so, they desired me even more.

'They were both married too. Though neither was still having relations with his wife. So I felt no guilt. Didn't think impropriety was involved. Though the wives may have thought otherwise had they known. Had they seen the welts on their buttocks.

141

'And they liked to be set tasks too. To execute my whims. And when I lost my temper with them, their fawning would increase. Which, in direct opposition to my more sympathetic inclinations, would make me more irritable and more demanding. The colder and more assertive a line I took with them, the greater the affection they showed me, and the greater their excitement. Each man was also very generous.

'By the time I had reached my late twenties, I had quite a court of generous and servile men in tow. Respectable, clean, decent men who required me to do things considered indecent at the time, when dressed in a particular style. Always high heels with Aristoc harmony points – usually black or charcoal – foundation wear and strict, formal outer wear. I was the aunt, governess, teacher, matron of their dreams. Their secret desires were as yet unsatisfied. I turned fantasy into reality.

'Of course, I still have many associations with the older man, but I now perform a far greater range of ritual and service to the younger submissive too. Increasingly, women come to me now. And men dressed as women or longing to be dressed as women, fill my schedule. And the nylons and heels, as you can see, are always a part of my regimes and routines. Though as much as a matter of my personal preference as from request.

'Which I know you are very curious about. You have never been dominated, have you, Al?'

I shook my head. 'No. But I can understand how a man would let you do anything to him. Instantly, the very moment I saw you today, and what you were wearing, I had a much clearer idea of male submission and female domination. But for the website, it is a submission to your legs that is important.'

'A popular preoccupation, darling. Where shall we start,' she said with a smile.

'I'd like to introduce the gallery with some establishing shots of your legs.'

'I see. Then let's begin.'

On my knees, and using the zoom function, I took thirty pictures of her sitting on my couch with her legs crossed. Closed in with the focus until the actual square knit of her nylons was discernible over the smooth flesh of her calves. Snapped away at the dark creases about her ankles, contrasting beautifully under the light with the transparent veneer of the taut nylon that stretched around the broader surface of her leg muscles. Took a wonderful shot of her pale toe cleavage, just visible as she dangled a spiky shoe over my polished wooden floor. Then I photographed the soles of her feet. Broad, glossy feet, wrapped in the reinforced soles of her nylons, but left so sheer on the upper part of her feet. As I worked, my mouth watered at the thought that soon I would be granted permission to touch, to stroke and adoringly caress her legs. For a while my fascination with the Nylon Dahlia was forgotten. My indecision about Sam mercifully removed.

Lillian had powerful legs. It was easy to imagine being crushed by them. Pinned down on the hard floor by these long silky columns. Driven to the floorboards by her weight, pressing through her silky, tickling soles. Yes, it was not an unappealing thought to actually be hurt by her legs in some way. Caused pain and not just from longing, but through the actual spikes she wore as well. Her feminine weight pressing down, transmitting its power through two stiletto weapons. Shoes so feminine. Such elegant plinths to display her ample curves, but so spiteful too. So cruel.

There is something cold, I thought, about a shiny high-heeled shoe. An indifference that in itself increases longing in the admirer. The beautiful, crafted lines and obsidian gloss of the leather attract a man's eye and down go his defences. But could such a seductive and intensely erotic object be tamed? No matter how much it is kissed and licked and sucked, no, it will always walk away, or sit in a corner of a wardrobe, or perch upon a shoe rack, and ignore you, while its shape holds so many secrets, so many stories that you can only guess at.

Of course my face would be slightly obscured, but I eventually surrendered the digital camera to Lillian, of which she had already had some experience. I had tracked her down through her home page on the Internet – that eternal sea that washes outsiders together with its swift tides – so she was skilled at capturing the pale and prostate shapes of her anonymous lovers.

'I have a hunch you might be eager to touch my legs.'

I swallowed. Nodded. They were precious to me already. Something to admire, to dream about, but to touch? Her legs possessed an aesthetic and sexual quality that seemed out of reach. A sensitive man can feel so unworthy before the perfectly presented object of his fascination.

Perched on the end of the couch, she crossed her legs slowly to produce a loud rasp in the airy silence of my lounge. A gritty nylon melody that I felt inside my gut. A sound that shortened my breath and increased my pulse.

Peering at me through her smoky veil, she raised one imperious eyebrow and nodded her sleek head. I sunk to my knees, before her outstretched foot. I watched my hands approach the delicate black nylon, the soft skin and hard, sharp onyx of her shoe. Gently, I stroked four fingertips down the seam on her calf muscle to the rounded slipperiness of her heel. Then opened my hands and cupped her leg. Stroked it. Supported the pale leather sole of her shoe with my other hand. Brushed my thumb about the pointed toe. Felt my jeans fill out with rigid muscle. Inhaled the perfume she had sprayed down her shin. Let it fill my head like an opium mist. Caught a trace of the scent of expensive, new leather, sharp beneath the cloudy musk of her perfume. A narcotic combination.

With my knuckles, I caressed the top of her foot. So soft, while the hand below her foot pressed against the unforgiving spike of her heel. Contrasting sensations my overwrought mind struggled to process.

'Take them off. Rub my feet,' she said without a hint of a smile on her face and in a voice bereft of warmth.

I never hesitated, but eased the tight leather shoes from her feet. The action created a little gassy whisper as the softer leather inners of her court shoes slid across the warm nylon. And I was offered my first complete glimpse of the empty insides of her shoes. A creamy leather colour, looking as vulnerable as naked flesh. And for the briefest moment her stockinged feet felt damp. A slight and fine moistness that quickly dried and disappeared, leaving the vaguest trace of a musty female foot perfume behind.

Through the dark toes of her stockings, I could see the red nail polish. Perfectly applied and defining her nails in a striking way. Not so much as a millimetre of nail was left uncoloured. Cupping her heel, I raised her inert foot and lowered my face at the same time. Kissed her toes softly, then the top of her foot. Felt myself falling into a desperate animal need for her. I gripped her calf muscle tighter and was about to passionately kiss her instep when the foot was withdrawn.

'I said rub my feet.' Her stern voice shocked me. I apologised. Couldn't meet her frosty gaze with my own shamed eyes. Felt guilty, foolish. Was too accustomed to having my deviant way with Sam and other models. Lillian was different. A man only existed to adore her, and to receive punishment for it if he were lucky, and here I was already crossing boundaries and making love to her leg like a horny dog.

Carefully, I stroked her feet. Massaged the soles of her foot with the ball of my hand. Rubbed the heel and sides of her feet that received the most friction from her shoes. 'Better,' she said. And allowed her eyes to lid. 'But it's always better if I work my feet on a body. A face. So take off your shirt and lie on the floor.' The instruction was given with such a nonchalant assurance that I would obey. And I did, of course. Just to be granted a few more minutes in the presence of these shimmering legs and royal feet, I realised I would have done almost anything for her.

Beneath my shoulders, the wooden tiles felt cold, uncomfortable. I kept my hands at my sides and looked up. At the length of nylon-wrapped shin on display. So close. Parts of her stockings shimmered white. There was a whole universe of tiny bright lights and colours flashing in the fabric, reminding me of petroleum floating through clear sea water.

And down came her feet. On to my chest, my stomach. And she ground her slippery feet against the hard bones of my sternum and shoulders. Pressed down with the balls of her feet. Ground her heels deep until my breath caught in my throat. 'That's good,' she murmured and took photographs of me; a man prostrate and used as a comfort mat for her tired feet.

But then I was surprised by the sudden shadow that fell across my face. Followed by the weight of a foot. A soft foot, both slippery and wrinkly in nylon, that covered my mouth and nose. Hampered my breathing for short periods; sometimes stopped it altogether. Forehead, cheekbones, nose, lips, chin, she ground and stroked with her slippery soles. Clenching her toes about my lips, she then forced my jaw down and forced her toes inside. Filled my mouth with salt and the synthetic taste of warm nylon. Pressed the underside of her toes on the other foot under my nose, so I could take in no air other than the hot oxygen filtered through the fabric of her hose. My lungs gulped at thin streams of tainted air, sucked in between her hot toes. Effectively, I was gassed by her feet.

And then they were gone, leaving my face damp and feeling smudged as if my features had been altered by her weight and toes.

'Texture is important for a man at my feet. I follow soft with hard, hard with soft. Confound his expectations. It is best if his vision is taken away or at least obscured. Anticipation heightens his dependence upon me. Increases his trust in my control of his body. Lift your head up.' From inside her bag she unfolded several snakes of nylon.

I obeyed and allowed her to wrap a long nylon stocking over my eyes and around my head. And another, again and again in silky coils. A fragrant bandage that gradually subdued the bright white light before sealing me inside a tomb of nylon. Once it was in place, I felt her strong nails and cool fingertips indenting my cheeks as she slipped a stocking between my lips. Around the base of my skull she wound it and tied it off. I could neither speak nor see.

At first I felt foolish. Then nervous as if expecting a blow. But her gentle voice, her soft shushing sounds calmed me, and I accepted her dominion over me at once. Outside my nylon mask, I heard her subtle shiftings and whisperings as she prepared herself for the next stage of my submission to her legs.

When the first heel touched me, I sucked in my breath. Cold, hard, inflexible, it touched the flesh of my stomach. Pushed down. Sank in. Pulled my skin tight about it, squeezed my breath shallow. A second heel took me by surprise and settled, then dug deep on my pectoral muscle. I heard a squeak from the leather sofa, as she shifted forwards. Bracing myself, I waited a second, two, three, and then tensed my body to take more of her weight through those black spear points.

'You are so weak for me. You lie before me and let me walk on you. I prick your flesh with my heels. Wipe your proud chest with the soles of my shoes.' Her tone of voice was derisory, but commanding. 'Your accomplishments, your intelligence, your free will mean nothing. Not anymore. Not when you lie like a pet dog at my feet. Open yourself. Show me your cock.'

The sound of the word 'cock' from such a cultured voice, from such a lady, made me feel a swoop of electrifying desire. She said 'cock' as though she found it dirty. An unpleasant but necessary task to even mention it. I was unmentionable, untouchable. But out of curiosity she wanted to see it, but could so easily dismiss it. Ignore it.

I obeyed at once and felt myself flop out into the cool air. Stripped, floored, unencumbered by decency or dignity, I lay exposed for her. The camera clicked and whirred.

'Ohh, that's better. It was dying to come out. Such a nasty big thing, all thick so near my legs. My feet. I couldn't possibly touch it with my hands. Not even with gloves on. And definitely not my lips. I would never smudge my lipstick on such a dirty thing. Or let something so foul and disrespectful and undisciplined enter my mouth. Never. It's the kind of thing I would kick away with my shoe. Or squash as an irritation.'

I tensed, my cock and balls suddenly feeling particularly bare and undefended as she mocked them. And the first touch of the pointed toe of her shoe against my cock forced me to cry out. But it was a touch so gentle and controlled. Lillian's other foot then bumped my cock. Between the hard leather toes of her feet, she soon held me. Pulled my cock from side to side, as if she were inspecting a joint of meat. Flattened it against my belly and filled my head with the image of her pale leather sole. Then raised it upright, its length more rigid than ever before.

'And we can make it harder. Make it weep. Lift your head.' Her voice had gone deeper and become hoarse from excitement. 'You never expected this, did you. But it's nothing really. Just a taste of how far I could take you. Silly boys who flirt with strong women should be taught a lesson they won't forget.'

And suddenly, a thin, slippery, whispering sheath was stretched over the crown of my head. Another stocking. I began to struggle, but a heel swiftly placed above my navel held me still. Pinned me down. My arms dropped again at my sides. My face flushed hot with shame. This I had never experienced but only seen on the more depraved quarters of the World Wide Web. Nylon enclosure.

The camera clicked and whirred. And then down over my entire head, the stocking was tugged. Flattening my face. Already blindfolded and gagged with hosiery, but she added another layer. A bond with greater restraint.

As I steadied my breathing, my head and mind in a funnel web of silky nylon, her spiky toes rolled me on to my front. I heard her heels clatter on the wood, on either side of my head. Move down my body. Pause at waist-level. Long fingers then gripped the waistband of my jeans and yanked them down to mid-thigh. I tried to get up into the press-up position as the cold air rushed in to inform me of the exposure of my anus to this beautifully dressed woman. But a high heel and flat sole pressed me back down, face first into the floor. None of this was in the script. I thought I'd get close to her legs, touch. Possibly even seduce her.

In my dreams.

She'd read my thoughts and dropped them in the garbage. And taken control.

A cool hand rubbed my buttocks. Made them tense. A smooth hand slipped about my hips, ventured between my cheeks. Made me gasp. Tickled the base of my ball sac. Slapped my arse. Once. Hard.

'Yes,' she said. 'Get up. Up!'

Bound by my own jeans, blind and gagged in her nylons, I struggled to find my feet. A fierce grip seized my elbow, held me steady.

'Bend.' The command was swift, impossible to query. 'Put your hands down. Out in front.' I did so and they found the unmistakable slick curvature of nylon-wrapped thighs. She must have sat down and pulled her skirt up, or even removed it. My head twisted; I longed for a peek at her firm and magnificent legs, but she had poured nylon into my eyes. She had drowned me in her stockings.

'Still!' she called from close by. 'Now kneel. Over my legs. Put your stomach on my thighs.'

Humiliated and disorientated, I obeyed. Ashamed but unable to resist the contact of my bare and sensitive stomach against her broad and glassy-nylon thighs.

I let them take most of my weight. Swished my naked torso back and forth, as if getting into position. A hand wrapped in a leather glove seized me over the kidney and forcefully pulled me from side to side, so that my own body whispered against her legs so tight in nylon. I dropped my head, allowed this expanse of rasping leg to heat my flesh with friction, to electrify every nerve inside my suit of skin. Appallingly, my cock jutted out between my unwrapped thighs, as if I were some hooded farm animal excited by the smell of a female I was to stud.

But I was not in my own living room to stud anything. Rather to be disciplined.

As her hand fell and stung my naked arse, my head filled with clouds of shame. But to be draped across her shiny legs, and so have my entire body, my being hanging from what I loved most in the world, no amount of shame could have compelled me to move an inch. I stayed still and took her wrath. Palm flat. Leathered hand lathering my rump. I hissed and took sharp breaths in turn. Felt curiously unencumbered of all control and responsibility. Euphoric in my total abjection. Couldn't help my hips from rotating, as if they were preparing themselves for penetration. Hooded and debased I achieved a far greater understanding of her world and of the complete devotion lavished upon her haughty image in that world.

When one finger pressed against my anus, I shrieked. Jolted. Gripped her feet. Curled my fingers around her spikes.

And had my photograph taken.

I wriggled. I writhed. I was held down. The intrusive finger left my puckered disgrace. The hand slipped down and between my thighs.

'Look at this,' she whispered. 'Is this for me?'

'Yes,' I said.

'Yes, what?'

I took a deep lungful of nylon-filtered air. The nylons had not been laundered; they were fresh with the scent of her big busy legs. 'Yes, ma'am.'

Leather-gloved fingers circled my cock. And began to squeeze, then rub its rigidity up and down.

Above me, out there, beyond the sheer hood and blindfold and stocking gag that choked me, I could hear her heavy breaths. I could sense her excitement at gripping this hard muscle, that had grown to its furthest reaches for her. For the sight of her and the sound of her voice, and for her control.

'That's it, lad. That's it. Let Lillian see it. That's it. Let Lillian see all of it.'

So I did. I let her milk me into the warm air and all over the floor. I made a sound like a crying baby as I came.

Eight

'You were talking about the separation of love and sex in your life.'

Was I? This doctor cannot be underestimated. She knows more about my secret life than anyone: my early crushes and dreams, my leg journal, my lovers, my investigations into female sexuality, my indiscretions, my deviancy, my perversion. And yet she has sat silent and still as a beautiful sculpture. Said little. And I have found her silence and patience appealing. Conducive to unburdening myself of so many memories. But that comment? I find it typically female. Verging on a judgement. But is my fetish so easily reduced to a distinction between love and sex? I've always seen it on more epic terms. It has become a sense of purpose in life. All of my eggs have gone into one vocational basket, so to speak. To love something so much, I had to know it well. Thoroughly investigate this thing that causes time to stop ticking when I am in its presence.

The search for perfection in any fetishist is no easy burden to carry. Not if you pause and reflect on the places it has taken you and the actions you have been compelled to execute. Filling you with a restless, relentless energy, the fetish can also interfere in every relationship with a woman. For the leg man it can manifest in a reluctance to settle for even a girl who bewilders with her legs, because they are not those legs; legs on other girls you see around who might represent, to an even greater degree, the ultimate pleasure, the end of the anxiety and the exhausting process of fantasy.

A fetish is not dissimilar to the artist's vision. Initially, the youthful passion is both a torment and an inspiration. A constant tyranny of images inflict themselves upon the senses with a force that can be paralysing. But the fetish is also something that transports the mind to another place, a place of bliss.

Out of this avalanche of visual delectation – the teacher's pretty legs in something dark and smooth, the mother of a friend who favours high heels and painted toenails, the flashes of stocking tops on television, smooth, tanned youthful legs in a summer dress, legs in magazines and newspapers, the notorious underwear section in a family mail-order catalogue – he begins to specialise in the same way an artist finds his voice, his style. The mind of the leg man begins to focus upon particular shapes of legs and shades of hose and cuts of shoe. Looks to refine his passion. Distil it into a particular range of immediate stimulation, that is both aesthetically pleasing and erotically charged. I know men who are solely interested in patent spike heels with fully fashioned stockings, with an emphasis on the thin wrinkles or flexes of the nylon about the ankle; others are enslaved by glossy tights with conventional office wear; another cannot sleep with a woman unless she is wearing red nail polish and the type of stockings with a flesh tone, called illusion, or desert sand, or tan; there are those almost traumatised by a desire for pencil skirts and thin heels; thick calves and knee boots crop up repeatedly in my online discussion forums; small-feet enthusiasts abound; long-feet devotees search for girls to whom their worship will remedy her self-consciousness about having big feet; bare-feet connoisseurs are legion;

hirsute lovers rise increasingly from the shadows; and many are compelled to re-create the woman of their dreams by dressing as her – by actually reinventing themselves and creating a new gender to get their fix of nylon and heel: if *she* won't come to me, then I will become *her*.

And the journey, the passion, is lifelong; either adapting with changes in fashion, or becoming marooned in an endless celebration of one style, one all-important look, from one formative era.

If he is lucky enough to find his holy grail, and she is willing to indulge his ardour, then a long and happy union can be the result. But some of us refuse to allow ourselves satisfaction with one particular girl, whose legs and feet, if we had any sense at all, we would be willing to spend a lifetime exploring and studying and ultimately knowing. There is something epic about our need for conquest and stimulation – a desire to consume forests of legs, presented in an infinite number of variations. And no matter how strong the emotional attachments that form with certain individuals, the curse will emerge time after time and lead eyes and inner eyes astray, to seek the next pair of pale feet, or slender legs mounted on a spike heel. Fetishists of this inclination may stroke more calves, kiss more toes and caress more shaven thighs enveloped with diaphanous nylon, but they may ultimately be the more dissatisfied and always risk the final desolation of loneliness.

Perhaps the doctor is angling at this. Maybe I have my first glimmer of her mindset. Love and sex. Mutually exclusive.

Conscience in an endless struggle with need. Reduced to a sniffing hound at the sight of shiny shoes beneath a restaurant table. Beggared by the gloss and whisper of crossing knees in an office. But ultimately, we still search for epiphany, when the flesh and the divine meet, until the end of our days on this earth. Where is she? The saviour and angel who will deliver me from the exhilaration and despair of the journey? And how many times will my eyes lower in the street or bar, then rise and be met with invitation by a stranger, until I know the search is over?

Sometimes I think a dip in the male sex drive is not a bad thing for a man to endure in mid-life. It can clear the head. But breakthroughs in pharmaceuticals have remedied any chance of that.

But if it is love my doctor wants, then it is love she will get.

'Your store is beautiful.'

'Thank you.' As the Nylon Dahlia teetered about Sheer Delight, my eyes moved to take in a panoramic view of her, both in the flesh and provided by the reflections in the mirrors on the wall opposite the counter.

Spike-heeled sandals, made from red patent leather, cracked a delightful staccato across the tiles. My chest was tight with excitement at the sight of her slender feet in black nylon. She'd opened up her feet for my admiration. Reinforced soles and the startling glassy uppers of her stockinged feet, visible through the thin straps of her shoes. Long and slender and tinted dark, every sinew and thin bone moved beautifully on the expensive pale soles of her shoes. Now and again, as she turned to peer at something, her nylons flexed or twisted slightly about her slim ankles. My eyes burned from staring so hard.

To complement her charcoal pencil skirt and tight-fitting jacket, she wore red gloves and a red hat with a wide brim. Outrageous. Too elegant and classic to provoke derision, but an outfit too large for life, even in London. But she had dressed for me. For our date. I was instantly lost in her.

'But it's not only a store, is it?'

I cramped with a brief seizure of embarrassment. Of course she is right. My store has many uses. Including the same function as the towers and traps hunters use to observe and capture wary, slender deer. It is better to admit such when questioned, but the remaining and stubborn remnants of my English reserve, or was it an innate Protestant aversion to anything sexual, could still surface. After all this time. Especially before a woman I was attracted to. And despite all I had done – the depravity I'd immersed myself in, the behaviour that could easily be classed as weird, perverse, dirty, even creepy by a woman – I had still failed to desensitise myself to unflattering scrutiny.

But my relief was instant the moment I realised the Nylon Dahlia was referring to something else. Something else entirely.

'It's a monument, is it not? To the beauty of female legs. A tribute to the height of sensuality a woman's legs can achieve in the right pair of shoes and stockings. I admire that. In a way you are an artist.'

I blushed. Laughed the laugh any reserved man makes when given a compliment by a beautiful woman.

The Dahlia cast me a disapproving look. 'Don't be so modest. This store is more than just a place to sell things. You know that. It is a beautiful creation. Everything is consistent here. All the different parts make the whole beautiful. The walls and mirrors and marble floors. The lighting and the plinths and the mannequins. They have a harmony together. And a resonance. It's an exhibition space. Designed in celebration of one man's muse. And your muse is not just one woman, but many. The many women you have seen with pretty legs and feet. Perhaps every woman's legs you have ever desired are in here. I think this is wonderful.'

I could barely speak. I felt forgiven. Proud. My entire life had been a battle between reason and my fetish. An endless conflict of shame and desire. And this living high-heeled icon had blessed me. She understood me. My hopes built to a dangerously high level.

She laughed as she stroked the nylon-covered leg of a mannequin, tracing three fingers from the knee to the slender ankle. 'This is a temple. A church. A place of worship for you. Women are so lucky to have such places to go.'

I'd never thought of that. But I liked the sound of it. Perhaps she was right; my perversion had created a stylish and irresistible paradise for female consumers, even if they were wholly unaware of the perverse concept behind its creation.

'Mmm,' the Dahlia moaned, after eating one of the sweets available from the blue bowls on the counter. 'You even lure them in with candy. Chocolates in squeaky, shiny wrappers. You are a bad man.'

'I truly am.' I took my digital camera from the case on the counter. 'May I? It would be a real coup to have a picture of the world's most beautiful legs in my temple of legs. For the store and the store's website. I wouldn't put them anywhere else.'

She smiled. 'All things are possible.'

'Of course, I would pay you.'

She waved the suggestion away with a gloved hand. 'Your website has many, many hits. This would be good for my profile. But you will give me your word as an English gentleman not to sell them anywhere else.'

'Of course.'

She sat down on the central couch, on which customers tried on shoes. It had been specially cast in iron. Each leg of the sofa shaped to resemble a woman's calf, ankle and foot. The seat cushions were made from sumptuous leopard-print silk.

Crossing her legs, she struck a pose I recognised from several of her modelling shoots I had collected. I knelt before her and began to adore her with the camera. And she purred with delight when I began to bring out the props. She loved the tiger-striped mules, so I let her keep them. Wrapped them in a red gift box. Did the same for the black sandals with gemstone heels and peep toe. It felt like an honour to make gifts to a goddess, to seek her pleasure, her favours.

All the time, I knelt before her, as she changed shoes. I assisted and held my breath as she slipped her long feet into virgin, pale-leather inners, toes pointed, and sliding with a rasp between soft leather. Of course, the security camera was running; the cur in me whispered, *if nothing else, you will have a film of your most triumphant moment as a shoe salesman.*

'Help me with these. My nails are too long,' she would say, so that I could buckle her foot into a sandal. And my fingers would brush her feet. Skim the fine gauze that webbed the delectable curves of foot and ankle. I felt dizzy, over-stimulated.

Once, after I had finished easing her heel into a black velvet Bruno Frisoni sandal, she turned to pick up another shoe and her calf muscle slid between my open palms. She didn't seem to notice the sudden intimacy of the contact, but my hands and arms tingled with a curious static for several seconds afterwards.

At times, she would place a foot, either exquisitely shod in spaghetti straps, or shoeless and vulnerable in just her black nylons, on the floor between my legs as I knelt before her. And I would look down and stare. Attempt to comprehend that the Dahlia's foot was so close, so real, so alive. I fell for her. I became convinced we had a real connection, an empathy. This model and I; this internationally renowned fetish queen and I, the artist.

We talked about the design of shoes, and the best retro cuts in clothes to complement her nylons. She said so many things that I took to be signs of her growing affection for me:

It is so nice to meet a man with such an enthusiasm for shopping.

I would love to come in here every week and be pampered by you.

You have such a nice touch.

I became drunk with her. Anaesthetised by the tangy perfume drifting off her long shins. Mesmerised by the quick glimpses inside the shadowy, whispery places inside her skirt as she moved and crossed her rangy limbs. And to see her walk the length of the shop, as if it were some catwalk, while admiring her reflection in the mirrors, gave me a pleasure the equal of any physical contact with a suitably attired lover.

'I am hungry now,' she said, momentarily breaking my reverie as my eyes were locked to the point of stinging on the seams clinging to the rear of her legs, as she marched, tottered, strode through my world.

'I have a table booked at Criterion. We should make a move soon.' Tonight I would dine with the most glamorous woman in London. I dared to dream that the occasion would be repeated many times in the future.

'One more chocolate.'

'Don't spoil your appetite.'

She turned on her heel and narrowed her eyes. Slowly bit into the sweet. Let me see her thick red lips move over the brown shell as she sucked the praline from its core. With one hand, I supported myself against a shoe rack. Then, unsteadily, rose to my feet.

The first bottle of wine was empty and we were waiting for coffee. Her eyes were as alert and intelligent as ever, but a smokier, softer expression had transformed them.

On the chair beside her she had stacked her gifts: two wrapped shoe boxes and a rectangular parcel containing three pairs of rare vintage nylons I had given her. I felt like Cary Grant with a Hollywood starlet. Dressed in my best suit with cufflinks and a handmade shirt, and sitting opposite an exquisite, exotic, elegant woman.

Even though this was only the second time I had seen her, we had instantly moved into the realm of familiarity and comfort and intimacy that I had always associated with the beginnings of a relationship. I hadn't dared to allow myself real expectations until that night: she was only in London for a few days; she was the Nylon Dahlia! A supermodel, photographed by the world's best fashion and fetish photographers on a weekly basis. I only ever saw her face or legs on magazine covers or in advertisements, not sitting across a table from me. But as the evening progressed, I had no power over the formation of expectation.

And despite the repeated and sudden return of my sense of wonder, which would shorten my breath at times, the Nylon Dahlia and I were becoming immensely comfortable with each other. Even superstars marry someone, I thought. Why should it be such a preposterous notion for me and this girl to be together?

'You spoil me, Al.'

'The greater pleasure is mine. To even be sitting here with you is incredible. I can honestly say this is one of those moments in life when a dream has actually come true.' I couldn't help myself, but instinctively felt it was a mistake to say so much. What about a bit of male indifference? Wasn't I supposed to cultivate that? Didn't I usually?

She laughed and shook her head. Then peered down at the table. For a moment she looked sad. The imperious woman from the burlesque show and night-club seemed to have stepped behind this new character

– someone young and vulnerable. 'You shouldn't be so in awe of me. Maybe I am just a little girl with long legs.'

'You're perfect. In every way. It's not just about the way you look.'

'Isn't it? But you are so impressed by the stockings and shoes. I wonder what else you see.'

I swallowed. 'Which doesn't mean so much if there is nothing beside them. No presence. No character. A woman's beauty becomes something else entirely when her thoughts and motivations are revealed.'

'Maybe. But you don't know me, Al. Not very well.'

'I know. But we've made a good start. Don't you think?'

She smiled at me in a melancholy way, but then the arrival of the waiter with the coffee closed the brief channel between us, when flirting was put aside and words that would be remembered were said.

Once we were alone again, the old Dahlia was back. Proud and perilously aloof. Her alabaster face poised and sharp. Flashing her eyes at me over the gold rim of her coffee cup, clearly enjoying my infatuation.

When I lit her cigarette, I looked into her eyes in an attempt to draw the vulnerability out again. These brief episodes of the susceptible girl hidden under the immaculate chic made her more desirable and increased my longing. Twice I stopped myself from saying something truly desperate.

'I do like you, Al. You are sweet. And handsome. I think you would make some girl a good husband. Or some family a kind father. But you must be careful. You take risks.'

'Sorry? What do you mean?'

'You and I are alike, I think. We both like to be in control. And we are lucky to be indulged. By others.'

'Maybe. But?'

'But will we ever be content, you and I? Is our tragedy not the very search for the impossible?'

'So maybe we should put each other out of our misery.' I smiled, playfully, but meant every word. 'I think we're a perfect match.' Since she arrived at the boutique earlier, I had already imagined a dozen different future scenarios in which we were together. My fascination in her physically would never cease. Of that I was certain. And I could never imagine getting to the end of her beguiling character. And if I did, so what? Would it not be better to know one woman thoroughly than two hundred fleetingly? It would be one of those rare unions in which we would be eternally inspired by each other's thoughts and words.

The Nylon Dahlia laughed. 'You are such a romantic. And I am flattered. But would you and I not tear each other apart?' The comment stung me. A sense of rejection must have shown on my face. She reached across the table and held my elbow. Smiled. She was in control. 'I am so lucky to meet admirers like you. What is it you all see in me, I wonder?'

Exactly what you have tried to be, I wanted to say: the femme fatale. Morbidly beautiful. The 1950s gothic. A heartbreaker and tormentor of souls. Siren and executioner. Irresistible. Unobtainable.

I raised an eyebrow. Wondered if all her power came from our slavish devotion. Perhaps this was narcotic. Too addictive for her to release herself from. Ever. Maybe even heartbreak enriched her. We'd put her beyond our own reach and she had begun to believe it too. I felt frightened. Suddenly aware, so acutely, of the dementia and desolation and self-loathing that could result from rejection from her. Would I ever recover from such a blow?

And at that precise moment, when an instinct for self-preservation gripped me, I felt the slow brush of her foot beneath the table.

'For your kindness this evening. And for your wonderful gifts and thoughts. And for your admiration that has never faded, I have something for you. In return, I want to do something for you.'

Inside my flimsy trouser leg, I felt the cool brush of leather against my shin. Then the prickle and tantalising abrasion of real nylon behind my calf.

I couldn't even swallow. And, for a while, the restaurant and its multitude of voices, noises and faces vanished into silence. I could hear nothing beside her words and the beating of my own heart between my ears.

'You can photograph me. For the Leg Lover website.'

Of course my flat is an extension of Sheer Delight. If she thought the boutique was an exhibition space, what would she think of my home?

In the cab ride to Notting Hill, she sat close to me, her hip warm against mine, her legs crossed, one knee shimmering every time sodium lamplight washed through the windows. When I stretched an arm around her shoulders, there was no resistance. On the contrary, her long, feline body relaxed into my ribcage.

Pausing my rushing thoughts and impressions of the night, I made myself comprehend the situation: the Dahlia and I in a cab, going back to my place for a Leg Lover session. She had seen the images on the site. She knew what happened during the shoots. She had seen the heels entering my mouth; the close-ups of my tongue on a silky or bare and pink sole; toes disappearing between my lips; the protuberance of my erect cock between the insteps of strange women's feet, as they held and pumped me; the same organ, thickened to maximum rigidity by a coating of sheer nylon, wrapped about its dimensions by pale fingers and glossy red nails; spike heels indenting my genitals; long feet covering my face; shocking white splashes of my come over painted toenails, red beneath shiny flesh pantyhose. Trodden on, spiked, on all fours in subjugation to long feet in strappy sandals: a naked exposure of one man's obsession revealed online to the world, recorded, downloadable. And despite all this, she wanted her own gallery on Leg Lover. Faceless, her identity concealed, her feet only recognisable by the devotee. Of course she had modelled softcore many times – I was intimately familiar with the moist pink folds of her sex, opened by her ghostly fingers in *Leg Galaxy* magazine; I had another three *Foot Licker* magazines in which she sucked her own toes and showed the camera lidded eyes above bulging lips and cheeks.

I felt dizzy. Excited but wary of danger. If I touched and tasted the most perfect legs and feet I had ever seen, where could I go afterwards? What would remain if she left me? What left but longing and regret?

To hell with that, I chided myself. Live for the moment. The holy grail of a leg fetish is about to be worshipped by my mortal hands.

'I guess I better warn you,' I said outside the front door.

'Oh. Not so good with housework? Or maybe you are a maniac?'

I laughed. 'No. People often think I've been in the military. I like clean spaces and right angles. It's just . . . Well, what you said at Sheer Delight. If you think the store is a tribute, wait until you see what I have inside.'

'I am waiting. It's cold out here.'

'Oh, sorry.' I plunged the key into the lock and let her into the communal hallway. The only thing on my mind as we mounted the stairs – her first, of course, so I could watch her legs on the way up – was the high proportion of photographs of the Dahlia festooned about the walls. Earlier, I'd thought of taking them all down, but then dismissed the notion as foolish as I never expected her to end up back here. That would have been presumptuous, but here we were.

'You know I'm quite a fan,' I said, attempting an explanation.

'Al, why are you so nervous? Stop it before it becomes contagious.'

I apologised and let her into the flat. She looked around, smiling, as I switched the lights on and revealed my hallway and kitchen.

'You have a beautiful home,' she said, and walked inside. Despite my Betty Page tea set, the kitchen ornaments in the shape of black patent stilettos, and the cabinets full of shoes and nail polish, the main body of evidence of my obsession existed in the living room and study.

I made drinks – vodka tonic for her, brandy and ginger for me – while she looked around the kitchen, her gloved fingers occasionally stroking shiny chrome or polished steel. She leafed through my vintage Pirelli calendar, and paused to study the covers of American paperbacks and girly magazines from the fifties I had framed in the dining room. 'I like your taste. Modern with just the right twist of retro. I don't know what you are so worried about. Most men would love to show a woman such a place.'

'But you haven't seen the living room yet.'

She turned and looked at me. Frowned. 'Show me.'

I carried the drinks back down the hallway and heard her heels following me. I opened the living-room door and turned on the light.

I cleared my throat and was unable to look at her. 'As I said before, I'm quite the fan.' In total there were twelve portraits of her legs, or feet in high-heeled shoes, arranged around the room.

I placed the drinks on the table, then finally turned to assess her reaction. Her eyes were wide with a mixture of concentration and surprise. At first she said nothing.

Then the surprise vanished from her eyes and her face appeared inscrutable. I thought of filling the silence with small talk, but could think of nothing to say. The Nylon Dahlia walked into the lounge and stood beside the coffee table. Sipped her drink. She made the room silent, still but oddly tense. 'You have always lived alone here.'

I nodded. 'Not many girlfriends would understand.'

'You are right.'

'I hope . . . I mean to say, I hope you don't find this too weird.'

Silence. She took another sip of her drink. 'Weird? Am I not weird also?' She turned and looked at me. 'Do I look like a conventional life is enough for me? Or could ever be enough?'

I looked down, unable to withstand the full force of those icy eyes.

'I am flattered, Algernon. Touched even.'

I exhaled. Took a swig of my drink. 'Thank you.'

She shook her head. 'No, I should thank you. This place is beautiful. A home. And you fill it with me. Why would I not be pleased?'

'Well, I don't want you to think I'm some kind of stalker. I mean, it's an odd thing for a forty-year-old man to fill his lounge with – pictures of a woman he's never even met. A bit adolescent maybe.'

'Maybe you should not be so quick to estimate what others think.'

'Thank you for understanding.'

She sat in the centre of the couch. Crossed her legs and spread her arms along the back. 'You should see my apartment in L.A. You would like the bathroom. I have an original 1950s tub and shower head. Along the rail I hang my nylons. My bathroom is a jungle of nylon and lingerie. In so many different shades.'

I swallowed hard. A picture of such an emporium was clear in my mind. It was exactly the kind of bathroom

I wanted her to have. I imagined her applying make-up. Her beautiful, tight bottom stuck out before the sink. Face close to the mirror as ghostly fingers lacquered her eyelashes up into black, dollish curves. Followed by the circling of the waist with a black garter belt. And a girl should always slip into her underwear once the make-up has been applied; a pretty, painted face seems to complement the delicacy and care with which they arrange their flimsiest apparel, so tight to the skin. I could see her in there. Californian sunlight falling through a small window and making the white tiles gleam. Her seated on a stool, upholstered in leopard print. Reaching out to snatch a pair of nylons from the steel shower rail. A cursory inspection for snags as she pours them through her fingers like sand. Then the swift ruffling of the first stocking to produce a roll; or does she slide her legs into them when they are drifting at full length? One pale knee drawn up to her breasts. Pinky-white toes pointed down for the nylon to envelop her feet with a second skin of translucent wonder. What I would have given at that moment to see such a display. The preparations. The transformation. The beginning of her day as a retro pin-up goddess. So maybe my fetish is all about transformations; the reality of a woman becoming something else through specific accessories. Becoming more than she actually is to enter into a dialogue with my dream life.

'May I?' I asked, after retrieving the camera from my satchel.

'How do you want me?'

'Just as you are to start with. You don't even have to try.'

She winked at me, reclined further into the sofa cushions and crossed her legs again, slowly. Pulling one calf tighter against the knee of the other leg, she filled my living space with a tantalising rasp.

She didn't want her face shown on Leg Lover, nor her identity revealed. But I could show parts of her. She liked the thought of her fragments spreading gentle shock waves out there, in the privacy of gentlemen's quarters. 'Put some music on. I see you have Chris Isaak. That will do nicely. I used to do a routine to "Wicked Game". Then let me undress for you.'

And so she took control. As the music crept through my rooms, she left the sofa and began to sway, to gradually perform an effortless, languorous waltz. I knelt down and took pictures whenever she came near me to discard a red leather glove, or to release her zip, her pouting face so close, as if to offer a kiss before drifting away on spike heels that barely made a sound. She was a magnificent dancer, combining burlesque stripping routines with two-step dance moves, then a little three-step jive. Her balance perfect, poise effortless. And it was always those slender legs that drew the eye as she moved and swayed about my lounge. The only thing I would be able to use, so I made sure the camera focused on them. The remainder would be for me. She knew that. It was her gift. A private audience with a collector. Her collector.

Slowly wiggling and gyrating out of her dress, she revealed a black satin brassière and matching panty girdle, four suspenders to each leg. Her pale flesh between the shimmer of nylon and dark gloss of her retro lingerie briefly startled me. I longed to taste her soft belly. To kiss it while stroking the seamed rear of her thighs. She giggled. Then kicked one leg high. Between her thighs and beneath the girdle, I caught a glimpse of a sheer gusset covering something dark and trimmed.

Sashaying back to the sofa, she beckoned to me with one long finger. Placed the tip of her tongue on her top lip. Moved it in a circle to make her full mouth wet.

I went to her. Knelt down. Gave her the camera. Collected the foot offered to me. Gently held it by the heel. Cupped my hand around the thin leather strap and smooth nylon. She pointed her toes at my mouth. My breath never left my chest. With the camera, she captured the image for all time. The long foot made dark by black nylon. The whole shape made more compact and streamlined by its shadowy covering. I lapped away at the sole of her shoe, as if I were dying of thirst and her instep were coated in a film of cold dew.

I asked her for the camera. Peeked along her shiny thigh with the lens. She widened her thighs. Revealed the long slit of her sex. Pale meat wet between the soft folds and cultivated pelt. My mouth watered.

'Take my shoe off,' she whispered, then took another sip of her drink. I put the camera on the floor beside me and brought both hands into play.

With careful fingers I unbelted the thin manacle of leather around her slim ankle.

She lit a cigarette. Drew on it until her cheeks hollowed. Then let a thick curl of white smoke rise from between her cherry lips.

I removed the first shoe. Eased the weightless artefact from the long sole of her foot. It consisted of three leather straps, a sole and a steel heel. Simple, elegant, devastating. Genius and devotion combining to craft a perfect pedestal for her pale foot. Each nail was perfectly shaped within its cuticle and the taut flesh of her toes. They were lacquered scarlet. Had been painted recently. I could smell the ether of nail polish through the toe of her stocking. Pear drops.

Slowly I stroked one hand over the top of her sleek foot, then turned the hand up on to the slope of her glazed shin and around to her Achilles tendon, where the nylon was slightly loose and the seam just detectable by the most sensitive nerve endings in the palm of my hand. She pulled her toes back and showed the alabaster tissue underneath her long toes. Untouched by sun or rough ground, and filtered and screened through the reinforced toe of her stocking. I decided this was one of the most beautiful parts of her entire body. Despite the rigours of dancing and the punishing elevation of her high heels, the balls of her feet were surprisingly smooth, the skin even tender. The fine bird bones of her feet had slightly parted and splayed to support her energy and height, and immediately appeared broader without the shoe to hold her foot closer together. Her instep was creased with thin wrinkles that I could admire through and around the darker nylon of her reinforced sole, and through the cobweb-sheer knit of the finer nylon that webbed about a centimetre away from the surface of her skin. I kissed her instep. Inhaled. She sighed.

'I like having my feet played with.'

I moaned an acknowledgement through my nose. Was incapable of verbal communication at this point. Placed my lips and nose and chin inside the curve and tasted the Nylon Dahlia's foot. A wonderful sensation: the soft pressure of the foot's flesh, under the synthetic gauze of nylon, tight around the foot. I kissed her heel. Bent her toes back and licked the livid skin.

She offered me the second foot. Drew on her cigarette. Within the circle of ice green, her pupils were large and black and shining. Her cheeks flushed with the beginnings of arousal. I lowered her unshod foot. Without my guidance it settled in my lap. Pressed the wooden bulge. Spread its toes inside the fine net of black silkiness, and rubbed. Slowly, up and down my length. Her big toe touching the sensitive tip lightly. Causing my breath to pause. My skin to shiver. My stomach to fizz and needle in an exquisite blend of excitement and anticipation.

I exhaled noisily and looked down. Wanted to watch, but the Dahlia had other ideas. 'My other shoe. Take it off.'

I obeyed, but my fingers were trembling. It took four attempts to open the buckle and draw the strap through. My mind was overloading. All the time her other stockinged foot kneaded my lap. Toe tips with hard semicircles of painted nail pressed the top of my sac. Pushed the very root of my shaft. Made it tent out my trousers and dampen my underwear. This foot had done this before in other laps. The thought hurt me. And thrilled me.

The second foot rubbed its sole along the inside of my thighs. Long toes clenching and straightening in turn, wrinkling the nylon sheath about them. 'Open your pants. I want to put my feet on your cock.'

I lashed my belt away and yanked the zip open. Was relieved to see my best Bjorn Borg underwear, black and tight on my groin. Her feet immediately found the shiny surface and added another sensation of slick, electrifying slipperiness to my crotch. Real nylons slithering over my lycra shorts. I held her calves and stroked them slowly. Finding the thin indentation of the seam with my middle finger and running my pads the length of her lower leg to the hot ligaments behind her knees.

'Pull your shorts off. Let me see what you have in there. It feels nice. Big.' Her eyes were half-lidded, and her mouth seemed thinner, tighter, verging on the savage.

Cool air embraced my hot groin as I peeled my shorts and trousers down to the top of my thighs.

'Ooh,' she cooed at me. 'Now take a picture of my pretty feet on your big cock.'

Concussed with arousal, I fumbled with the camera, then forced the right level of concentration into my mind in order to zoom in on her shapely feet working around the stem and middle girth of my cock. I caught the minuscule wrinkles, the criss-crossy squares within the fine knit of the very material of her hose. Even the slight smear of pre-come on the side of her foot, that had been squeezed out and then dropped on to her busy feet.

'That good? Mmm? You like that?' she said breathlessly, her voice thin then thick with excitement. I looked to her pussy and saw a wet sheen on her transparent panties, at the base of her slit, where it clung to the fabric.

'I want to see your white cream on my toes. Go on, pump it out. All over my feet. Do it, baby. Come on. Do it.'

I had a curious notion that she was in some way masturbating her own cock. Deriving pleasure from wanking my cock, as if she could feel what I was feeling. As if it was actually connected to her body and nervous system. And then she extended one long finger down to her sex, and began to swirl it about quickly on the outside of her panties, directly on to the little part of her that could immobilise the greater part of her with pleasure.

I swallowed. Could this actually be happening? I blinked twice. Three times. Watched that clot of blood-lacquered fingernail, its smooth beetle-bonnet gloss twinkling under the bright-white ceiling lights. She started to make soft panting sounds, and her feet jerked harder against my cock. Pulled it up. Then her insteps would quickly glide down the sides of my shaft, until her feet struck my pelvic bone. I was not long in coming.

'Now,' I said.

'Yes,' she cried out. Rolled her eyes up and thrashed her finger hard, up and down her clit. 'Do it on my feet. Fuck my feet.'

With two fingers I held my throttling, jerking cock. Grabbed her left foot by the heel, and pumped one string of oyster cream after another across her toes and the top of her foot. Then I gripped my shaft with my whole hand and choked the last two spasms on to the helpless foot. Wet it. Desecrated its nylon sheen with dollops of seed.

The Dahlia's body jolted very quickly. Three times. Each shudder smaller than the last. Then she shivered, breathed out, relaxed her long body. And before I had time to collect my thoughts, she lay back on the sofa and pulled her left foot up to her face. A long tongue extended, big lips sucked, and she ate my come from her smeared foot. Moaned through her nose as she lapped like a big cat with its eyes closed. Devoured and swallowed every drop of me, her ballerina throat working furiously to take me down. Inside her. The Nylon Dahlia.

The goddess had accepted my sacrifice and I was blessed.

When I think back to that night, I wonder if she was indulging me or herself. Could it have been a thank you for dinner and the gifts? Or a reward for so much adoration? Or was she one of those girls with a high libido and sense of adventure whose sexuality had come to mirror what is perceived as a male sexuality?

I'd met women like this, or interviewed them for the archive, with an increasing frequency. Roles had somehow been reversed. Perhaps a desire for a more conventional or traditional approach to relationships – say marriage and kids and longevity – lurked somewhere at the back of their psyche, but for the meantime, which was often a long time, they freely indulged their desires with a whole plethora of men without a shred of emotional attachment forming. It was never about working your way by process of elimination through an eligible crowd of peers to find that perfect man; it was about erotic satisfaction. About sex, and an unrepressed delight in getting as much as possible, with as many men as possible for a certain period of time. Often calculated in advance. *Right, I'm thirty. I'll settle down when I'm thirty-five. Until them I'm going to have fun.* Every philanderer wants to meet one of these women; but the reality is often different to the fantasy. Sure, it will be intense and uninhibited. Soup, main course, dessert and cigars all on the same plate. But if you fall for one – an inevitability considering her indifference to commitment – the end can be like stomach surgery without anaesthetic.

Which is a hint as to where this story is going. The Nylon Dahlia's brazen enthusiasm for my own kinks that night was a defining moment in life for me, when the fantastic and the real blended seamlessly. That long and torrid evening, and the affair that followed, empowered me, completed me, but also blinded me and completely fucked me up. Like the tourist who steps into a busy city road, looking the wrong way, there was little in the way of a warning before the bus hit and time stopped.

After the foot-wank and her dextrous cleaning routine of her sticky feet, we drank more, changed records, lay together on the sofa and talked until the late evening became early morning. We fought for airspace, each having so much to tell the other. It seemed a lifetime would never be enough to share our ideas, stories, thoughts. And each comment by one could lead the other off on another engaging tangent. We formed a closed circuit that never seemed to lose momentum. The time of silences, repetitions and pauses was over. It was what dating experts call a connection. A real live one: absolutely humming with empathy and sparking with a mutual fascination, each to the other. And of course my physical obsession with her returned with a virility and force I'd not experienced since my early twenties; I

175

suddenly remembered what it was like to ejaculate and return to form three times in one evening. Unprecedented and wholly down to the Dahlia.

'I like my feet sucked. I mean really sucked,' she said to me, when her eyes were glazed from drink and while my erection pressed into her thigh as I lay behind her, kissing her ear. 'I insist upon it.'

She let me rearrange her on the couch, which was wide, deep and could sleep two comfortably. Kneeling between her thighs, I raised one leg. Stroked its silky contours and then unclipped her stocking. Eased it up her leg, over her heel, before pinching it off her toes. She smiled when I pressed the damp ruffle of dark nylon against my face and inhaled deeply. I repeated the process with the second leg, then draped both nylons over the back of the sofa, where they would still be visible. Just seeing an empty, discarded pair of sheer hosiery near the girl I'm fucking can intensify the entire experience. Especially if they're still tangled in a pair of skimpy panties. Once her legs were bare, I slipped one of her big toes into my mouth.

It was cold. And briefly my mouth was enriched with a strong salty sting. This melted away to the tastelessness of a well-sucked thumb. And the purest enjoyment arose from the shape of her toes in my moist, hot mouth. Kneading the cool flesh of her instep and looking down at the milky whiteness of her slender feet, I sucked until my tongue hurt. Replaced her big toe with the longer, thinner toes. Replenished my mouth with the musky taste. My cock was as hard as it had ever been within minutes.

A thin tracery of bluish veins marbled the top of her foot. The skin above so soft – softer than the skin of her legs and hands – was a delight to lap at, with broad sweeps of my tongue. I painted the ceiling of her foot with saliva. Made her writhe. Her cheeks flushed, she slipped long white fingers inside her sheer panties and made a faint squelchy sound. The ball and heel of her foot were as pink as ham, and as briny as slices of that same meat, when peeled apart and sniffed. I cleansed every inch of that first foot; dissolved all of its taste and spicy minerals and swallowed them. Not once did she stop looking at my face and into my eyes while I ate with exuberance and thoroughness.

When I made time for the second foot, she placed the pads of both feet on my chin and pushed as many of her toes into my mouth as she could. Crammed my mouth with fresh toes. Toes that had been bound in a second skin of nylon all day and presented on a tray of pale leather sole. And as I sucked and lapped to appease these eager digits, the Dahlia groaned and slapped at her pussy. Slapped her own sex. Only ever pausing to beat three fingers very quickly against her clit, to work herself towards another peak.

'When I start to come, fuck me.'

'OK,' I said, feeling a cool sweat break across my forehead. Inside her. I'm actually going to be inside her, I thought to myself. And then remembered becoming terrified that I might suffer a stroke or heart attack a few moments before I made it inside her. Once I was inside, right up inside, it wouldn't be so bad if I had a fatal seizure. I suddenly wished I'd never smoked so many cigars in case some thin arterial wall suddenly sprang a red leak. Crazy thoughts. Crazy infatuated, aroused thoughts.

But after a few more minutes of my passionate sucking of her toes, combined with the speedy lashing of her fingers against her clit, she started to come. Opened her big red mouth and fluttered her eyelids right back. Her body locked before me and she started to shake. Her shoulders became rigid against the sofa cushions. 'Fuck me,' she said, though it was more of a breathless gasp than a clear instruction.

I pulled her wet toes from my mouth and dropped her legs over my shoulders. Fisted my cock and shuffled forwards on my knees until the head of me touched her long sex lips, now soaked and pleasingly fragrant. The first few inches of me were immediately swallowed, and then I met that resistance further inside that always makes a man feel his cock is large. I pushed against it and she moaned. And diminished somehow. Looked smaller. Felt weightless beneath me. Utterly vulnerable and submissive to the act of penetration. Is there anything better? I thought to myself.

And then, inside her sex, something gave way. Soundlessly tore apart and through her I sank, to the very back of her. She closed her eyes. One tear slipped from under a dark eyelid. Hands behind her pale knees, I pulled her long body further apart and began to thrust into her.

With scarlet fingertips, she tore at her nipples through her bra, and moved her head around on the leather padding beneath her long bones. Gulped and moaned and cried. The full force of her reaction sobered me slightly, then incited me to harder, faster, deeper thrustings until the frame of the sofa shook and jolted. Together, we made a fleshy clapping sound, like fresh fish, slapped down on a marble chopping block. And I would turn my head, every once in a while, to study her long feet: the thin bones, ghost skin, blood-red varnish, contour lines of blue vein within the white flesh, and I would instantly feel the rise and scorch of semen through my organs. Her feet were wonderful. I was sure I'd never seen anything so beautiful before, so closely.

And I came while digging my entire body into her. Pressing her down into the sofa until she could sink no more. Face red and teary and screwed up, she made soft grunting sounds from the back of her throat. Bit at two fingers, then let them fall from her smeared mouth as if she had lost all the feeling in that hand.

'Coming. I'm coming in you,' I said, and it felt as if my skeleton had turned to mercury and then drained away. It wasn't just a climax; I loved her. And it felt as if I'd fucked those strong feelings into her along with my cream. Something she could feel beyond the physical sensation.

'Fuck me,' she whispered. 'Fuck it all into me.' And then she winced and jolted one final time before lying still.

Leaning over her I covered her face in kisses and found no resistance at her mouth. Just slipped my tongue inside and kissed her until she had to break away and breathe.

'Mmmm. That was nice,' she murmured, and ran her fingers through the hair at the back of my head. 'I think we'll be doing that again.'

It was exactly what I wanted to hear.

Nine

And here we are again. Doctor Kim sitting on her chair: trousered legs crossed, notepad perched on her thigh, her thin features angled down to spare me the unflinching gaze, the inquisition; and me, across the room, slumped into the bigger of the two armchairs in her study. Barely aware of the synthetic carpet smell, or the vague stuffiness of the air and the silence in which it swells, I close my eyes and look deep inside myself.

All I wanted to do was talk about the Nylon Dahlia. I was brimming with enthusiasm for her and that part of the story. Hadn't slept properly for the four nights that followed our last session, and as a result found myself nodding off every afternoon. Was listless at the store. Dreamy when alone. Stricken with an inertia and a pain that felt like ice cubes melting in my colon. Love remembered. Love.

'It was a beautiful story. But it's not the whole story. It is a part of a much bigger story,' Doctor Kim says, with a patient smile on her lips; she wants to go backwards again. We were on a journey. We had touched upon the early genesis of my fetish, and now it was time to talk about where that led me in adolescence. What it made me do. How I learned about the strange self-loathing that comes to a young man compelled to indulge his needs, and the exhilaration of shame that accompanies his actions.

The risks I took.

And Doctor Kim wants me to talk while, as ever, she listens. Her slender body relaxes, but still maintains an enviable posture. Her handsome face and intelligent eyes inscrutable, irritatingly bereft of judgement, half raised and watching me in studied silence as I pour myself out; open a door into my memory and subconscious and let it all escape. And I'd taken an oath with myself to leave nothing out. Nothing.

It was time to tell her about Mrs Clark.

Who lived across the road from the house my family lived in for seven years. I was nine when we moved in – a boy; sixteen when we moved out – a young man.

Her son was my best friend. Someone I probably saw, beside family holidays, every day for that entire period of time. But although I remember every den we built in the wood, the time we set fire to the wood, the long summers of cricket, the endless war games with 72nd-scale soldiers from virtually every military campaign in history that Airfix manufactured, I think of his mother more often. A woman I doubt I ever had a conversation with that consisted of more than a few words in a few seconds. But a woman three times my age who had a profound impact upon me. Much of this influence was due to changes in fashion.

Something happened at that time with female style. It was the end of the seventies and the dawn of the eighties.

I clearly remember the women in my life during the seventies and the majority of them didn't dress in a way that particularly excited me. Lots of flares and trouser suits, floral dresses and hippy skirts, plastic sandals and long socks. Tights were worn with short skirts, which I liked, but I was still young and able to find myriad other distractions more engaging than staring at women. And the pointlessness of a dedicated pursuit of a girl was obvious to me until my late teens. It was not something I had the confidence, or style and status to do. I was a geek. And a painfully shy geek whose father disapproved of any fraternisation with the opposite sex until my education was complete. He was old school. And I thought I was a loser. So it wasn't hard to avoid so much as a kiss until I was sixteen.

But when the seventies turned into the eighties, a great deal changed in the way the women around me presented themselves.

New Romantic music was embraced at school, and for a couple of years, the girls at school and in the neighbourhood indulged themselves with Duran Duran, short skirts and sheer dark tights, and even stockings. Their mothers and older sisters rediscovered glamour and what was to be a reinterpretation of the 1940s and 1950s – my favourite decades in film from an early age. High heels, tight skirts, two-piece suits, sheer hosiery and heavy make-up all became fashionable again. Striking haircuts and colours transformed their straight seventies hair into extravagant permed creations. Their lines changed. Tighter-fitting clothes made them look both straighter and yet more curvaceous. The female body was reshaped. Not so loose and freely swinging, it became more compact. Calf muscles bulged over stiletto heels. Painted fingernails flashed atop pale fingers. Red toenails began to make a reappearance at the end of peep-toe shoes. The aesthetics of Kim Novak, Bette Davis, Garbo, Dietrich and Monroe, that I had become smitten with on wet Sunday afternoons in front of the television, were back.

Teachers at school, working women I passed on my way to and from school, and the mothers of friends began to look a whole lot more interesting to me. Especially Mrs Clark from across the street. I was sixteen when this style revolution occurred. Coinciding with it was the sudden availability of adult magazines. *Penthouse* and *Mayfair* I managed to read on a monthly basis, due to another friend whose father read every issue and then threw them out. Only for them to be salvaged from the dustbin by his son, Grant, and passed on to the others in our group. And I was usually the last to receive the well-read edition. And I hoarded. I kept scores of them under the bungalow we lived in; stacks wrapped in polythene and well hidden under timber off-cuts. A stash. It might still be there. The women in the magazines reflected the fashion of the times, but gradually removed the outer layers as you turned the pages. Stockings galore, in every shade and style imaginable. Complemented by high heels – court shoes or spike-heeled sandals with their feet on display. And that is what I looked at. Maybe their breasts and bushy genitals got a cursory inspection, but it was the legs I obsessed over. I would have been happy just to look at photographs of legs and feet, suitably attired, in these magazines. Of course, in later years when the American girlie mags specialised, my periodical library began in force. I have every copy of *Leg Show*, *Hustler Leg World* and *Leg Sex* ever published in the archive.

But back then, not a day went by when I didn't see a real woman or girl wearing the accessories I desired on whatever portion of her legs she desired to reveal. I was visually over-stimulated. Endlessly frustrated, baffled, prowling, day-dreaming, and masturbating with a ferocity and regularity I thought pathological.

And of all the women who surrounded me in this glorious renaissance in which legs were rediscovered and re-dressed and displayed, Mrs Clark was the recipient of my biggest crush. My best friend's mother. My own mother's friend. A friend of the family. A woman newly forty with the most attractive legs and feet I was sure I had ever seen. And through her son, Stephen, my access to her was not insubstantial.

Mr Clark was a lawyer, and Mrs Clark had been a housewife for as long as I had known her son – through junior and secondary school. But when we hit sixth-form college, and all three of her kids were in school, she wanted to return to work. And did so with style. Quickly becoming someone important in sales for a fitted-kitchen company. And with the new position came a new wardrobe.

Overnight, it seemed to me, she transformed herself from the mum in nondescript jeans and tracksuits and long skirts with flip-flops, to a dominatrix to whom I was ever willing to succumb and serve and please.

I remember the exact moment of my speechless, dry-throated discovery of her transformation. It was a school day. And the worst of all school days, it was Monday. The sky was grey and the air drizzly enough to make me instantly melancholy. As I meandered up the steep hill our street was built around on my way to college, their family estate car pulled over to the curb just inside my line of sight. I heard my name called. I looked to the right and saw Mrs Clark leaning across from the driving seat to wind down the passenger-side window. 'Hi Al. Jump in. I'll give you a lift into town. You'll get soaked, love.'

I hesitated. Smiled weakly. Blushed. Her lips were bright red with lipstick. Her eyes attractively made up with a soft charcoal eye-shadow and her eyelashes were lacquered. It made her green eyes look so clear, so alluring. My last heartbeat seemed to pause and cling up near the back of my throat. Instinctively, I took a step to the rear door of the red Ford Cortina. I'd been in the car hundreds of times, with Stephen, and we had always sat beside each other in the back. His mother had never worn make-up like this before. Mrs Clark laughed. 'You can sit in the front seat, you know.'

I did some kind of stupid chuckle and said, 'Yeah. Sorry,' or something; at the time, I used to apologise every time anyone spoke to me. I moved to the front door and that is when I saw her outfit, through the open window. The radio was playing in the car too. My head filled with noise and the reddish static of arousal. I went dizzy.

She wore a dark-grey suit with a white pinstripe and a white, silky blouse with some kind of high, fancy collar. But my gaze quickly and inevitably fell into the foot well. Black sandals. High heeled with a thin ankle strap and three straps across the bridge of her toes. Toes capped with painted toenails. Red varnish. Her hose was grey and very sheer. My cock was hard and pressing into the tissues, polo mints and loose change in my left pocket. I climbed into the car, my forehead and armpits and lower back wet with perspiration.

She asked me questions about college. Told me about her job. I grinned and nodded and grunted. Conversation was stilted. She was no longer talking to me as if I was the kid her son played with. But that is exactly what I felt like. I looked down, repeatedly. Couldn't help myself. Whenever she looked through the windscreen and into the rear-view mirror in order to perform a manoeuvre, I dropped my eyes down and to the right and took in her legs. Mesmerised, I watched the bones and sinews of her long feet moving inside her stockings and within the thin spaghetti straps of her shoes as she depressed the pedals. The car was full of the smell of her perfume. It made me swoon. The fragrance of an attractive, glamorous woman, her feet on the pedals, her painted eyes, the red fingernails on the leather steering wheel, her wet lips pursing and moving as she talked, the glimpse of a shiny black underskirt moving over sheer grey nylon, the roundness of her solid knees, the sheen-line on her kneecaps, her white hand on the black knob of the gear stick, the smell of rubber foot-mats, car upholstery – all combined to produce a powerful multi-sensory and erotic experience I would never forget and would crave thereafter.

She dropped me off outside the dour college gates. 'Thanks for the lift, Mrs Clark,' I said, like a nine-year-old with an iced treat from the fridge in hand.

She laughed, looked right inside me with those jade eyes, and said, 'It's about time you boys started to call me Angela.'

Angela. I'd known her name for years and not thought much about it. But now it took on a new significance. It seemed to develop a new sound, and one heavy with glamour. A word evocative with a sensual melody when spoken. One that made my stomach flip over whenever I heard it mentioned.

And with any infatuation, you remember anything you hear said about this person, recall every word they speak in your presence for the duration of the spell, and can easily revisualise anything you ever saw them wear. I noticed everything – the times she came and went from the big white house across the road that I could see from my bedroom, the changes in her hairstyles, the new shoes and outfits she bought, the offhand comments made by my parents about their friends and neighbours, Peter and Angela Clark. And, of course, my imagination was filled with her.

Under the covers, cock in hand, I shot and then replayed my own adult movies featuring Angela and myself. For two years I am certain I ejaculated over my memory of her, or the idea of her, the very thought of her, more than once a day. All banal and predictable fantasies. No more imaginative than the fictional letters of 'real' sexual experience I read avidly in *Fiesta* and *Escort* and *Razzle*. There was the fantasy about me going over to call on Stephen and he being out but his mother inviting me in to wait, soon followed by my seduction; the one about me helping her in with bags and her commenting on my muscles and physical development, before I was whisked on to the living-room sofa and ridden into experience; the one about the house party and her drunken seduction of me outside in a darkened garden, my parents and her entire family only a few feet away, behind a wall. And of course, my favourite – the ride in her car that became a ride into the country and then a ride on the back seat, her spike heels making indents in the vinyl ceiling as I plunged between her thighs, so slick with black stockings. Of course, in these fantasies she was always, always dressed in stockings and heels, like the women in *Mayfair* and *Penthouse* had been.

In reality, if I ever saw her walking from the porch and down the slant of the drive to her car, I would feel weak with desire and fatigued by the powerful flushes that left me dizzy. If I was out in the street, she would smile and wave, before swinging her glossy black court shoes into her shiny company car, her curvy calves and slightly thick ankles sheer in something dark and glossy, drawing my eyes.

But I wasn't in love. I had crushes on girls at school who were barely aware, or totally ignorant of my existence. And those feelings for those girls had an exaggerated courtly or romantic angle to them. Invariably in my fantasies, I would appear heroic to these individuals. I rarely thought about having sex with them. They were on pedestals, too precious for my grubby beastliness. But my feelings and thoughts of Mrs Clark were purely sexual. The utter banality and mawkish sentimentality of my mind back then is still cause for considerable shame. As is the extent of my obsession with Mrs Clark's legs.

I still have the pair of sheer black stockings I took during my first terrifying, exhilarating visit into her bedroom. They were the first pair, captured in the field, that began the actual exhibit section of the Leg Library.

Stephen may have suspected me of behaving strangely – he certainly saw more of me. I called on him more than I had ever done, though was curiously preoccupied in his presence. He did wonder, I am sure, why I had sought him out with such regularity and determination, only to be distant and somehow bothered by something else. Of course he never knew how my hearing stretched itself out and into the warm spaces of his house, searching for the click-clack of his mother's heels on the kitchen floor. Or the slightly husky but feminine voice on the phone at the bottom of the stairs.

I became sneaky and stealthy. I learned that to go and call on him, moments after his mother arrived home from work, there would be a good chance that she would still be in the process of removing her coat in the hallway and would open the door. If I was lucky, she might even have kicked her shoes off, and as I walked in, red in the cheek and tight in the throat, I could look down and admire her full, long feet stretching her sheer tights. If she was on the phone in the hall, I would slip out of the rumpus room they had made for the kids downstairs, beside the door to the garage, on the pretence that I needed the toilet, and I would linger and peer at her legs as she sat on the stool, talking to a friend. Much the same as Mrs Skinner, Angela Clark had a habit of absentmindedly stroking her legs as she sat on the stool. Running her whole hand up and down her glossy shin with a whisking sound. And she was a shoe dangler. Liked to wear black open-toed mules with a kitten heel indoors, instead of the terrible slippers my own mother wore. Her feet bare or reskinned in dark nylon, she would bounce that front foot up and down as I passed. And I would move slowly and stare down. Squint so hard until I could see the little freckles on the top of her foot and the minuscule criss-cross of the knit of her stockings. Of course, by the time I made it into the bathroom, I would be unable to pee, even if I had actually wanted to, because my urethra would be strangled by the solid, engorged muscle of an erection.

And almost as soon as my infatuation took full control of me, I began to rifle through the laundry basket in the bathroom. In there went dirty towels and the kids' laundry, but nothing that belonged to Mrs Clark. That she deposited in a separate basket in the master bedroom, the dark and terrifying and utterly irresistible marital suite.

It was not long until I was compelled to go in there. Into a thrilling darkness I still dream about.

When only Stephen and I were in the house, I would instantly volunteer to get us drinks and snacks from the kitchen, or a fantasy role-playing aid from his room upstairs (like most hapless male virgins of the 1980s, in their mid to late teens, we were inveterate players of Dungeons and Dragons). Add these sorties out of the games room, as it came to be renamed once he and his brother were older, to my relentless visits to the toilet, and I found plenty of opportunities to steal through the silent and empty upper storey of his house. To start with, I would just approach the door of the master bedroom, then turn back, my heartbeat swelling into my throat, my skin covered in a frost of panic. And I would return to Stephen downstairs, silently vowing to never even consider such a depraved and intrusive act again. But like most addicts, we can but lie to ourselves. On the matter of our fix, our word is as good as worthless.

I went back. Again and again, I returned to the bedroom door. Sometimes partially ajar, or left wide open, and I would peer through the doorway and into the perfumed gloom. Sometimes, from the doorway, I would spot a pair of her high heels discarded on the floor, or her clothing thrown over the chair beside her table and mirror, and I would rush away, the image logged and filed in my data banks for future bedtime fantasy. And, eventually, I took a step inside. Then a few more. Closer to her underwear drawers and the wicker laundry basket with Mr Clark's freshly ironed shirts piled on top.

The first time I opened it, my entire body was shaking and my vision jolted. The bile of terror and rising panic scorched my throat and mouth. But I persisted, looked down, reached in, broke the soft surface, sifted about, and then saw the unmistakable, tell-tale sign of discarded hosiery. Shrivelled and wrinkled and wrapped around other things, and yet still possessing part of its erotic appeal in this lifeless, static and innocuous state.

My trembling, moist fingers dipped in. Thumb and finger pinched a black curl of hose. Then plucked it out, batting a cream-coloured brassière and one of Mr Clark's vests away. And, to my surprise, it wasn't attached to the crotch of a pair of tights. It was an individual black stocking. An electrical shock of instant arousal jolted through me. Angela wore stockings. Under her suits. In the bedroom too. Did she leave them on when Mr Clark's hairy body moved slowly on top of her? Did she wear them because he liked them? Or was it her choice? Absolutely none of my business, but I couldn't be stopped. I retrieved the second stocking, panicked, replaced the lid on the basket, put the pressed shirts back on top of the lid, then fled.

I made my excuses to Stephen and ran home, my left trouser pocket bulging with Angela Clark's worn black stockings. Straight up the stairs, into my room. Record cases against the door. School trousers unzipped. Under the duvet with my treasure.

Beside the strong odour of perfume, she was curiously absent from her stockings. I inhaled every inch of them

190

until I couldn't smell anything anymore. But one detail that thrilled me to my marrow was the evidence of red toenail polish on the reinforced toe of the stocking, where she had put them on before her glossy toenails were completely dry. But the pear-drop fragrance was long gone.

They were very sheer, but not real nylons. Stockings made stretchy with lycra. I believe they were made by Elbeo, because of the thin blue thread that was woven around the tops. Something I discovered on a pair belonging to a girlfriend a few years later, in a moment when once again my head was filled with Mrs Clark.

Of course, I was ashamed of the act. A line had been crossed. Trust had been broken. A betrayal of sorts. I was disgusted by the very act. Felt squalid enough to believe myself worthy of life imprisonment.

But I went back.

I stole another two pairs and then stopped in case she became suspicious. I wonder if she ever noticed. She must have done, though she bought many pairs of stockings and wore a new pair each and every day – even at the weekends. Angela loved stockings. And from her I stole a pair of shiny white stockings and a pair of dark mahogany stockings with a high sheen and see-through toe. Both from the laundry basket. The white ones had the smallest trace of her toe scent, but it vanished quickly, becoming overwhelmed by my hot nose breath. I was sorely tempted to take a pair of shoes, but knew it was far too risky. Instead, I compromised and settled for licking the pale-tan soles of her high heels, where her soft bare feet, or warm hose-slicked skin had been for hours the day before. I actually did it in the marital bedroom. Put them to my mouth and tasted this residue of her.

I also rifled her underwear drawers and fondled her suspender belts. Inhaled her panties. Touched the flat, square packets of quality hosiery, stacked neatly behind her camisoles, waiting to be opened and for the flat, weightless hose to be stretched to fit and reskin her muscular calves and broad thighs.

Stephen nearly caught me twice. After the second near miss, I never entered the bedroom again. Both times he'd ventured up the stairs undetected, wondering where I was, what was taking me so long, and I managed to conceal myself behind the bedroom door, a black high-heeled sandal clutched to my chest. My favourite pair of her shoes. The ones I had repeatedly slipped my erection inside, through the open toe, in the bathroom with the door locked. I knew the time was fast approaching when I would be caught. He never said anything, but I knew he was becoming suspicious of my long absences from the games room, and from the game.

And when Mrs Clark was promoted and began to go on business trips, I became insanely jealous, but somehow exalted by the betrayal. You see, I was convinced she was having affairs. Fucking businessmen in hotel rooms. Picking them up in bars. Sitting on barstools, her long legs crossed and shiny in stockings, her face painted sluttishly, her sultry green eyes assessing and then selecting her lover for the night. I began to imagine her doing the most depraved things with other people, and wondered how Mr Clark could allow such repeated infidelity. I began to believe it myself.

Shortly after this, and perhaps mercifully for me, my family moved house, moved to a different town, and moved me away from Mrs Clark. I often wonder about her. Was even tempted to look her up, when I was a few years older, and try to instigate an affair. Just confess my infatuation. Though I never did. All I have left of her are my memories of those thrilling times in her bedroom, and three pairs of worn, unlaundered stockings – the foundations of the collection.

But it was the start of something. The beginning of the collecting. Years of intelligence and artefact gathering. An inevitable next step for the enthusiast.

'So you began to take women's underwear?'

Oh, be careful here, Doctor Kim. Are you curious whether this is the beginning of a criminal pathology? A first step on the road to flashing or stalking? I wonder how she disguises her disgust. Practice? Desensitised to the madness of men? Probably.

But I guess this one pursuit of sexually aroused men may always seem too deviant for most women. Something squalid and creepy. Not something that actually fits into the idea of what well-balanced, adjusted adults should do. But in our defence, how can we be blamed?

Female underwear, hosiery and footwear is usually designed with us in mind. And predominantly by us. Something to enhance their beauty and arouse our interest.

And we are emotional, impulsive creatures. We are not always content with glimpses and dreams. Sometimes we actually need to hold, smell, taste and explore their flimsy cast-offs. We become hounds hungry for the scent of a mate. Baffled, frustrated, excited animals who must have some intimate thing that has been close to the skin of the desired. It's irresistible. And it's ironic how human ingenuity in design and fabric refinement can instantly trigger the beast in man.

But apply the sentience of humanity and, of course, our attraction to these insubstantial items of female clothing, that are so loaded with symbols and meaning, will become more complex. A fetish.

'Took underwear? No. Hosiery, yes. I stole hosiery. And lots of it. Shoes too. Though they are more noticeable when they go missing from a woman's wardrobe. Especially good ones. But hosiery, and the odd pair of panties, if I was that way inclined, from a basket or under a bed, are more disposable. Or consumable, I should say.' You'd be surprised, doctor, some of your lovers may well have done the same thing to you. If not actually removed something, then fondled something flimsy that you had worn close to your soft skin when you weren't looking, or when you weren't around. All men have their moments, regardless of social background or education or our better instincts. We can't help ourselves. For most of our lives we are sexually frustrated. In fact, I would hazard a guess that the more sensitive and academically intelligent men Doctor Kim meets would be more prone to keeping a well-ordered collection of underwear or shoes or photos than she probably gives them credit for.

'Were you ever caught?'

I thought on this. I'd had close shaves and knew some girlfriends must have become aware of disappearances, or disordered drawers, but I had never been challenged. 'No. Not really. In fact, you'd probably be surprised at how many of my lovers encouraged me, or indulged me.'

'How so?'

'Well, they would send me things. In the post. There are few non-contact thrills more intense than the arrival of a padded Jiffy bag, rustling with . . . items. Perfumed secrets. I had one girlfriend in my twenties for three years. A record. She lived in another city between her university terms, and sent me a pair of worn stockings every single week. With a letter attached telling what she had worn them with, how she had looked, felt. What she had thought about me while wearing them. It never bothered her. It was just a part of our sex life. Two other married women I knew did the same. I've had girlfriends who send photos of their feet to me. Or their legs. I have hundreds of photos. Sam –' I pause '– Sam used to send me pictures on her phone. She would take her shoes off at work and photograph her feet, or pull her skirt up and take photos of her stocking tops. She did it for fun. And to arouse me. And to get me to go into the shop when she needed my help with something. Kind of like a homing device. A beacon to the pervert.'

The doctor nods: if she has made a judgement, she's not going to share it. 'But that is different to actually taking something.'

'True. Stealing is more exciting. Your kleptomaniacs will tell you the same. It has a vicarious thrill all of its own. Especially when the theft involves something intimate. I have taken outrageous risks. The worst being gym bags at school. I once snuck into the female changing room and stole four pairs of sheer tights from girls I fancied. Imagine if I had been caught? I wasn't. I was lucky. They were lovely. Very sheer and flesh coloured. And very aromatic. Nothing was ever said. They must have thought other girls had pinched them. Or maybe they had suspicions about the P. E. teacher. Who can say?'

'Were you ever tempted to break into houses or take from washing lines?'

'Are you nuts? That's not my style. Though I did fantasise as a youth about wandering around a strange woman's house and enjoying her things. But washing lines? Hosiery is dried indoors, and why would I want anything laundered?'

'I see.'

I hope she does. For some reason I feel irritated with her. It seems banal for her to think of me as dangerous. 'You know, making a woman uncomfortable is the last thing on my mind. I would never want that. It's actually a form of worship. Stealing the fire from a goddess if you like. Especially a woman you can't have, like Mrs Clark. And for a woman to think you're a creep or deviant or unpleasant, that is just about the worst reaction a fetishist can imagine. You want approval ultimately, and a willing confederate.'

'But do you tell women about your fetish?'

'Sure. Sometimes on a first date. Or I make it obvious fairly quickly. I mean, how can you repress it? If my fetish is going to be a problem for her, I don't continue with the relationship. There's no point. I guess I made a decision, once I left home and my teens were behind me, that I was through with denial.'

She nods. 'Is it often a problem to your partners?'

I shake my head. 'It's only contributed to the end of one relationship. The girl was lovely but absolutely refused to wear skirts, or hosiery. Or heels. Ever. Of course I asked her on numerous occasions, but she wouldn't. So I broke it off. I couldn't face a life without my kink. It's not usually a problem. If I wanted to cover women in custard or flour, or to bind them and cane them, maybe it would be more so. I've often been accused of being in love with their legs and feet and hosiery, and not them. I've heard that a lot over the years.'

'And how did that make you feel?'

'Bad. What do you think? Some of them were right too. I was infatuated with them physically. Only what they wore really mattered, and the sex when they were wearing it. But most – I would say over half of my girlfriends – have been OK with it. They've told me they find it flattering. And that they like to wear it because it gets me so excited. Makes me love them harder. Makes me more passionate. Those are the girls I like. The ones I hope to meet, like Sam. But of course, you hold out. Part of me held out in the barely acknowledged hope that I would meet a woman like me. As much like me as a woman can be. A woman for whom legs were a major part of her sexuality too.'

'Like the Nylon Dahlia?'

'Exactly.'

'You want to tell me what happened next?'

'Yes. Yes, I do.'

Ten

The Dahlia left London for Germany one day after our first date. It was a month before I saw her again.

Over the next two weeks I called her several times. Left messages mostly, but only twice did she call me back. Our longest chat lasted for about fifteen minutes. She was back in LA. A new tone of intimacy and affection warmed her voice and it proved a tonic for the exhausting nervous excitement that kept me up all night, and unable to swallow a mouthful of anything but water. I was starving, but gorged on infatuation. Dizzy with emotion, but completely focused on one face, one pair of legs. All around me, while I sighed and dreamt away the hours, her portraits on my living-room walls displayed her in black and white, in pencil-thin heels and nylons. Her arresting eyes peered through the mist of veils; followed me around the room; summoned me back from fruitless forays into the kitchen when I felt light-headed with hunger.

'So you'll be back in two weeks?' I asked her on the phone, the second time she called.

'Maybe. If I have a good enough reason to be in London,' she teased.

'Take some time off. I'll send you the plane ticket. And you can stay with me.'

'I'd like that, Al,' she said in a soft, husky tone of

voice that turned my legs to melting wax. 'And maybe we can take some more photos. For the collection.'

'Yes. In every shade and style of stocking known to man. And in the most fabulous shoes ever made.'

'Mmm. You spoil me. I like to be indulged. But you'll go out of business if you keep giving me so many gifts.'

'It's a temple in your honour.'

'And in return, maybe I'll send you some photos of my bathroom. The nylon jungle.'

'Baby, I'd like to see what you have hanging in there.'

'Maybe you will. Soon.'

'I'd like to come and see you too.'

'That can be arranged.'

At the boutique, I was next to useless. Distracted and lethargic, then suddenly euphoric and animated. Too happy for words. Too generous for my own good. Cecilia and Lucy, welcomed the change in me, found me amusing, especially Lucy, who extracted further favours from me like a naughty child working one parent for permission when the other has said no. Samantha was cool. Suspicious. Displeased with the missing stock, and unconvinced by my excuse that I had taken it away for a promotional shoot. Instinctively, she was attuned to even the most marginal vagaries of my moods. We had become close; spent time together; grown comfortable. And now, I was unrecognisable. Lovelorn. In love with someone else. I hoped she wouldn't notice; I didn't want to hurt Sam, and tried to convince myself that she and I were never having a committed, conventional relationship anyway. But she did notice, and she did hurt. I never knew how much until later. Until it was too late.

'Al's like a lovesick schoolboy,' Lucy joked, while we all stood in the shop during an idle moment, free of customers, after I had returned from the sandwich shop down the street, carrying lunch for everyone. On me.

My startled reaction, followed by the immediate

colouring of my face, confirmed the accuracy of her loose, teasing comment. Samantha looked away, her face briefly stricken, stiff and pale-looking. I saw it in a mirror.

Cecilia cried out, 'Lucy!' and slapped Lucy's arm.

What did they know? Was I so transparent?

'What?' I said, once I'd recovered from the initial shock.

Cecilia frowned and took her salad from the plastic bag. Lucy mouthed 'sorry' at me, then winced. Samantha turned around. Looked herself again; composed, sweet, smiling. She thanked me for the roast chicken ciabatta sandwich, then walked to the office without another word. The other girls watched me with vaguely challenging expressions on their pretty painted faces, before they followed Samantha to eat their lunch in the back of the store. I heard three pairs of shapely legs cross with a whisking sound. The kettle began to boil. Uncharacteristically, they ate in silence.

Uncomfortable, I left the store to do the banking. I felt uneasy. Guilty even. It was spoiling my mood, my absorption with the Nylon Dahlia. And as I walked away from the shop I also experienced a brief but powerful sense of loss. It made me slightly panicky. As if I had just made a decision and embarked on a course that entailed a great personal sacrifice. I felt an urge to go back and say something reassuring to Sam.

The feeling passed. I thought of the Dahlia instead. My tummy rolled over, pleasingly. I felt short of breath. Instinctively, I felt that one of life's great opportunities had presented itself to me. This was a girl I had waited my whole life to meet. Had even sought her in every other lover. Found shining fragments of her in other women, but never the whole. The missing parts I had invested into girls with my imagination, but these parts were never really there. I had wasted a lot of time –

theirs and my own. But then no one wants to be lonely, for long.

But I also felt close to something dangerous, though terribly exciting. I am a reasonably well-travelled and worldly man, but not a glamorous character, despite my good fortune with women over the years. In cinematic terms, if I were honest, I would never truly empathise with a Steve McQueen or Paul Newman; but the characters created by Woody Allen or Peter Sellers I instantly related to, though begrudgingly. Whereas the Dahlia represented a world I felt excluded from. One that was filled with airports, photographic studios, burlesque nightclubs, film shoots, celebrities, society parties; something totally removed from the conventional world of routine and responsibility. It took a certain kind of personality to enter this world of strong sunshine, silver jets leisurely crossing the blue sky overhead, and martinis in hotel bars. To operate successfully within it, to offer something to it and to create a momentum that continually opened new doors denied to the ordinary, one had to be a certain kind of person with a certain quality that was as much inbred as acquired. To inspire others, to win confidences, to be accepted; I sensed all of this in her. And yet I was a bit player. A minor peripheral character with suspect leanings. Smut hound, pornographer, businessman. A Jack Ruby, a minor nightclub owner obsessed with film stars. A press agent infatuated with Lana Turner. Could the two ever really mix successfully?

Of course, I wanted into this world of the Nylon Dahlia. The close proximity of its presence through her thrilled me to the marrow. And I could learn fast. But I would always be a contender and someone forced to punch above his weight. I never had the glamour, nor the money to buy a season ticket, nor would I be able to offer the right opportunities to cultivate the contacts. I was an outsider. It worried me. How could I compete?

But perhaps she wanted someone a little different, eccentric for sure, but also more earthy. And didn't we have a connection? A vital attachment at fundamental emotional, physical and cerebral levels? When I re-played out every minute we spent together in London, I could convince myself it was so. It was possible. But then I would get glimpses of this world and would feel a sharp pain in my stomach, as if anticipating a colossal wound or downfall. It might be the sight of a plane, high up, travelling to some distant place I knew to be hot and filled with white buildings facing blue water; or the sight of a beautiful woman stepping from a cab and into a good restaurant in the West End; or the momentary glimpse of an attractive, expensive head behind the tinted glass of a high-performance car, tearing through West London. I would suddenly feel excluded, vulnerable, indecisive. And would quickly try and think of something familiar and safe which I could retreat to, cling to. I would think of Sam.

During the last two weeks before we met again, the Dahlia answered some of my emails, briefly. Acknowledged the gifts I sent her, eventually. And attached to an email she sent me photos of her bathroom. Of six pairs of nylons hanging from a metal shower rail, lit up by dusty, yellow Californian sunshine. The photo looked like a Polaroid taken in the seventies and left to fade inside a shoe box, hidden under a bed. But it was a beautiful snapshot into her world. An intimate insight of her props. Strips of smoke they looked like, drifting in the air and magically transforming the world behind them into something indistinct but with a silky soft focus. Three pairs of flesh RHT nylons. One pewter-grey pair of fully fashioned stockings I had given her. And two pairs of black RHT stockings with crumpled toes. They all looked so long, the welts stretched wide. Well worn and still containing the impression of her slender limbs. Within the email were two words: 'my world'.

So I assumed it was now incumbent upon me to chase her. Why should she make much of an effort? She was the Nylon Dahlia, an international supermodel; a fetish queen; she had a book coming out taken by Delpeche, the renowned French photographer, who shot for *Vogue*.

Every few hours I checked my email account and phone messages. Launched hopeful, cheery messages off into the communications void. Her phone was mostly switched off, or she was screening calls. And I was suddenly in pain. The kind of pain you feel in your stomach; that turns every solid that passes your lips into water. The dysentery of love. My sleep was fitful, light. I would spend hours with my eyes open, not quite asleep, and not fully conscious. She exhausted me. Or rather, my infatuation for her burnt me out. Had she lost interest?

And then, four weeks after our solitary date, she called.

I was editing photos for a series of new galleries destined for Leg Lover. There had been complaints about my failure to update as regularly as before. I'd had my mind on other things; my eyes on other legs. But I was responsible for placating the needs of fellow enthusiasts. I understood their disappointment at logging on and seeing the same 200 galleries they had seen before. Never enough. 2000 would not have been enough for men of our persuasion. We wanted new material all of the time: new toes, feet, legs, stockings, pantyhose. A production line of instantly electrifying stimuli.

But the phone rang in the living room. And I actually didn't jump, or race to catch it with my thumping heart swelling in my throat like all of the other times. I rose from my chair with a tired sigh. Ambled down to the living room. And missed the call. A red light appeared on the phone to inform me of a message:

'Al darling! It's your favourite legs here. What a shame you're out. You must be entertaining a new pair, you frisky tomcat. Ciao.'

She sounded drunk. I scrambled for the receiver and tried to return the call. My fingers were shaking so hard I had to redial three times.

I got her answering service. Wanted to scream with frustration. Tried to remain calm, to control my voice, to sound light-hearted, cool. But I stammered some nonsense in between clearing my throat. She had made me inept.

She picked up as I fumbled.

'Al darling, I just called you. I've been thinking about you today.'

'Really?' I said, trembling from the sudden current of hope that expanded through my entire body.

She was drunk. Had been out somewhere called the Coconut Teaser. Had been so busy; had been to so many parties and shoots. Had been in Paris three times. So close, but she never called.

'You should have said something,' I muttered three times, but she didn't hear me or chose to ignore me. She was the girl from the party again: self-assured, quick-witted, strident, aloof. Our original roles had been reassigned. It was my role to listen. I couldn't keep up with her flitting thoughts and changes in direction. There was no time to answer her questions. Any pause, she filled with a new story or question.

'Oh Al, I thought you'd be thrilled to hear from me. You're no fun.'

'I am. But . . . I am. I am. You . . .' Fine comeback. But she was on something. Sounded like coke. I flopped on to the sofa. It was helpless. My head emptied of jittery, flighty thoughts. My body felt numb and heavy. I didn't try to speak again.

She slowed down to let me catch up. 'Sorry, darling. I'm teasing you again. Guess what I'm wearing?'

Stubbornly, but surely, she had my attention again. All I really wanted to say was all of the boring, needy stuff about why she hadn't called. But this was a dance she was leading. Her screen may have dropped briefly in London, but it was back in place now.

'Go on,' I said.

'No, you have to guess, otherwise it's no fun. I want to see how well you know me. You should be able to guess.'

How? 'OK. Let me think. Mmm. I know. I've got it. A pink bathrobe with stains down the front. Frumpy slippers. No make-up. And men's pants. That are too big.'

Silence. One, two, three seconds. And then a shriek of laughter, followed by a deep, dirty, unrestrained laugh that sounded too old for her.

'Oh, you bitch!' she said. 'Well you're quite wrong, darling. Imagine this. High-heeled mules with a leopard print. Black fully fashioned nylons. A brand new pair. A tight animal-print pencil skirt that matches my shoes. And a sheer nylon blouse so you can see my bra through it.'

My head felt hot. My throat had closed. I cleared it. 'Really?'

'Of course really! I am the Nylon Dahlia! I look like this every day, darling.'

'Wish I was there to see it.'

'I know you do, darling. I look so nice. So beautiful today. So trashy. So sexy, darling. I just had to tell you. It made me think of you. Where are you now?'

'On the sofa.'

'Mmm. Where you fucked me, you naughty boy. And sucked all of my toes.'

'The very same place. But you're not on it with me now.'

She laughed, teasingly. 'Pretend I am. Crossing my legs and dangling a spike-heeled mule.'

'I don't believe you. Sorry, all I can picture is the bathrobe.'

'Oh!' she shrieked at me. 'I'll prove it.'

'How? We're on the phone.'

'Listen.' My ear filled with a rasping sound I knew only too well. Abrasive but still managing to sound sensual – one nylon-glazed leg rubbed hard against another when crossed. 'Now do you believe me.'

'Yes.'

'Mmm. It gets me so hot, Al. Rubbing my legs together. Makes me feel so sexy. Do you know when I walk in a tight skirt my pussy gets so wet. It does. You don't believe me but it does. Just putting them on makes me think of fucking. You don't believe me.'

'Yes I do. Which is why we should be together. We are the same, baby.'

'I know. I think I'm the only girl in the world like this.'

And it wasn't making me feel any better having her remind me of this.

'Is your beautiful big cock hard for me?'

'It is. So hard it's starting to hurt.'

'Mmm. Wish I could put it between my feet. And stroke it. Then suck it.'

Phone sex? I wish I'd put a tap on the line. I took the bait. 'And while you sucked me I'd suck your long toes.'

'Oh don't.'

'And lick your instep. Kiss and suck and lick your feet so thoroughly. Through your stockings, and then without your stockings. I have a nice tongue.'

'Mmm. My hand is in my panties. Tell me more.'

206

'And I'd eat you. Put your long legs over my shoulders and just eat your pussy. Use my lips and teeth and tongue and chin. All of my face between your legs and I'd make you come.'

'Yes . . .' Her voice was breathless. Some of her words started to quiver. 'Would you fuck me?'

'Oh yes. Really hard.'

'Yes. I like it hard.'

'Harder than you've ever had it before. So hard it would almost hurt. Maybe bruise you a bit.'

She let out a little shriek and her breath saturated the line. My ear even felt wet.

'Fuck you so hard. Make your whole body shake. I'd hold you down. Hold your hair and just slam myself against you.'

'Yes. I'm coming. Yes.' And she sounded exactly like she had when she lay on the very sofa I lay sprawled across, cock in one hand, phone in the other.

'You would have teased me and made me so hard in your stockings and heels, I would just take you. Be so turned on I would even take your ass.'

'Yes.' She gulped and whimpered. 'In there?'

'Mmm. Really hard in there. Right up inside. You'd feel me inside your stomach.'

'No.'

'Yes. I'd stretch your lovely ass wide and fuck it so hard, you wouldn't be able to breathe, let alone speak.'

From the other end of the phone, from the other side of the world, I heard her moan and shiver and sob. Not only did she have the most beautiful legs in the world and actually get aroused wearing stockings, she was also completely submissive. It didn't get any better.

'I'm coming to see you,' I said.

'Yes.'

'Very soon. I'm coming over there to take your tight ass with my hard cock.'

'Oh, yes. Come quickly.'

'You've teased me so much. You've made me wait for so long. It's going to be hard and fierce. As soon as you open the door, I'm going to be inside you. Hard. Hard and quick. I'm going to hold you down and punish you with my cock. Wear your highest heels and sheerest stockings. Be ready for when I get there. I'm coming.'

It sounded like she was crying. She mumbled things to me, but I never heard much of it. 'Fuck' a few times. 'Bastard' twice. Not much else. But we were back on.

'So that's settled,' I said. Understanding somehow that I had to be firm and take the initiative. How had I become so whiny and desperate and clingy? I thought. She wanted me to make the moves. To just go and take her.

'You in town this weekend?'

'Yes,' she whispered. 'Yes I am.'

'Then be ready. I'll call you from the airport. You got that?'

'Yes. Yes.'

So I went. I flew to LA to turn a dream into a reality. Anything that's worth having, you have to work hard for. I reminded myself of this. It's the same for everybody.

Only, nothing is that simple.

The day after the Nylon Dahlia sent me a brief email: *Thank you for last night. You were wonderful.*

I booked a flight to LAX to get there Friday afternoon.

On the Thursday before I flew out, I popped into the shop to steal more stock as gifts for the Dahlia: a pair of Jaguar-print stilettos by Le Silla and two pairs of vintage nylons in her size – one pair in coffee, the other in pale blue. But after I had craftily snuck my loot into a case, Sam asked me to work Saturday with her at the store. It was an emergency. Lucy hadn't been in all week; she claimed to have the flu. And Cecilia had already booked the day off to take an aromatherapy course in Brighton. She couldn't manage on her own. Which was true. Someone had to watch the shop and deal with the customers, while shoes were fetched from the stockroom. A rule I had absolutely insisted upon.

I told her it was impossible. That I had to go away. On business. For the business. I started to sweat.

'What business? You never told me.'

I swallowed. 'To set up a promotional deal that will really put us on the map, internationally.'

I could have said, I was going to Glasgow to look at a huge stock of real nylons discovered in a factory warehouse. This had happened before, and I'd bought every single pair; the resale value was immense. But I didn't. I said 'international'.

Her eyes narrowed. She smiled. But not in a pleasant way. 'I see. You're going to see her, aren't you?'

'Who?'

'Don't fuckin' who me, Al! You're going to see that Dahlia. Who you're so crazy in love with. Some fuckin' model you're kidding yourself you got a chance with. She's so fake. She's freaky. She's trouble.'

'What?' I tried to look astonished, exasperated, bemused. Instead, I just looked like a guilty fool.

'You're such a liar,' she said quietly. Cecilia was out front, behind the counter; she must have heard the exchange. Tears quickly welled around Sam's pretty eyes. She tried to blink them away. One ran down her cheek. She dabbed at it with a little finger; the nail was immaculate and polished a glossy plum colour.

'Hey,' I said, and reached for her hand.

She took it out of my reach. And sniffed. 'You do what you like. It's not like I'm your girlfriend anyway.' Her voice broke on the 'anyway'. She turned on her heel, to hide her freshly wet eyes from me, and teetered into the stockroom. I watched the twin, perfectly symmetrical seams on the back of her calves disappear.

She'd worn black fully fashioned stockings from GIO. We had a pact that she would only wear those when she wanted really intense and filthy sex with me. She had worn them that day to get my attention. To get some attention after I had ignored her for a whole month, while I pined away with my fixation for the Nylon Dahlia.

I couldn't swallow the lump in my throat. I don't think I'd ever felt so bad. I hated myself. Loathed myself. Despised my wretched self. I closed my eyes and leant against the fridge door. If I went to LA and left her to manage the shop alone, Sam was lost. For ever. The very idea appalled me. My mind suddenly filled with a different kind of gallery. Thumbnail pictures of every time I had made Sam giggle, or given her a real belly laugh; of how her eyes, framed by dolly lashes, had looked at me with admiration, with love, or narrowed with desire. Of the dinners we had enjoyed. The old films we had been to see together at the NFT festivals. The retro clubs we had gone jiving in. Her always dressed like a curvaceous fifties pin-up queen, her hair styled like Tippi Hedren. I remembered with a hot flush of shame, how many times I had held her hand.

Despite my faults, and my perversions, she adored me. Was genuinely accepting of everything that I was. Could I honestly ever say I had experienced that before? She was special.

I left the store. Cecilia never even looked up at me from her magazine, or said goodbye.

I flew out to LA the next morning.

Eleven

But before I can continue towards the climax, my therapist wants to know how my fetish (we use this term freely now) 'affected my early relationships'. I must go back again before I can take myself to the end and relive the inevitable results of my actions.

Waiting, her body relaxed, a kind smile on her violet-red lips, she crosses her trousered legs. Still covering herself from toe to thigh. I wonder if she paints her toenails. Almost certainly. I wonder if she thinks differently about her legs after meeting me.

So, I must pace myself. Take us back before I am allowed to rush to the end of the story that brought me to her surgery, where all the various parts could be examined. And so I tell her about my first adult relationship – the final consummation of my desire to love legs, to actually touch them, to fuck them. The defining moment. I tell her about Margaret.

Margaret always said something to make me blush, before she paid me a five-pound babysitting fee, and released me through the porch of her house to walk home.

Friends of my parents – what rich pickings they were in retrospect – I would watch the kids, Cathy and Richard, on Thursday evenings if Margaret was at her dramatic society and when her husband Eric worked nights at a power station – every week for a month sometimes. And in those short intervals before Margaret left the house at seven, and returned tipsy around eleven, we developed a friendship.

But for a painfully shy eighteen-year-old, working through his second year of A levels and one year away from university, who had yet to have a girlfriend, I took some warming up.

In the early evening I managed Cathy and Richard – listened to their stories, assisted with homework, watched television, examined their toys – while Margaret rushed up and down the stairs, applying final touches to her make-up and hair, grabbing things she needed. She was always a little frantic and harried, but I never saw her lose her temper. A good woman, mother and wife. I loved their house.

But later, after a few drinks with the other players in her theatre group, she was different. She had more time for me.

And she would always laugh at the effect of her flattery on me – 'Mmm, if I was twenty years younger, I'd snap you up.' 'God, haven't you filled out, Al.' 'You have turned into a very handsome man.'

Blushing, silly embarrassed giggles, averted eyes: my inevitable reactions. Had I not desired her so intensely, I may have reacted differently. And the more familiar she became with me, her final comments in the evening became more salacious. 'You'd better go, Al, before I seduce you.' Three times she said that to me near Christmas. And I took it home with me, that comment, and inevitably built an entire fantasy life around it.

Of course, instinctively, I knew a married friend of my parents was never going to sleep with me. She was just a gregarious, extroverted, playful character who liked to push her luck and try and bring bashful, introverted Al out of his shell.

But she was a woman for whom I developed a deep and lasting fascination because of her legs and how she presented them. Margaret was never a great beauty, but she was glamorous. Loved fashion. Took care with her appearance. And had shapely legs. Of average length, but verging on a pleasing thickness that developed an attractive shape in heels. Of which she had a fondness. Margaret was a real shoe woman.

Eyeing her final preparations from the living-room floor or dining table, I always remember her strapping her feet into a variety of high-heeled sandals before she went out. Earrings and shoes last, every time. Very sheer stockings – white, grey, nearly black, or black as fashion dictated in the early eighties – to complement a smart dress or skirt. Red-painted fingernails buckling her long, pleasing feet into the elegant cage of patent spaghetti straps. Black, red, white, pink, blue, cream – she had so many beautiful shoes. I knew them all intimately, and everything she wore with them. Had made many visits up to her room when my charges were sleeping. And many forays into the laundry basket they kept in the little annex next to the kitchen.

It was the first time I'd handled and fondled corsets, or discovered a woman who owned so much lingerie, or 'sexy underwear' as it was called then. And I immediately knew that Margaret was probably dressing to please Eric, and being pleased in turn by Eric as a result of her sexual underthings. Eric and I had a lot in common.

Drawers filled with purple, red, black and white lace; see-through French knickers; lace-upholstered corsets; tangled froths of suspender belts, and more stockings than I had ever uncovered in one place before. In her bedroom, I unravelled and handled and adored Aristoc Harmony Point stockings for the first time. And was electrified by the very sight of them. I'd never seen anything so enchanting – so sheer and long and slippery and instantly sexual. Made flat with a seam up the back, completely from nylon, tailored to the leg to produce an immaculate colour tone throughout the garment. Stockings I had idolised on actresses in the films that formed a backdrop to my youth. In my hands they slithered and slid, practically weightless. I used to hold them up to the light and see how they changed the world on the other side into something sultry, mysterious, achingly erotic. A world of pleasing shadows and dark hazes I wanted to pass into so I would remain forever aroused and tingling with anticipation.

And so, inevitably, my obsession with Margaret grew. I thought of a hundred lines I could say in response to one of her cheeky remarks, and imagined a hundred different scenarios that would be the result of my not being paralysed by self-loathing, diffidence, shame and reticence for the first time in my young adult life.

And eventually I did say something that changed things between Margaret and me.

She was drunk. And came home reeking of wine and perfume and cigarette smoke. Wearing a dark-purple suit, with a silky pink blouse and matching high-heeled sandals. Her stockings were dark and shiny, nearly black. I opened the living-room door when I heard her key jabbing at the lock in the porch, and then again at the front door. She smiled, her eyes mischievous as usual, but full of drunken mischief.

Whispering frantically about her evening – the various characters and politics of rehearsal – she tiptoed clumsily into the lounge: I wasn't really listening. Instead, I was devouring her with my eyes. Trying to keep them up and off her legs and feet, but failing.

Deep-purple nail varnish on her well-formed toes, visible beneath the sheer toe of her stockings; toes that turned up slightly at the end, which I always found pleasing.

A cold hand with sharp nails slipped around my bicep. 'Ooh, my feet are killing me,' she said. Then placed both hands on my chest. Her face close. Hazel eyes looking right into mine, flirtatious, sexual, challenging eyes. My throat closed and one eyelid trembled. She'd never been this physical, this drunk, before.

I helped her into the room and she flopped down on to the sofa. Stretched out her legs, that shone and glistened under the overhead lights and flicker of the television. I shut the living-room door.

'Be a love and take my shoes off. I can't see straight.'

I swallowed the lump in my throat and hesitated. Froze. Couldn't move at all, but inside my head all was frantic and flitting. Panic. A woman had actually asked me to touch her legs, her feet. A woman whose legs and feet I endlessly masturbated over while alone in bed and in the bath. A woman whose most intimate underwear I had touched and pawed and adored and tasted with nose and tongue.

My look of shock registered with her. 'No, perhaps you'd better go, or I really will disgrace myself.'

I smiled. Managed to force some clarity into my mind; to stop things racing about in there for a moment. I said, 'In that case, I think I'll stay.'

She was smiling and looking surprised at the same time. 'Oh, Al.' She crossed her legs, and her skirt and slip slid down her thigh. 'No, you better go before it's too late.' I still couldn't decide whether she was fooling around with me or not. But the sheer force of my frustration and desire compelled me to linger. Years of fantasising and self-pleasuring over just such a woman finally prevented me from skulking away to imagine what might have been. Instead, encouraged by the effect of my first comment, I continued. 'Would you like a massage. I've got warm hands.'

She laughed, loudly, then clapped a hand over her mouth so as not to wake the kids. Shook her head in surprise. I smiled at her. Approached. Knelt down before her feet. She played along. Stretched her right foot towards my chest. Rotated her ankle. I nearly choked. Thought I was having a stroke. Then went cold all over from the most pleasing shudder I can ever remember experiencing.

I could see every detail of her legs up close: the grain of the leather of her shoes, the freckles of her skin beneath the tiny square mesh of her stockings, the faint pleasing creases between two toes. I cupped her ankle. It felt big. Filled my palm. The fabric of her stocking not as slick or soft as I'd have guessed it would be. But slightly abrasive.

I picked at the tiny golden buckle of her ankle strap. Then freed her foot. She let me withdraw the shoe and take her foot into my hands. It was large and soft and warm.

'Don't worry, they don't smell,' she said. 'My feet get a lot of air in these shoes.' For some reason this innocuous, obligatory remark from her filled me with a peculiar sense of revulsion combined with a sharp thrust of arousal so intense I felt dizzy. At the time I was still ambivalent about the fragrance of women's feet. I liked it but felt deeply ashamed of liking the very idea of it. In time I grew to adore it in the same way a vintner examines a bouquet from a rare Pinot. I embraced it. But this sudden comment about imperfection and mortality in something so iconic and idolised in my imagination made me want to simultaneously remove my hands and also press the soles of her feet against my face.

I stroked the top of her feet, gently. She sighed, and said, 'Oh, that's nice.' Her stockings swished inside the palm of my annoyingly damp hand, which was interfering with the sensation. I pressed harder and her stockings tugged on her toenails, creating a resistance in the webbing I found pleasing and had never expected.

216

Then I rubbed her heels and let my hand stray up her Achilles tendon where the fabric of the stocking wasn't so tight to her flesh. She closed her eyes and purred. I stroked the pinky soles of her feet. They felt slippery. I kneaded the ball of her foot because I thought that was the thing to do. It was. She bent her toes back in my hands, then curled them. I had never experienced such an erection; it felt like a girder of tempered steel that would never soften.

'The other one.' She gave me the left foot. I repeated the manoeuvre, and this time stroked the foot with more confidence and added more pressure. Really massaged my fingers into her hose and skin and then interspersed the more forceful rubbing with gliding caresses across and around the curves and lines of her long, middle-aged and married feet. 'Ah. I like having my feet rubbed,' she whispered to me. I smiled at her narrowed eyes. There was something dangerous in them. Primal even. A woman's lust coaxed to the surface by disinhibiting alcohol and a man's touch. A man she found desirable. It was almost too much to process into fact. But I knew I was close to something life-defining.

Holding my stare, she said, 'Do you fancy my legs?'

I nodded. 'Oh yeah. Can't take my eyes off them.'

A slight smile formed around her mouth that was also beginning to bewitch me. 'I know,' she said. 'You always watch me walk.'

'Can't help it. They're beautiful.'

'Really?' she said, in a much softer, earnest voice.

I nodded. 'I like ... I like ... what you wear.' I couldn't say it. I couldn't say 'stockings and shoes'. I was unable to give a sound to the signifiers of the signified that was dominating my entire life.

She saved me the trouble and asked, 'You like stockings?'

'Oh yeah. More than anything.' I stroked my hands up her broad calves. Both hands working up and down

217

at the slippery curvature; so compact, so streamlined in black stockings. My hands grew warm from the friction.

Margaret winked and slowly pulled her skirt up to the top of her thighs.

I swooned. I actually swooned. My head felt heavy and filled with a violent pumping of blood. My vision darkened and I was unable to breathe or swallow for a few seconds. I choked on my own desire.

I saw an expanse of thigh stretching her hosiery to a slightly paler colour than the fabric on her calves and feet; opaque bands of black stocking top beneath two inches of skin so pale it almost blinded me; two thick suspender straps dividing her milky flesh; a triangular pouch of female sex coated tightly in purple and black silk. All of this confronted my eyes and produced a kind of physical surge through my body that made my jaw shake.

She let me look. 'You like that?'

I nodded, mesmerised.

'Touch me if you want to.'

It was actually happening. It could have been any one of a thousand fantasies I had lovingly created for myself. Not ephemeral anymore now it involved real flesh and the actual fabrics I adored. Real words, an actual tangible location, but involving all of the conventions of my fantasy narratives: the tipsy housewife, the ordinary living room, the transgressive element of infidelity, the secret life of a woman revealed. But more significantly, I was in the presence of a real woman. An actual human being. The true goal of a lifetime's fascination. Dressed to please.

Tentatively, I laid my hands on her knees. Cupped the slippery mounds. Stroked upwards to her softer, thicker thighs. Allowed my fingers to stray on to her inner thighs. She parted them slightly, let out a little groan. I never touched the pale skin at the top, just indulged my eyes and let my insistent, exploring finger tips stroke her stockings.

'Come with me,' she said, and suddenly stood up. Took my hand and led me out through the dining room, then the kitchen and laundry room I knew so well, and into the playroom built behind the double-car garage. She closed the door and turned to face me, looking much shorter without her heels.

I remember her leaning into me for a kiss. And then we became tangled. Sucking and licking and tugging on each other's lips. I remember the sensation of so much softness pressed into my body. At how wide her hips felt, and at how it took so much of my arms to encircle her waist. Something fantasies never reveal: the true dimensions of a lover.

I liked the taste of her lipstick, and was surprised by the force of her tongue as it jabbed into my mouth and thrashed around. Against her belly my erection pressed and rubbed, almost of its own accord; calling out to her, demanding her ministrations. And she willingly took the lead. I had a sense of her really wanting me. Of wanting a man. Of needing sex. I was astonished.

Once she unbuckled me with those swift, strong fingers, she fell immediately to her knees. Yanked my jeans and underwear down, and paused for only a moment to stare at my cock. Her eyes actually widened. She gritted her teeth. Looked slightly savage, despite her glasses and elegant hairstyle. Then took me into her mouth.

Held my cock by the stem and moved her whole head on and off my erection quickly. Sucking hard and moaning through her nose. She enjoyed it. Actually liked having a cock in her mouth. She did it for me, and she did it for herself. Spread her painted nails on my groin and pumped her head on and off my erection.

I expected more sensation from her mouth. It felt so soft as to almost be imperceptible. And watery. The real

219

pleasure I realised was in watching a woman do it and knowing an actual lady had your cock inside her mouth.

As she tugged at me with her thick lips, she stripped her jacket off and unbuttoned her blouse. Her heavy bust was supported by a black and purple bra that matched her panties. And the skin of her shoulders and belly looked so white it shocked me. She was plump about the middle. I liked that – the maternal, matronly aspect to her waist and hips and bust. And especially as it was carved in two by a black and purple suspender belt. It was a real, definable body; not unobtainable like the girls in *Mayfair* magazine I studied. A body that had given birth and been married in church; that lay in bed with a husband, that was respectable and fenced in by convention and propriety in a middle-class suburb; I couldn't have invented a better scenario in my private bedroom reveries. It was too much to comprehend. My reason seemed to go numb.

'Ooh, you have a lovely cock,' she said, after pulling her swollen, slightly puffy mouth off my erection. I could smell my semen on her breath. Her eyes looked skewed, drunken. But with lust more than wine. She pulled my jeans, pants and socks off my feet as I hopped from foot to foot. Then rose up against my body and turned around so I could unzip her skirt, which dropped to a puddle at her feet as soon as I smoothed it down over her hips. Without a pause she hooked her fingers inside her cream slip and bent to push it to the floor; a floor covered in Lego bricks from her son's extravagant but crumbling spaceship creation. Without a pause, she lay down with her shoulders and head supported by a large red beanbag. She said, 'Come here. I want you inside me. Quickly.'

Easing her panties down to her shimmering knees, she showed me her wide, bushy sex. I had to take my eyes from it for a while and concentrate on peeling her panties off her ankles and feet. But I could smell it. A salty, briny thickness filled the air.

She was wet. Curls of pubic hair had gone dark and were stuck to the long purplish-brown lips of her sex. I couldn't speak.

'Come here. Come on,' she said, and put her feet on my shoulders. I shuffled forwards which pushed her legs back, opening that nest of curls and silvery dew between her thighs. It was only a few inches below the engorged head of my own grotesque sex.

Thick fingers, heavy with gold rings and jewels, opened the moist folds and creases so I could see a small dark hole. She was shameless. Her other hand snatched at my length and lowered it to the heart of her. I pushed forwards. Missed. Slipped in and out in my furious eagerness to be inside her. Without a condom, I thought, and felt like ejaculating.

But the bright light, the toys on the floor, the coloured bricks I kept kneeling on, the very physical reality of Margaret's house, provided enough of a grounding to prevent me succumbing to a pure ejaculatory release.

Eventually, with her coaxing and steering, she planted me inside herself, and I leant forwards and slipped all of my length inside in one long descent. Biting her fingers, she swore. Said, 'Bloody hell, that's nice.' And after a few over-enthusiastic withdrawals that had my wet erection back out of her fleshy sheath, I eventually found a rhythm and prevented myself from repeatedly slipping out.

Constantly, I stroked her legs. Kissed and sniffed at her silky toes. Eventually growing bolder and licking my tongue into her instep while hammering my groin into her. At one point I put her stockinged toes inside my mouth and sucked them wet. I never touched her breasts once, I only realised after it was all over. But she did.

With her eyes closed, she pinched and tugged at her nipples. Had pulled them over the top of her bra, while I covered every inch of her silky legs with strokes and kisses and licks.

It took me a long time to come. This surprised me. I thought it was inevitable for male virgins to ejaculate straight away. But it was hard to get to my absolute peak – my point of no return. I didn't want it to end. I held back on the more intensely pleasurable ripples in my cock, by clenching my muscles. And this delaying technique, combined with an unpredicted sweating exhaustion at the physical nature of fucking, and the residual self-consciousness at what I was actually doing to one of my parents' friends and neighbours, enabled me to thrust and grind into Margaret for forty-five minutes. I checked my watch with a sense of pride and triumph. I think she even had a climax. Her feet had locked twice against my cheeks and she had rolled her eyes. Though it was not solely from the amateur but enthusiastic stabbing of my virgin cock. I will never forget how fast and brazenly she rubbed at her clit the entire time I rammed myself into her. She made herself come with her rubbing fingers and from the thought of having a young man's cock inside her. Nice.

Her hair was now damp with sweat, and the air in the room thick and cured with the saltine of sex. Eye make-up running, face flushed red, she asked me to stop. I pulled out reluctantly, eager to finish.

'You should go. Your parents will be wondering what's happened to you.'

And sure enough, the phone rang minutes later. It was my mother. But I heard Margaret cover like a pro. 'Oh, I've waylaid him. I'm afraid we've got on to J. B. Priestley and *An Inspector Calls*. We're doing it next year. OK. Bye, Jen.'

She came back into the playroom, smiling. I looked disappointed, having realised that my fun was over. My sense of completion, of definition, of confirmation and relief at the end of my virginity thwarted by not having actually come. Was I still a virgin?

'Come here,' she said, reading my thoughts, and taking me into her hand. 'Did you like it?'

I kissed her on the mouth. 'So much. Thanks.'

This made her laugh, as if she had provided a service and was being shown gratitude by the recipient of her skill and experience.

I'd grown back to a fullness in her hand. 'I bet given half a chance you'd keep me up all night at your age.'

This made me sink back into the dizzy vortex of quick-fire male arousal. I wanted her again. Desperately.

Stroking me with one hand, she started to unclip her suspenders from her stocking tops. 'Don't take them off,' I said.

'Darling, you have to go now. Your mum's expecting you.'

'Just a little bit more. Please.'

She frowned, then smiled. 'OK. But be quick.'

Twenty minutes later, I finally came. Into her mouth. Lying on her side, like I asked her to, and sucking me. While I lay the other way, stroking her legs, kissing her feet and sucking her toes wet through her stockings. It was the only way I could climax, the first time. I needed my fetish maximised. And I never saw a drop of my ejaculation even though there was so much of it. Margaret swallowed all of me.

By the time I left, I'd grown bold enough to even ask for, and be granted, her used stockings as a souvenir. 'You're a strange, boy, Al,' she'd said, with a shake of her tousled head, while pulling them down her pale legs.

'Did you ever see her again.'

'Oh yeah. I carried on looking after those kids until the following spring.'

'But did you continue to have relations?'

I nod to the doctor, and contain a smile at her eagerness to know, her curiosity at how others live their lives. How we carry on.

'But only a few times more. Eleven to be exact. I can remember each occasion vividly. What she wore. But it started to give her too much to worry about. Weird thing was, her husband knew. The next time I visited, Margaret said, "We better not. Eric and I are worried your parents might suspect something." He sanctioned it. Thought it was funny. Probably liked to hear about it.'

'But you did carry on?'

'Yes. Given half a chance, I'd have been around there every day. I assured her no one would ever know. Was I going to jeopardise the best thing that had ever happened to me? A private exploration of my fetish? With an older woman? No way. So, she came home early from rehearsal a few times to have sex with me, in the playroom. Always in there. At the front of the house, in the extension, because there were no bedrooms above.

'But it became too risky with the kids. The boy came down for a drink once and nearly caught me fucking his mother doggy-style over a beanbag. A woman who had dressed in black seamed stockings, high-heeled sandals and a corset for the babysitter. So then we switched to days, when it was mutually convenient. When the house was empty and I had half-days at college. That was better. Then I could come over and over again. Four times some mornings. And she always dressed to please me.'

'What about her husband?'

'On the rare occasion I saw him at someone's fiftieth party, or something like that my family was invited to, he would just smile at me. Shake my hand. Sometimes give me a wink. But my parents to this day remain clueless about the whole thing. It stopped when, surprise, surprise, my parents moved house again, just before I went to university. Damn that property ladder. I've never seen Margaret since. But God knows I've been tempted to call. Even now, and she must be over sixty.'

'So did your fetish then become a part of your sex life in all other adult relationships?'

I smile. 'You know me so well, Doctor Kim. Yes, always.'

So I tell her about Trudy, my first real girlfriend at university. Who indulged me. Like so many of the young and older women who gave me experience, who cultivated my passion. Trudy must have worn every single brand and type of hosiery in the three years we were together. She never had sex completely naked. She liked what it did to my eyes when she pulled her skirt up or down, and when she peeled her trousers off and showed me the shade of her legs, and how they shone under sun or lamp light. I must have spent half of my annual student grant on hosiery, shoes and boots for her. I still have every empty packet and about forty pairs of her laddered stockings. They hold memories. Sensual memories I am unable to let go of.

I've since experienced as many types of female leg and foot as I have been able to, and experienced varying degrees of erotic stimulation from them. Have had lovers' legs coated and shod in as complete a spectrum of accessories as opportunity and resources have allowed. And, finally, I narrowed the epic nature of my fetish to a particular kind of leg and foot for which I can never tire. Unconsciously, and then consciously, it is this shape and length of leg that stops time for me. When I see it a stillness and immobility is created inside and about me; all extraneous thought is paralysed; an intensity of focus, of all my senses, on the legs and feet occurs immediately.

Legs that are long, but not skinny. Full legs that have the qualities of being both slender but also defined by a pronounced musculature. Legs with a tiny gap between the thighs at the very top. With defined ankles and long feet in which the sinews, bones and muscles of the foot are visible. The feet must have long varnished toenails and soft unblemished, pale skin that has the potential to go honey brown in the sun. Simple, really. The Nylon Dahlia has those legs, Sam too.

'And the Nylon Dahlia represents a sexual fascination that you think will never fade, as well as companionship?' Doctor Kim is almost condescending as she says this. As if she's getting close to a judgement, to closing the file on me. Crazy, predictable me. 'Tell me what happened in California. I think we're ready to talk about this now.'

Twelve

Things started to go wrong as soon as I was through immigration at LAX.

I called the Nylon Dahlia's number four times from the airport in the first hour. No answer. Tried her cell phone twice. Ditto. Was she screening me?

The previous day in London, I'd sent an email confirming my arrival time, which she acknowledged briefly: *Hi hon'. Gonna be fun.*

Sure, a real barrel of laughs.

She'd said, albeit drunkenly once on the phone, that I could 'crash' with her. But the actual details of my stay this weekend were never confirmed. Was she unsure, or just too busy?

My body told me it was midnight, London time; my time. It was one p.m. in LA and the sun turned the air to a dusty haze, like someone had just split a Hoover bag over the city. But the white stucco and metal of the buildings still managed to burn white spots into my retina if I stared too long.

Crumpled from the ten-hour flight, dehydrated and feeling like I was walking through molasses, I found a cab outside and gave the tired-looking Sikh driver the Nylon Dahlia's address – the one I'd sent all of those gifts to. It looked like both of us hadn't had a good night's sleep in a while. I could speak for myself; since the night I first met her, my sleep had been fitful, my stomach a mess, like a torn bag.

Couldn't remember being so nervous on the ride to Santa Monica. It had been ten years since I'd been in LA, and out here I was at her mercy. The euphoria of escape – of escape from myself – I usually experienced travelling was stifled at birth by a double-header of romantic anxiety and fear of just being lost in an unfamiliar place.

The one-storey building she lived in on a quiet suburban street was set back from the road and almost entirely concealed by palms and tropical bushes drooping over the white concrete wall. When the taxi pulled away I felt like my only friend in the country had abandoned me.

For a while I stood on the pavement, my case and suit cover beside me. The linen jacket and trousers I was wearing began to feel like a suit of armour on a crusade through the desert. Sweat clouded my pits, drenched the channel of my spine and dripped with a salty sting down my forehead and into my eyes. There was no shade. I felt exposed. Felt like I was burning from inside and out.

I opened the gate and walked down the narrow path, brushing back palm fronds and large waxy-looking leaves the size of dinosaur tongues. The windows were shuttered with blinds against the light. Standing on the porch, I remembered a newspaper story about a confused British businessman in Florida who was shot fatally through the front door of a private house while fumbling with the wrong keys in the wrong lock.

I dropped my bag on the small porch and opened the mosquito screen. Knocked. Knocked again loudly. Listened out for a pistol being cocked. Or even better, the clip-clop of spike heels on a wooden floor. Nothing.

Beyond the closed front door I sensed a cool, private and perfumed darkness and hoped I was welcome inside it.

Again, for the hundredth time since I landed I recalled her frenetic, excited, salacious and drugged words the last time we spoke on the phone. She must have been high in the afternoon. It's a terrible and fruitless ordeal to continually analyse and deconstruct a few lines of dialogue from a woman who may or may not be interested in you. It produces a particular type of exhaustion that is bound to make you feel foolish months later. But at the time, it's everything.

I swallowed. Headed back down the drive, tripping on a paving slab and scuffing a shoe. I couldn't even walk in a straight line. Co-ordination was on the way out. A knock-kneed clumsiness was setting in. My tongue felt swollen and a headache was kicking in like a bass drum. Weeks of sleep deprivation seemed to be catching up on me. Maybe it was sunstroke. I was confused, tired, disappointed.

Back out on the street, I started walking back to the main boulevard. On the ride in, from the cab window, I remembered seeing a kind of staple-shaped car park with a range of one-storey businesses built around it.

It was much further away than I remembered. The heat and the weight of my luggage added another layer of discomfort. One old man in an electric wheelchair passed me. I came across no one else on foot. Even on the pavement people were driving things. The traffic was relentless, the air hot and dirty. I began to feel that a layer of grease had coated my entire skin. I thought my shoes were melting off my feet. Wished I'd bought a hat. And a handkerchief to wipe my face. I felt pink and English and stupid. The pointy corners of the shoe boxes in my luggage banged against my knees. The irony didn't escape me. I kept walking. One mile, maybe two. No one looked at me in the passing vehicles. An ambulance screamed past. Briefly, I felt cold, but not in a pleasant way.

Eventually I reached the shops: a 7-Eleven; something called Little Caesar that sold pizza but had no chairs and tables inside; a drug store; a dry cleaners; and something that was a cross between an adult-magazine shop, a liquor store and a sweet shop. I bought Gatorade and chewing gum. Nowhere to wait. I loitered for twenty minutes outside and slurped at the cold liquid. Walked another 200 metres down the same road to something called Jack in the Box. A fast-food burger restaurant with seats inside.

I suddenly felt hungry and bought all kinds of things, but lost my appetite after taking one bite of the steak sandwich. This wasn't weather to eat in. The place was air-conditioned but the sun was still blinding through the glass. There was lots of glass.

I tried the Nylon Dahlia's home number and cell phone again. No answer. The battery level on my phone was low. I had to turn the phone off to save juice – in case she called later. I had a fear of the silver pay-phones; they looked so complicated but curiously anti-quated at the same time.

What was I thinking? What kind of a man would have flown to another country on a whim to visit a fetish model? A desperate man was the only answer I could come up with.

I ate half of the sandwich slowly. Picked at the curly fries. Waited another two hours. My head felt abnorm-ally heavy and my vision started to pixilate. Without my even being aware of precisely when it happened, I fell asleep.

And was woken by a Mexican boy wearing a Jack in the Box cap. He smiled. 'You fell asleep,' he said. 'You got somewhere to go, sir?'

He thought I was a bum. I looked like a bum. Shabby, down at heel. Dragging a case. Killing time in a burger joint until the next hit of Seagrams. Humiliation clashed with shock. It was late afternoon. Gone five. I scrambled for my phone. Turned it on. Waited for the signal.

I had a text message from my network informing me of call rates while visiting the States. *Welcome to the USA*, it said. At least the phone satellite cared. It didn't make me feel any better.

The skin on my face felt tight. Sunburn. The Mexican youth wiped down my table.

'My friend's not home,' I mumbled. 'I was waiting for her call. Is there a bar near here?'

Wrong thing to ask. His suspicions were confirmed. He began to wipe down the next table, smiling tightly. He had two colleagues, both Mexican. They watched me from behind the brightly lit counter. Must have been watching the sleeping bum for hours. I reddened with shame, but doubt whether it would have been visible through the scorched colour of my facial skin. How long before the cops showed up? I imagined being deported for falling asleep in Jack in the Box.

'Better get going,' I said, having nowhere to go. Briefly, I felt like crying. Cleared my throat. 'Hotel? Motel? Is there a motel near here?' I asked the youth, now three tables down.

'Plenty, plenty,' he said, and pointed behind me. Outside.

I could take a hint. Said goodbye and left, sensing ridicule and relief behind me.

I went back to the drugstore and bought sun cream. Briefly checking out my face in the strip mirror by the sunglasses stand. My eyelids were white as uncooked pastry. The rest of my face was pink as a half-cooked sausage, and looked sore. Ridiculous.

I pounded the pavement. Lowered my head as I passed Jack in the Box. But at least the sun wasn't so fierce now. Getting on for six p.m. After about another mile, I came across a dirty-looking motel that offered cable TV, a swimming pool and water beds. It was called the Palm Inn. Of all things.

I checked in. The fat, balding clerk was suspicious when I said I had no car. He scrutinised my passport and made a phone check on my credit card. 'Folks come here to rest,' he warned me. 'Not to party.'

I felt hysterical laughter rising up my throat, but just managed to hold it back until he handed over the keys to 22.

In my room, I drew the orangey curtains, undressed and climbed into bed, too tired to wash. But had to get back out of bed, put on my rancid clothes, and go back to the clerk to buy a plug adapter to recharge my phone. My head felt like it was going to burst like a boiled tomato.

Back in bed, the sound of traffic was relentless. Eerie voices and sounds drifted through my mind, like I'd put my head under water in the bath. They stopped when I fell into a coma of exhaustion.

It took me a long time to haul myself from a dreamless concussion of sleep when the phone rang, and rang, and rang.

Eventually, I sat bolt upright in bed. Then scrambled hopelessly about the floor looking for the phone. I calmed down and followed the sound. Found the little screen glowing yellow-green under the window. Hit the answer button just in time.

I heard music. Loud music and loud laughter. 'Hello,' I said three times before the Dahlia answered. Her voice was slurred. Party girl. But still my hopes somersaulted. I filled and then sagged with relief and the pathetic pleasure of the briefly acknowledged. 'Al? Hey, Al? Where are you? Why aren't you here?'

I jabbered something about the Palm Inn, about her not being home. She wasn't listening. Instead she talked over me. 'Come out to the Roxy. It's so cool. The bands are coming on soon.'

'Where?' It took three attempts to get the address of a place on Sunset Boulevard. 'How are you? You OK?' I asked.

'Darling, I'm just divine. I'm the Dahlia.' The line went dead.

I stumbled into the shower. Shaved and fought a scream when I scraped my tender top lip. Put on new clothes and headed out to reception to get a cab.

It took twenty minutes to arrive. The clerk had changed and I preferred this one. An old hippy type who asked me questions about The Who, and about London, as I paced and shivered from nervous excitement in reception. He started every question with the words, 'I hear over there you got . . .' At least I felt better after seven hours of sleep. It felt like about nine in the morning but was now nearly three a.m.

Outside the Roxy, I joined a long queue of young people with lots of tattoos and quiffed hair. Two of the women were tall and beautiful and had haircuts like Betty Page. They were both wearing high heels and fishnets. Suddenly, the trip was looking up.

I called the Dahlia from outside. Got an answering message. One I was very familiar with by this time.

I paid twenty 'bucks' and entered a very small, dark space packed out with more tattoos, muscle shirts and girls with very red lips. The music pouring from the direction of the small stage was so loud it thickened the air with an electrified, distorted sludge-wall of sound. A relentless cacophony.

I secured a drink – they sold bottles of Budweiser in sets of four for twelve bucks. After admission, two cab rides, Jack in the Box and various sundry items, I had thirty dollars left from the stash I bought with me from London. I'd expected it to last the weekend.

I scanned the crowd for the Nylon Dahlia. People jostled me and bumped into me. I apologised. Then started to get irritable.

I found a damp black wall to lean against and realised I was just about at the end of my tether. Was practically broken and in danger of being consumed by a dark cloud of self-loathing. How did I get here? How did it come to this? I kept telling myself over and over again. And then I saw her. In a crowd. Mostly male with retro haircuts, engineer boots, braces, tight T-shirts on muscular torsos and tattoos to their chins. They looked tough and effortlessly cool; I had a swollen face the colour of an Oompa Loompa in Willy Wonka's chocolate factory, and was wearing neutral clothes. A pinstriped suit with an open-necked shirt. I looked like a yuppie and hoped to pass for a record exec. Did they still look this way?

I was disoriented by the noise, too much sun, and the oppressive heat was back. Moist, humid, acrid. Even the walls were slick with sweat. Jesus, someone open a window. There were no windows and everything was painted black.

I approached the group. Stood by them. Went unnoticed for several seconds. The Nylon Dahlia was swaying to the music and being watched keenly by the guy close to her. Hair razored bald up the sides of his head to a huge oily quiff. On the side of his neck he had a tattoo of two chequered flags, crossed. His biceps were bigger than my thighs and were completely inked a greenish-red colour like the pages of a comic glimpsed from a distance. The Nylon Dahlia looked sublime: a sleeveless, red gingham, patterned shirt, a red chiffon scarf about her neck, black pencil skirt, tan nylons, high-heeled shoes with Minnie Mouse bows before the peep toe. She held a bottle of water in one slim hand. She looked at me twice with glassy eyes but didn't seem to see me. She was loaded. I waved a hand filled with beer bottles in front of her eyes which got everyone's attention.

'Daarling!' she screamed and fled to me. Wrapped her arms around my neck and kissed my cheek with a loud, smacking *mwah* sound. My joy was offset by the evil stare of the rockabilly psychopath with flags on his bullock neck.

'You came. You came. I can't believe you came to see me!' she shrieked.

'I've had quite an adventure.'

'I got your messages. I was in Pasadena. Work.'

'OK. OK. No problem,' I said. She was forgiven, instantly.

But she didn't hear me, or anything I seemed to say after that either. I felt like just one more gift, one more temporary distraction at a spoiled girl's birthday party. She twirled around and started jiving by herself.

'Anyone want a beer?' I asked the scowling men with Elvis hair and Kirk Douglas chins. Two of them warmed to me instantly and snatched up wet bottles from my fingers. Flag-neck just stared, and stared, and stared.

'Dude, what happened to your face?' the one in a Social Distortion T-shirt asked. 'I can like feel it from here. It's like so fuckin' hot, man.' He and his friend went into peals of laughter.

'They don't like get sun in England, dude,' his friend said. 'But I hear your beer is like killer strong?'

Here we go. I should have stayed home and talked to the hippy nightwatchman.

The Nylon Dahlia was back. Her pupils the size of black olives, her pretty face looking thin and tense. 'Come, come, come with us to the party. It's in the hills.

235

It'll be so cool. We've got to go now,' the Dahlia said. What happened to the cool, irreverent woman I had met in London, who could transform in a heartbeat to a vulnerable girl? It seemed to me there were other characters inside that beautiful long body. My disappointment felt like the mumps. I couldn't speak. Or smile. Just developed a rictus grin that made me look nervous and uptight. Because I was.

'Yeah, man, you're all right,' Social Distortion guy said. 'You should like hang out with us and shit.'

I nodded until the grin ached on my face. Flag-neck just stared and stared and stared.

Cramped in the back of a 66 Chevy, clinging on to the side to prevent myself flying out and on to the tarmac behind our rattling tailgate, I was driven into the hills by the two rockabilly guys who drank my beer. My suit jacket became a balloon, with creases. The knees of my trousers were soiled. They should have dropped me off at the nearest Jack in the Box.

The Nylon Dahlia drove ahead with flag-neck in a Mercury with the top down. She wore a head scarf and sunglasses. Jackie O.

The party was at someone's house I was never introduced to. I felt acutely self-conscious having brought no bottle, and also resentful at her treatment.

I just couldn't assimilate into the drugged and loaded discourse on fast forward all around me. The Dahlia cruised the room kissing everyone on the cheek. A mixture of film types, rockabilly guys and surfers. At least I think they were, but my knowledge of American subculture was not what it used to be. Some of the women were astonishing to look at. All adult-industry blondes with big lips and long legs. Two of them took in my face and smiled. Another giggled. I wanted to drown myself in the pool.

Every time I tried to speak to the Dahlia, flag-neck hovered nearby. Twice he pushed past me, into me, deliberately. Knocked me back. It was hopeless; she was hopped out of her head, too happy for words, jabbering. 'Do you like my shoes?' she asked me four times. 'Wasn't the band fucking great? I went to school with the singer.' She dropped a lot of names. Told me to lighten up. Twice. Said, 'Is that sore?' and pushed the tip of my nose. I didn't recognise her. Didn't know who this girl was that I had travelled across the world to see. Everyone else knew her. Wanted a piece of her.

'So like what's your fuckin' story?' Flag-neck asked me at one point. 'Why are you here?'

'I'm a friend.'

He glared at me. Then at her as she shrieked at a joke a small Jewish man in a pink polo shirt told her. 'She's everybody's friend.' He was also loaded, cocked and looked ready to fire. One punch to my face and the skin would surely split like orange peel.

Thirty minutes later he and the Dahlia were having a tense conversation by the stairs with no banisters that grew from the living-room floor. Then she was crying and he was holding her elbow tight. She pulled away and walked outside. If I followed, it was certain death. I dithered by the kitchen counter and got cornered by a drunken film agent with a hair transplant. Near the electric lights, he looked like a Barbie Doll. The whole time he talked at me, I stared at his scarred scalp. 'So what do you do in London?'

I told him quietly about the boutique. It seemed to be the funniest thing he'd ever heard. He told three people that walked past that I sold, 'Longereyyyy in London.'

Flag-neck scowled in a corner. Watched me, keenly. The Nylon Dahlia never looked at me again. She disappeared for long periods. Outside. Upstairs.

One of the rockabilly guys who drove me out must have felt sorry for me as he walked past. He stopped to ask me about Camden Town. I steered the conversation on to the Dahlia. Asked him if she was OK. 'Man, she and Tray. They have this totally fucked-up relationship. But they'll be fucking later. They always do. I mean, she can be an asshole. So can he. They're like totally into coke and shit.'

The temperature of my head suddenly refrigerated. I managed to swallow. 'Dude, you know she's like with Tray?' Tray? I think that's what he said. 'She's been like with him for ages.'

It was all I needed confirmed.

I checked out.

The guy with the hair transplant proved useful enough to call me a cab – he knew a number off by heart.

I waited outside the strange house in the hills until it arrived.

Went back to the Palm Inn. Lay on my bed. Wide awake and wired with misery. Looked at the television. Watched a business report on NBC with the sound down.

I knew when I was beaten.

The Nylon Dahlia was gone for good. How much of her I actually saw and got to know well I wasn't sure. In London she had been the femme fatale of my dreams; in LA someone I didn't recognise. But I'd seen enough instability and darkness and capriciousness to know she was on a self-propelled, self-absorbed journey of which the best I could hope for was to be dragged along the asphalt behind whatever she was driving, very fast.

Step off. Let go.

Despite my bleak disappointment and self-pity and anger, I did again experience a curious relief. The relief of a man who stayed behind on the docks while watching his friends embark on a journey of which there would probably be no survivors. In the Dahlia I sensed an erotic euphoria and intensity capable of breaking me

238

out of the gravity that holds an ordinary life in place. But I also glimpsed a potential for the kind of heartbreak that would feel like a heated needle being pushed through my sternum, every day, for ever. She would have broken me. I had been spared.

But for what?

Because, as was my wont, in the absence of another consuming infatuation suddenly dispersing into a cloud of transparent gas, I thought of Sam. Loving, attentive, affectionate, loyal, uncomplicated Samantha. With those marvellous legs, always presented to my exacting requirements.

Unaware of what time it was in London, I called her mobile from my bed. Got her answering service. In a brief and explosive onset of white incendiary rage I hurled my phone against the wall of my room. It smashed into three separate pieces and dislodged a chunk of paint and plaster. I regretted the action immediately. It had a fast sobering effect.

People come here to rest.

Just to torment myself, I thought about her for the next few hours. Experienced a kind of epiphany I had been holding back for nearly a year. A big penny dropped, shiny and heavy, through the fog of my disillusionment with the Dahlia. I loved Sam. Had been in love with her and the Dahlia at the same time.

With Sam, I always secretly suspected that I had met and employed perfection in the very temple of legs, Sheer Delight. And yet, I had done nothing but offer the most fleeting and random form of commitment to her because I sensed my erotic journey was still incomplete.

I suddenly wondered if I'd been born stupid or just turned out that way. In that musty, hot hotel room with the cable TV and air conditioning I couldn't work out how to operate, her smile lit my imagination and my memory. When I closed my eyes I watched her walk

239

from behind, a delightful wiggle above polished calves and patent spikes.

But something was very wrong. Our connection had been broken before I left for the Dahlia. I could sense the severance, even in another country. Correctly, I assumed a decision had been made by the soft, warm blonde Samantha which would leave me, ultimately and deservedly, empty-handed. I was denied the anger, resentment, injustice and victim-status of the jilted. I'd brought the axe down on my own neck by being as selfish and single-minded as any other addict.

To torment myself and to throttle myself with a long-overdue guilt, I remembered how she had not only run the business, but made it a success. Streamlined the administration; ordered and worked out how to use all of the relevant software; the money she had saved on bookkeeping; on ordering the right levels of stock; on managing the staff; on organising and overseeing maintenance and fittings. I had been in receipt of her efficiency, style, affection, friendship and love, and had treated her like crap. I thought of her beautiful legs and feet and toes.

She was just a good woman who made me happy and who could have made me a good man. I'd taken her for granted, and now couldn't bear the thought of being without her. The realisation stopped the blood in my veins. I felt sick, but mercifully cured of my infatuation with the Nylon Dahlia.

I remembered Sam's tears.

I wanted to get back to her as soon as possible. Before the damage was irreparable.

I loved her. Why had it been necessary for me to push myself, and her, into such a desperate extreme to realise this? In a pit of wretchedness, failure, loneliness and despair, my situation suddenly became clear.

I was still the A-level student babysitter, the under-graduate spending what little money he had in the lingerie department. No different in mind or intent than the middle-aged hunter of legs creating online and retail traps to indulge his insatiable appetite. It was me who was loaded. High on stimulation. An addict. And my cravings were in grave danger of ruining a real shot at happiness with Sam, without my having to sacrifice any sense of the erotic stimulation or satisfaction that had driven me thus far in life. My fetish was a purpose; it was that simple. I would never be without it, nor would want to be without it. With Sam, I wouldn't need to be.

But now I'd gone beyond the pale and reduced myself to a sad, sunburnt, lonely and disappointed bachelor in a cheap motel room. It could go on for ever like this. I could end up here over and over again; waiting for models and married women and divorcees for whom my interest began at the top of the thigh and ended at the tip of the toes. Maybe I would never run out of variety, but there was something dangerously repetitive about my behaviour. I was risking the most colossal slumps for the briefest of ecstasies. I was tired of playing the lottery. And of disappointing good people who cared.

I used to dream of falling into a forest of legs. It was a premonition, because I did fall into those strange, silky and erotic glades. And then I explored every thicket and limb I came across in that forest. Mapped it, memorised it. But the forest went on for ever. It was there before I arrived and would be there after I'd left. It was eternal. A man could never know it all. But rather than endlessly traversing the enchanted wood, until I dropped from exhaustion, perhaps it was time to rest beside, love and nurture the most attractive limbs I had yet discovered within the forest. Life is long, but not that long.

Two hours later, before I felt myself slipping into insanity at the Palm Inn, I took a cab out to the airport. Called Sam three more times at the airport. Called the shop. Answering machines.

I flew back to London on Saturday morning. Paying eight hundred dollars for the early flight. I had no idea what time it was in England until I arrived.

Nodding in and out of troubled and exhausting naps, inhaling recycled aircraft air and just plain strung out from a rollercoaster of hope, despair, hope, despair, by the time I entered my flat I was in no condition to do much beside lie prostrate in bed. My immune system had been shredded by the last two days and nights. Stricken with a temperature and flu symptoms, I rolled in my damp pit, haunted by a legion of legs and faces and feet.

At different times the Dahlia was in the room, sitting on the end of the bed smoking, watching me with a cruel, knowing smile. At other times I saw Sam, in a nurse's uniform, teetering around me in white fully fashioned nylons. And I fell over and over again into the forest of legs. They kicked me. Or swayed apart to let me land upside down. Night turned into day, into night. I dragged myself to and from the kitchen to drink water from the tap and swallow paracetamol. My skin was oil and grit. Tarred and feathered by my own sickness and desperation.

Sometime early on Tuesday morning, I felt well enough to stand up and wash.

With a stomach full of angry stinging bees, I called the shop. Cecilia answered. 'Thank God you're back. We've being trying to call you.'

'Why? What?'

'You better come in.'

Shaved, showered, dressed in clean clothes, but still resembling a mummified corpse at the British Museum, I took a cab to the store.

Cecilia looked worried, Lucy amused. Cecilia led me into the staff room while Lucy watched the counter.

The news was beyond the worst-case scenario I had imagined, which had been a vision of a cold and indifferent Sam I would spend months, if not years, trying to win back.

Saturday had been terrible. Sam had worked alone. A fuse had blown in the antiquated fuse box and left the shop in virtual darkness, the till inoperative. The short circuit had also activated the alarm. Which rang until closing time. All on a day in which a sudden need for our range of spike-heeled sandals had filled the store with customers. Every time Sam left the shop floor to get boxes from the storeroom, the counter had been left unoccupied. A girl walked out with a pair of Alexandra Neel sling-backs; her kid took the bowl of sweets. Two drunks had then rolled in and made a nuisance of themselves for over an hour. The police had been called and not shown up. She'd been swindled by two fake fifty-pound notes and had to chase two hooded, opportunist kids out of the storeroom, who'd run in there and made off with her handbag. She locked up and left in tears. All this time I was in LA chasing another woman.

I wanted to put my head under the back wheel of a bus.

On Monday, she wrote her letter of resignation, taking her annual leave entitlement in one go to serve out her period of notice. A hosiery and lingerie distributor had offered her a position as a sales manager. She had taken the job. Had been considering it for ages, but was waiting to see if she and I had a future. I answered that question for her by the end of Saturday.

I called and called and called. She never picked up. Then an answering service told me it had been disconnected. I went to her flat three times that week and rang the bell. No answer.

The skipper had jumped overboard. We were leaderless and rudderless. Both the girls and I were afraid, and felt useless. We weren't sure who to call about resetting the till and alarm, or fixing the electrics. I'd forgotten how to do the admin work.

It would just never be the same again – we all knew it. I was the vision, Sam the business and brains. And her effortless and speedy administration was not the only vital component missing, but also her personnel-management skills. Lucy was never cut out to work and Cecilia was bored. Samantha had supervised the girls and their characters in a way I never could. I was like a hopeless, soft-touch uncle who spoiled his nieces and ruined them.

Enmity suddenly developed between the girls. 'You know Cecilia is a bit lezzy, don't you, Al?' a restless, mischievous Lucy asked me one day in the office. 'She fancies me a bit, you know.' I had suspected an attraction between them the day I caught Cecilia playing with Lucy's feet, but also guessed that for Lucy the sexual tension between her and her colleague merely presented an opportunity for her idle curiosity and manipulative whims to indulge themselves. She was basically straight; Cecilia more complicated. An unlikely union. But something had happened between the girls about two weeks after Sam left. They suddenly stopped speaking. The natural camaraderie had stiffened and the girls seemed to retreat into different corners of the store. Trade was slow at this time anyway, so there was ample time for each of them to indulge in indolent and slipshod habits while I retaught myself how to run the business. And out of this lethargic, restless and unstable period, something unusual occurred.

Something I discovered by accident.

Some stock was missing: twelve pairs of stockings, some nice Touchable foundation wear we couldn't account for and, more importantly, a pair of Rene Caovilla and a pair of Beatrix Ong high heels. Lucy had a infuriating habit of failing to return boxes of expensive designer shoes to the store after a fitting, and just leaving them on the shop floor by the couch. A grand's worth of stock had vanished and I wanted to know why and how.

Alone that Thursday evening after we'd closed up, as I tried to fathom and relearn the manager's job in the office, I played the security cameras back on fast forward from the previous week to try and locate the missing shoes.

I began with the hidden camera in the staff room and office to locate the departure of the shoes from source. After an hour of fruitless searching and stopping, I whizzed across a blurry commotion of white uniform and exposed underwear on the tape. I rewound and played the tape and was immediately confronted by the vision of Lucy and Cecilia kissing.

I rewound the tape further. Paused it, loosened my collar and blinked the fatigue from my eyes. Leant in closer to the monitor and restarted the performance.

The time-code on the tape indicated it had happened four days earlier and twenty minutes after closing time.

On the screen, a half-empty bottle of champagne that Lucy and Cecilia had purloined from the special occasions' cupboard lay on the desk beside the printer. They had been drinking and playing with each other's hair. Somehow this had developed into a compare and contrast session in which each girl unbuttoned her uniform and showed the other her breasts. Hands and fingers pressed and caressed. Bras were judged. Shoes were kicked off. Hair was down. Faces were flushed and laughing. They sat close beside each other on the table and drank. Stretched out their shiny legs and compared length of limb, toenail polish, hosiery, or some other delight I wasn't completely privy to without sound.

As this went on, I noticed that Cecilia had a habit of touching Lucy's smaller, muscular legs with her long feet, to point something out. But also to rub her friend's glossy shin with the long slippery sole of her left foot.

Hems were pulled up – Lucy first, she always led – and stocking tops and suspender fastenings were discussed, fondled, rearranged. Lucy straightened a seam on Cecilia's legs and then admired the taller girl's panties from behind. They were giggling. Often enjoying belly laughs and drinking the champagne like fizzy pop.

From their partially distinct facial expressions and body language, I do believe Lucy was both teasing and quizzing Cecilia over her sexual experiences with other girls. Asking how *this* felt and how she went about doing *that*. It's amazing how one sense is emphasised after the other main sense is removed. I could hear nothing but could intuit by sight more or less what was unfolding on the tape between two attractive young women wearing white uniforms unbuttoned to the waist, and shod in no more than a thin veneer of nylon on their delectable feet.

And then they kissed. Once tentatively, that resulted in peals of laughter. A second time, which again degenerated into hysterics, before Cecilia took control and held Lucy's pretty blonde head and got stuck in with a deep, open-mouthed and passionate kiss.

After a few seconds, Lucy clipped her arms around Cecilia's long, pale back and slid both of her smaller legs around Cecilia's glossy thighs. The kiss continued. I could see them partially from the side, at a downward angle. Their hands became busy about each other's nipples, and, perhaps for the first time in her decadent life, Lucy put her mouth on another girl's breasts. Which delighted Cecilia.

Lucy eventually sat back, looking pleased with herself and the expression on Cecilia's face, who then slid her uniform down to her feet and stepped out of it. Standing tall in her black stockings, garter belt and sheer black panties, Cecilia displayed herself to Lucy from the front, then slipped on to her knees and buried her face between Lucy's thighs, which were sheer in nearly-black hold-ups.

Lucy opened her mouth in surprise and lay back on the desk, but kept her head raised so she could see Cecilia's beautiful, slender face going to work on her pussy. For the first time in over a week, I slipped my cock out of my trousers and added a rhythmic, fleshy percussion to the silent movie running on the screen.

Two pretty shop girls in heavy make-up, with their hair loose, uniforms shed or half-removed, wearing sheer stockings and revealing their soft girly feet, were having sex in an office. I'd waited my whole life to see such a thing occur naturally. And to my eternal delight, Cecilia actually stroked Lucy's stockinged thighs with her long, broad hands while eating the girl's wet blonde pussy. She was actually enjoying sheer hosiery on her lover's pretty, petite legs.

I created this erotic world of feminine accessories to indulge myself, but it seemed the spirit was contagious.

I came before Lucy. Before Lucy shook and shivered and writhed on the spot where I ate my Greek salads (no wonder she'd been grinning all week). And Cecilia was insatiable. She devoured Lucy's big brown bust and stroked every inch of her colleague's body. I had every suspicion this was a long-held desire finally satisfied.

But Lucy played her part too. Didn't seem to object when Cecilia clambered on to the table and straddled Lucy's red, smudged face; made her lick and suck and taste and fully experience another woman's sex. Grinding and bucking about on her diminutive friend's face, Cecilia threw her head back at one point and looked right at me while plucking and strumming her hard brown nipples.

Between my legs, a recovery was in motion.

Cecilia kept Lucy trapped between her strong thighs, even used the blonde's face to push and rub her raven pussy, until she'd come herself.

After they separated, I believe Lucy wasn't so much uncomfortable about what had taken place but overwhelmed; she'd surprised herself. Again, I found this delightful. Cecilia was triumphant and affectionate with her lover as they cleaned themselves up and got dressed. But there was enough of a resistance and reserve about Lucy's quick, but stiff, movements to signify trouble between the two. Lucy had liked it, perhaps too much, and was not keen to try it again anytime soon. Cecilia had other ideas.

We were losing stock, the takings were down, an infestation of dust and small flies had arrived on a biblical scale, equipment was malfunctioning and my staff were misbehaving. The store depended on Sam: the girls needed her and I missed her.

'And have you see Sam since?' Doctor Kim asks.

I shake my head. Dig my fingers into my tired, strained eyes. 'It's been two months.'

'But are you still trying to contact her?'

I nod. 'Four of the best letters I have ever written. Flowers, cards, gifts, all sent to her flat. Nothing. But I won't give up. We were too good together. I have a hunch I'll see her again. On her terms. I hope to God I do.'

'How does her disappearance make you feel?'

'Exactly how I should feel. You see, I don't blame her. At all. This is exactly what I deserve. Exactly the kind of risk I have been running my whole life. But it's been hellish. I haven't slept or eaten much at all. I work to try and take my mind off her, and off the regret. So much regret.'

'Which is why you are here.'

'Yup. So what do you think of me? A degenerate? A hopeless, immature, pathetic pervert? A sexually undeveloped man who's managed to extend his adolescence

248

into middle-age? Do I have a pathological aversion to commitment? Am I a sexual cripple? A misogynist? Hit me with it. I want to know exactly what I am. Don't hold back. Let me have it. Right between the legs if necessary.'

The doctor smiles. 'Well, you're not short of powers of self-examination or self-interpretation. You have probably given your fetish as much objective analysis as anyone in my profession. I'm not going to classify you or persecute you for adoring women's legs or feet. And I think we both know exactly who and what you are. I doubt I can tell you much that may surprise you, or act as any kind of revelation.'

'That's it?'

She looks at me over the rims of her glasses. 'But what I will say is that despite being capable of identifying and understanding exactly what it is you desire, you have no intention of ever resisting it. Even slightly. As long as you photograph women for your website, collect their confessions and stockings, and run a hosiery and high-heel emporium in London, you will continue to immerse yourself in the same degree of stimulation you have always done. And the same cycle of longing and need and dissatisfaction that you suffered with the American model and Sam will continue. You are lost in the forest, Al, because you want to be in the forest. You are a never-ending voyager. I just think you wanted me to confirm this. And that is exactly what I am doing. The desire for legs and their accessories, as you put it, will never go away. Or your need to find them. And if I was capable of offering you medication now to remove your fetish, we both know that you would never take it.

'But twinned with your insatiable appetite to collect legs in every medium possible is an equally powerful impulse to find a companion who can be a part of your sexuality. The two are not necessarily incompatible. You found them before, I am sure you are best placed to find them again. Only next time, you have to be aware of her when she appears. You must resolve the conflict between the present you actually exist in, and the future you idealise.

'But you are not dangerous, or sick, or out of control. Your desires are ultimately harmless. Next time I see you, we will talk more about this.'

She was right. Instinctively, I do know myself. Too well, perhaps. Because if I have learnt one thing at my age, it is that I'm utterly predictable. Is this the dawn of the end of experience for me? Not that I have seen and done everything, but that I know in advance how I will react, and so I stick to the things that give me maximum satisfaction?

'Can I ask you a question, Doctor Kim? A frank and probably inappropriate question? But I have to know.'

She raises a thin, dark eyebrow, but her eyes are smiling. 'You may?'

'Do you like to wear sheer stockings and high heels? And if so, how do they make you feel?'

nexus

The leading publisher of fetish and adult fiction

TELL US WHAT YOU THINK!

Readers' ideas and opinions matter to us. Take a few minutes to fill in the questionnaire below and you'll be entered into a prize draw to win a year's worth of Nexus books (36 titles)

Terms and conditions apply – see end of questionnaire.

1. Sex: Are you male ☐ female ☐ a couple ☐?

2. Age: Under 21 ☐ 21–30 ☐ 31–40 ☐ 41–50 ☐ 51–60 ☐ over 60 ☐

3. Where do you buy your Nexus books from?
☐ A chain book shop. If so, which one(s)?

_____

☐ An independent book shop. If so, which one(s)?

_____

☐ A used book shop/charity shop
☐ Online book store. If so, which one(s)?

_____

4. How did you find out about Nexus Books?
☐ Browsing in a book shop
☐ A review in a magazine
☐ Online
☐ Recommendation
☐ Other _____

5. In terms of settings which do you prefer? (Tick as many as you like)
☐ Down to earth and as realistic as possible
☐ Historical settings. If so, which period do you prefer?

_____

☐ Fantasy settings – barbarian worlds

- ☐ Completely escapist/surreal fantasy
- ☐ Institutional or secret academy
- ☐ Futuristic/sci fi
- ☐ Escapist but still believable
- ☐ Any settings you dislike?

_____

- ☐ Where would you like to see an adult novel set?

_____

6. In terms of storylines, would you prefer:

- ☐ Simple stories that concentrate on adult interests?
- ☐ More plot and character-driven stories with less explicit adult activity?
- ☐ We value your ideas, so give us your opinion of this book:

_____

_____

_____

7. In terms of your adult interests, what do you like to read about? (Tick as many as you like)

- ☐ Traditional corporal punishment (CP)
- ☐ Modern corporal punishment
- ☐ Spanking
- ☐ Restraint/bondage
- ☐ Rope bondage
- ☐ Latex/rubber
- ☐ Leather
- ☐ Female domination and male submission
- ☐ Female domination and female submission
- ☐ Male domination and female submission
- ☐ Willing captivity
- ☐ Uniforms
- ☐ Lingerie/underwear/hosiery/footwear (boots and high heels)
- ☐ Sex rituals
- ☐ Vanilla sex
- ☐ Swinging

- ☐ Cross-dressing/TV
- ☐ Enforced feminisation
- ☐ Others – tell us what you don't see enough of in adult fiction:

_____

_____

_____

8. Would you prefer books with a more specialised approach to your interests, i.e. a novel specifically about uniforms? If so, which subject(s) would you like to read a Nexus novel about?

_____

_____

_____

9. Would you like to read true stories in Nexus books? For instance, the true story of a submissive woman, or a male slave? Tell us which true revelations you would most like to read about:

_____

_____

_____

10. What do you like best about Nexus books?

_____

_____

11. What do you like least about Nexus books?

_____

_____

12. Which are your favourite titles?

_____

_____

13. Who are your favourite authors?

_____

_____

14. **Which covers do you prefer? Those featuring:**
    (tick as many as you like)

☐ Fetish outfits
☐ More nudity
☐ Two models
☐ Unusual models or settings
☐ Classic erotic photography
☐ More contemporary images and poses
☐ A blank/non-erotic cover
☐ What would your ideal cover look like?

_____

15. **Describe your ideal Nexus novel in the space provided:**

_____

_____

_____

_____

16. **Which celebrity would feature in one of your Nexus-style fantasies?**
    We'll post the best suggestions on our website – anonymously!

_____

THANKS FOR YOUR TIME

Now simply write the title of this book in the space below and cut out the
questionnaire pages. Post to: Nexus, Marketing Dept., Thames Wharf Studios,
Rainville Rd, London W6 9HA

Book title: _____

NEXUS NEW BOOKS

To be published in February 2006

AQUA DOMINATION
William Doughty

Just why would Mary go back to David and his bizarre bathroom? What could be crazier than designing and equipping a luxurious bathroom for the soapy, slippery domination of women? Yet she has returned to submit to watery domination, while dressed in fetish garments of plastic and rubber. And having seen the bathroom, can her friends – Jack, Carol and Faye – resist plunging into such slippery submission?

£6.99   ISBN 0 352 34020 7

TOKYO BOUND
Sachi

James Burke's mastery of the Tao of sex made him a prince of the Excalibur, a Tokyo host club that catered to wealthy women with particular tastes. He brought intense pleasure through the universal force of chi. His world was sublime until a secret society learned of his skill and sought the dark side of his Tao, the power to inflict pain. They would have it or destroy him.

£6.99   ISBN 0 352 34019 3

PLEASING THEM
William Doughty

Robert Shawnescrosse introduces his young and beautiful wife to the peculiar delights he shares with his carefully selected servants at the most peculiar house in Victorian England. Yet he has an even darker secret which requires everyone at the manor to work harder to satisfy the strange desires of three men of dubious integrity.

Why does the puritanical Mt Blanking send young ladies into a muddy pond wearing only their hats? Can the wicked Sir Horace ever obtain the satisfaction he craves through cruelty? And why is David making such strange demands? How can Robert, Jane and their servants offer pleasures extreme enough to please them?

£6.99   ISBN 0 352 34015 0

If you would like more information about Nexus titles, please visit our website at www.nexus-books.co.uk, or send a stamped addressed envelope to:

Nexus, Thames Wharf Studios,
Rainville Road, London W6 9HA

NEXUS BACKLIST

This information is correct at time of printing. For up-to-date information, please visit our website at www.nexus-books.co.uk

All books are priced at £6.99 unless another price is given.

ABANDONED ALICE	Adriana Arden 0 352 33969 1	☐
ALICE IN CHAINS	Adriana Arden 0 352 33908 X	☐
AMAZON SLAVE	Lisette Ashton 0 352 33916 0	☐
ANGEL	Lindsay Gordon 0 352 34009 6	☐
THE ANIMAL HOUSE	Cat Scarlett 0 352 33877 6	☐
THE ART OF CORRECTION	Tara Black 0 352 33895 4	☐
THE ART OF SURRENDER	Madeline Bastinado 0 352 34013 4	☐
AT THE END OF HER TETHER	G.C. Scott 0 352 33857 1	☐
BARE BEHIND	Penny Birch 0 352 33721 4	☐
BELINDA BARES UP	Yolanda Celbridge 0 352 33926 8	☐
BENCH MARKS	Tara Black 0 352 33797 4	☐
BINDING PROMISES	G.C. Scott 0 352 34014 2	☐
THE BLACK GARTER	Lisette Ashton 0 352 33919 5	☐
THE BLACK MASQUE	Lisette Ashton 0 352 33977 2	☐